Outlaw

Outlaw

Book 2 in the Aelfraed Series

By

Griff Hosker

Outlaw

*Published by Griff Hosker 2013
Copyright ©Griff Hosker*

*The author has asserted their moral right under the Copyright, Designs and Patents Act, 1988, to be identified as the author of this work.
All Rights reserved. No part of this publication may be reproduced, copied, stored in a retrieval system, or transmitted, in any form or by any means, without the prior written consent of the copyright holder, nor be otherwise circulated in any form of binding or cover other than that in which it is published and without a similar condition being imposed on the subsequent purchaser.*

A CIP catalogue record for this title is available from the British Library.

Contents

Outlaw i
Chapter 1 2
Chapter 2 16
Chapter 3 29
Chapter 4 43
Chapter 5 57
Chapter 6 71
Chapter 7 84
Chapter 8 98
Chapter 9 111
Chapter 10 126
Chapter 11 140
Chapter 12 153
Chapter 13 166
Chapter 14 179
Chapter 15 194
Chapter 16 207
Historical note 221
Characters and places in the novel 223
Other books by Griff Hosker 224

Outlaw
Chapter 1

I am Aelfraed of Topcliffe, or at least I was for a while, and I fought with King Harold at the Battle of Stamford Bridge. Perhaps it was *wyrd* or my dead mother watching over me but I was not there, at Senlac Hill, close to the town of Hastings when Harold and most of my former comrades died in a final shield wall. I was recovering from a wound to my back, a wound which almost cost me my life but perhaps, ultimately, saved my life, for had I been with the other Housecarls then I too would have died for we had all sworn an oath to protect King Harold and my dear friends, Ulf, Wolf and Osgar, all died honouring that oath. It was the mark of the Anglo-Saxons that warriors took oaths which they kept until death. Ridley, the Thegn of Coxold and my oldest comrade, also survived for he too was wounded and, like me, he mourned not only our comrades but the end of the finest fighting force ever seen in England. I was just glad that my uncle, Aethelward, who had been strategos and advisor to King Harold, had also survived for he had been with me in my castle at Topcliffe.

Until my wife, Gytha, had finally arrived from London, escorted by my soldiers, I had feared for her life for she had been with Ealdgyth, Harold's widow and her twins. We had heard that Duke William had stripped Harold and his brothers of all their land. It had been an astute move for they had owned most of the best parts of southern England. I did not know what it meant for me. A few years ago, before the Confessor had given me my land and before I had met Gytha then I would not have worried about a new ruler but now I had responsibilities. I had a large estate and the people thereon, such as Thomas the Steward and his wife, Sarah, relied on me to ensure that they could continue to live and work the land.

As part of my regimen to improve my health and recover from the almost mortal wound, I had taken to riding my estate each day escorted by Branton, the sergeant of my archers. His brother Osbert, my sergeant at arms, was training new men to replace those who had fallen fighting Hadrada and Tostig. I enjoyed the exercise but it also gave me the opportunity to speak with my people and discover their feelings. The land gave me an income but it also gave me great responsibilities. Before we left the castle, I called in upon Ralph, the blacksmith. He was like Thor himself in his fiery smithy with two of his boys pumping the bellows for all they were worth. His knotted, heavily muscled arms, hammered out the sword he was shaping.

"How are the weapons coming, Ralph?"

He briefly paused and nodded to me, holding aloft his latest blade, "Well my lord but we are running a little short on iron."

"I will send to the Tees for more." I leaned down to speak to him a little more intimately. "I know not when the Normans will come and what it portends but I know that they will come and I would like all of us to be ready."

He nodded and I could see that he appreciated the confidence. "Do not worry my lord. I have repaired all the armour and weapons you recovered from the battle and we have fitted out all of your men at arms and we now have enough for another ten warriors to be so armed."

"Excellent. You are a good man." He beamed and I thought back to my half brothers and the man whom I had thought was my father until a week ago. They would never have praised any of the workers on the estate no matter what they did or sacrificed. Perhaps that was why he had had no loyalty from any of them.

Branton and I kicked our horses and headed south. "How many more volunteers Branton?" One advantage of my fame, some might say notoriety, was that warriors sought employment with me. There were many, for most of the northern lords had died at Stamford Bridge and Fulford whilst the southern ones had fallen at Senlac. The disadvantage was that men sought you in battle to gain honour from your death in combat.

"There are another fifteen my lord. My brother is assessing their worth and their skills even as we speak."

"Any archers?"

I saw the grin appear on Branton's face. It had been a sore point to him that he commanded fewer men than his brother. I saw the value of archers, of which Harold had had too few for in the battles I had fought they had been crucial to success. "I think we have twenty altogether my lord and some of them are good. The rest," he shrugged.

Outlaw

I understood what he meant. Even poor archers could be improved by a good trainer and Branton was just that. The memory of Aedgart came to mind. He had fallen at the battle defending me and he was even better than Osbert and Branton when it came to making warriors out of the rough clay that arrived to fight for me. I turned in the saddle and regretted it immediately as the pain lanced up my body but I continued my turn, Aethelward had told me that I had to get the suppleness back into my body if I wanted to fight again. The small motte and bailey castle, one of the few in this part of the world, made me proud. Built upon my uncle's advice it stood protecting the old Roman road and was a formidable obstacle to any invader, Norman or Scot!

Branton saw my look and smiled. "It is a fine castle my lord. You should be proud."

"I am, Branton." I could not confide in Branton that it would mean nothing if the Normans decided to take it. It might be a barrier to the Scots who raided the vale but not the Normans; I knew that from my uncle. "Tell me Branton will your arrows pierce the mail of the Norman armour?"

"A good question my lord." He looked off to the south and then took a goose tipped arrow from his quiver. "You see my lord that the arrows we use are intended to cause wounds." I could see what he meant for the arrow's tip was sharp and then broadened. "This works well on flesh. Sometimes it will pierce mail rings but not if they are well made. My men are trained to aim for the horses or the flesh of the warrior. But," he suddenly looked at me eagerly as though he has had an idea, "if Ralph could make the arrows so that they were narrower, all the way down then they would pierce the rings. The wounds would not be as big but they would penetrate."

"Well done Branton. When you return tell Ralph to make some and we will try them out."

He looked at me curiously, "On Normans, my lord?"

"Not at the moment but there may come a time…" our ride and our ruminations were cut short when a rider from the castle suddenly galloped up. "My lord, a messenger has come from the Queen. She is at Jorvik."

Reining our mounts around, we galloped back to Topcliffe. Our brief interlude in the backwater of the north had ended and politics was returned once more. Aethelward and the messenger were deep in conversation when we arrived back. Branton helped me down; mounting was easier than the dismount.

"Is she safe then uncle?"

He flashed me a look which told me to ask questions when we were alone. I might be lord of two manors but to my uncle I was still the small boy he had sworn to protect. "Thank you. Tell the Queen that we will follow you as soon as possible." As the messenger remounted and galloped south, Aethelward turned to Branton. "Send a messenger to Lord Ridley and ask him to join us."

"Sorry uncle. I forget myself sometimes and speak when I shouldn't."

He put his arm around me and led me inside. "These are dangerous times Aelfraed. I know you trust your people, as I do, but we are not playing for small stakes. This is a kingdom for which we chance."

Once inside he shut the doors so that the room was only lit by the fire which seemed very attractive at that moment. "Do we know…"

"Nephew, you have still to learn to listen more and speak less. I will tell you all that I know." Aethelward had that look which parents have with young children and I suddenly felt like a child again. "The Queen has brought the twins north for she has nothing left for her in London and Winchester." I opened my mouth to speak. "William had confiscated all the land of Harold and his brothers. Her brothers and the Aetheling are heading south even as we speak. The Queen thinks that they intend to submit to Duke William."

He stared into the fire. I was still young enough to have more questions and there was information I needed. "Will he be crowned King?"

"Now that is a good question. Probably. The Witenagemot is now purged of those who would oppose him and ruled by our old friend the Archbishop of Canterbury." We had had a run in with the wily and belligerent churchman in Winchester. Both of us believed that he was involved in an assassination attempt on King Edward's life. "I would expect him crowned by Christmas time."

Outlaw

"But that is less than three weeks away!"

"I know."

"Is there no good news?"

"Not really. The Queen fears that Edith will try to have her sons killed to enhance the likelihood of the Aetheling being crowned. Unlikely in my view but…" I suddenly realised that Gytha and my unborn child were in danger for I had recently discovered that I was the eldest child of Harold Godwinson and the King's consort for many years, Edith, the mother of the Aetheling, knew this. "I think, for the moment you and your family are safe although if the Duke discovers that information then things may change." He saw my downcast face. "Things are not all black Aelfraed. There are signs that there is trouble for William in Hereford and Exeter and you are fortunate in that you have one of the strongest retinues. Osbert and your men at arms can protect you and your family."

I had much to think about. I had thought I was a marginal player in this game but as I reflected on Aethelward's words I could see that I was not. Most of the northern support of Harold had died at Stamford Bridge and all of the Wessex support had perished at Senlac Hill. Morcar and Edwin, the Earls of Northumbria and Mercia as well as being Gytha's brothers had become very much self-serving and poor Edgar the Aetheling was still a child. "I will leave Osbert to protect Gytha, she cannot travel and I will take Branton and his archers."

"Good. I also think we need to make plans for the future."

I looked puzzled. "I thought that was what we are doing."

"The immediate future, yes but what about a future with William as King?"

"Then we would fight him."

"With your forty men."

"And Ridley's."

He laughed. "Heroic, noble and doomed to failure. You need more men and an escape route. If you fight William then you will have to find somewhere for your wife and child where they can be safe. And what of the monies and coin you have accrued? What of them?"

I knew that Aethelward had money and he had been careful to hoard it over the years. "What do you suggest uncle?"

"When we go to Jorvik we will seek out the Jews. We will arrange for them to watch your money."

I was shocked. "Christ killers?"

He laughed. "No, the money lenders. Since when did you become so Christian? You can have money anywhere if they watch over it for you and you do not have to carry it around. You need to plan and plan carefully."

When I told Gytha that the Queen was in Jorvik, she wanted to visit immediately. "No my love, for I want you and our unborn child safe here. I will be gone but a day and I will try to get her to visit us." When she protested I explained to her most of what Aethelward had said. She too had only recently known of my real father and the thought that our child might be hurt made her see sense. "I will tell Osbert and Thomas to keep a close watch."

By the time Ridley arrived, we were ready and I had told Osbert of the danger to my lady and impressed upon him the need to increase our warriors. He seemed quite happy about the whole thing. Looking back I suppose it was because that was his world, the world of war.

Compared with a few weeks ago Jorvik was like a ghost town. The military presence of the Earl was no longer there and many families had lost brothers, husbands, sons and fathers in the two battles fought within a few miles of the city walls. There were few guards but they smiled as we passed as the three of us were famous, not only in Jorvik but the whole of the north. The Queen had taken over the chambers of the Earl and I was pleased that she had retained some twenty warriors as her guards. It seemed a pitiful number when compared with the armies the King had commanded and it showed me the difference between victory and defeat.

She greeted Aethelward first and tears gushed from her eyes for Aethelward had been Harold's truest friend. My uncle had shed his tears in private but his face showed the emotion he felt. She whispered words in his ear and, pulling away, he nodded. She seemed to see me for the first time. Her face lit up when she did so and I remembered that we had always been close. Now I knew the reason; her husband must have told her I was his son and that made her see me differently. "Ah, Aelfraed. Your father was so proud of

Outlaw

you and yet he never had the chance to tell you." She grabbed me and began sobbing. "What must you think of me? Blubbering and carrying on, I am the Queen." She stepped back. "Not that I look like one."

I dropped to my knee and held her hand. "You will always be a Queen to me."

"Rise and thank you. And now we must talk." She looked at Ridley who stood, embarrassed behind us.

Aethelward closed the door and said, "We can trust Ridley but I fear that the only ones we can trust are in this room."

The Queen had more personality than any woman I have ever known, including Gytha and she glided across the floor to touch Ridley's arm. "Of course, I can trust you Ridley and how could I forget you after you were so kind to me on my journey from Wales." Ridley blushed his thanks and she gestured for us to sit at the table in the middle of the sparsely furnished room. "We are all in danger. Edith Duck-legs," Ridley and I smiled for she always referred to Harold's previous consort, Edith Swanneck in such disparaging terms and we no longer bothered to correct her, "is trying all she can to protect her son. She has told William that Harold had a bastard." She looked at me. It was the first time I had realised that was what I was. "Do not take offence Aelfraed for William is a bastard himself. She hates me and wished ill to come to my children."

Despite my uncle's previous admonition, I could not help myself, "But your majesty, your brothers?"

"I fear my brothers are too busy watching their own back and seeing what they can get out of Duke William. And you Aethelward, you have many enemies at the new court for all your friends died at Senlac and Stamford."

He shrugged, "Having enemies does not worry me. What does worry me is your precarious state for you have few guards should anyone attempt harm on your babies."

There was a silence as we all wrestled with the problem. When Ridley spoke and came up with the solution we all stared at him. He was the quiet one, the warrior but that day he showed us his innate wisdom. "Your Majesty should go to Topcliffe. It is safer than here and there you will be amongst trusted friends."

8

For Ridley this was his proudest moment for Aethelward clapped him on his broad back. "I have underestimated you Ridley and I thank you for the best solution."

The Queen did not look convinced. "Topcliffe?"

"My castle majesty. A little rough around the edges but secure and we could defend against a large army. It would give us breathing space to decide what to do."

"And this is not a safe haven. Your brothers will both have spies here and Edith knows it well."

"Mentioning that witch's name has decided me. We will leave for your home tomorrow." She leaned over and touched my arm. "And I will get to see your lovely wife again. Now I am hungry let us eat." She went to the door and asked her guard to tell the cook to serve the food.

"Where are the twins majesty?" Ulf and Harold had been born shortly before the cataclysmic battles which had decimated the ranks of the Saxon nobility and they represented the future if there was one. "They are sleeping hopefully, with their wet nurse." She leaned over to touch my hand. "A little advice, Aelfraed, when Gytha gives birth have a room for your child which has solid walls or everyone will hear the wails."

I had not yet thought of being a father. Other events had occupied my mind and I realised that I had given no thought to events after the birth which was but a couple of months away. I suddenly smiled for I knew that Gytha and Sarah would have done all the planning which was necessary. I still felt guilty, as most fathers would but I knew that all would be well.

The servants scurried in bearing fine dishes filled with steaming food. It had seemed a long time since I had broken my fast and ridden all the way to Jorvik and my grumbling stomach confirmed this. Politeness dictated that, as guests, we waited until Ealdgyth had begun to eat. One of the servants who had brought in the food saw us waiting and offered, "My lord, eat for the Queen will be eating special food."

My uncle's preoccupation with listening and not speaking began to pay off because there was something about the man I did not like. Perhaps it was his accent for he did not have the northern accent of the other servants. It might have been his nervous look

Outlaw

but whatever the reason I kept my wits about me and my attention on the servant. Ridley tucked greedily into the mutton stew and Aethelward picked at his. I tore a piece of bread and dipped it into the rich gravy of the stew, all the while watching and waiting. Other servants brought in more food, including three platters for the Queen and then the sly and furtive servant brought in a single bowl which he placed before the Queen. He did it very carefully and I noticed, again his nervousness, "Thank you, Egbert. This looks delicious."

He bobbed his head and said unctuously, "I know how your majesty likes fish stew."

She looked over at me. "I became fond of this when living in Wales for they have some wondrous fish there. In the south, it is not so good but here, again, I have the chance to eat my favourite food."

I felt bold. "I have never tried fish stew. Could I try some, your majesty?"

The Queen looked surprised; Aethelward looked intrigued and interested while Egbert looked horrified. "I will get my lord a bowl. There is plenty in the kitchen."

"I only want a spoonful. Your majesty does not object do you?"

The look I gave her was pleading and I think that she knew me well enough to trust me for she smiled and, glancing at Egbert, said, "Of course Aelfraed."

As I walked over to the bowl, spoon in hand I caught, in the corner of my eye, the sight of Aethelward slowly and silently rising and Egbert trying to edge backwards. Suddenly he turned to run from the room but my uncle blocked him. Ridley had been watching us and he too leapt to his feet and, with Aethelward, held on to the servant.

"I think nephew that I would like this servant to try the fish, with your majesty's permission of course. If there is plenty of fish stew in the kitchen then we can always get another bowl. Aelfraed, a spoon of the stew, if you please."

The man's face was a picture of terror as I dipped a spoon into the reddish liquid of the stew. The Queen's appetite was forgotten as she sat fascinated by the scenario being played out before her like a mummer's play. The closer I came to him the more he tried to escape. It was useless for Ridley could have held him on his own. He turned his head so that it was away from the spoon. Aethelward's words were cold and dripped with anger. "What is wrong with the stew that you will not eat it?"

"I do not like fish."

"There is no fish on the spoon; merely liquor. Taste or I will geld you here and now."

The knife which suddenly appeared in his hand made the colour totally drain from Egbert's face and he ceased struggling and sagged in Ridley's arms. "It was Edith Swanneck. She paid me to put the poison in the stew."

"And the twins?"

He looked in horror at Aethelward who had, it seems, read his mind. Like a cornered deer he looked from the Queen to each of us and then broke down. "I was to slit their throats when the Queen was dead."

The Queen did not show any emotion but her eyes were cold and hard. She looked at Aethelward and nodded. In one slick motion, he drew back his dagger and slit the throat of Egbert, the poisoner. I went to the door and called in the two sentries. Their faces showed their shock but that was their only reaction. The Queen's voice was cold. "Dispose of this traitor and then send the cook to me."

After the body had been removed, Aethelward began to question Ealdgyth. "Is he a new servant?"

"He was one of the house servants from our home in London but as he had served Harold I assumed that he was loyal. I was wrong."

"All of which adds impetus to our need to escape from this web of intrigue and take you somewhere which is safer than this place."

I was not unhappy about the Queen coming to Topcliffe but something was nagging in my mind. "Uncle if we leave Jorvik with the Queen then everyone will know that she is coming to Topcliffe. Surely we want them to be in the dark about her whereabouts."

A rare smile passed across my uncle's face. "They would indeed, chess player. Your majesty, if you and your retinue head north then we can follow a little later and meet you at Topcliffe."

"What if I am asked where I am going?"

Outlaw

"You are still the Queen. Tell them that you are unhappy with the accommodation and are going to visit your brother in Mercia. You would have to head west for a while anyway. Ridley, you can leave now and warn Osbert and Gytha of our arrival." He smiled wryly, "I dare say I will be in trouble with Gytha and Sarah for not giving them enough warning but…"

Grinning to Aethelward and bowing to the Queen, Ridley said, "I will smooth your passage my lord and I thank the gods that I am not entangled with a woman yet." Suddenly worried about what he had said he mumbled, "No offence your majesty," and backed out of the room as quickly as he could.

"I like Ridley. He is an honest man."

"Yes, majesty and there are many more like him in the north although many fine men died at Fulford and Stamford Bridge. There are still enough to resist the Normans."

"Thank you Aelfraed, I know, and I hope that I am not endangering your family by my presence."

"Since the King died we are all in danger and doing nothing will not save us. I fear the nights will get darker before they lighten."

While the Queen went to organise her departure Aethelward and I went to find the Jew he spoke of. The Jewish quarter was shunned by the Christian element of the city but those who were of Danish origin treated these foreigners well. Christians did, of course, visit the Jews, normally when they needed money. Aethelward had used Reuben of Jorvik before when he had first returned north and Reuben managed my uncle's money, for a small fee of course. The Jews kept to themselves and did not advertise their religion but, as we were visiting his home we saw that he was indeed a truly religious man and wore the dress of a Jew. I felt it a shame that he could not do so in the street for then he would have been reviled. He was tolerated as a necessary evil, in many people's minds but I found him to be a courteous gentleman with a mind as sharp as any.

"Welcome Lord Aethelward. It has been some time since you graced my establishment."

He bowed slightly and my uncle held his arm to include me. "This is my nephew Lord Aelfraed of Topcliffe."

Outlaw

The blue eyes were a little rheumy but they lit up at the mention of my name. "Aelfraed of Topcliffe! I am honoured for all in Jorvik know that it was you and your bravery that saved our people at Fulford. How may I be of service?"

Aethelward nodded at me. "Sir, you know that we live in parlous times and when the Normans get around to visiting us in the north then who knows what will become of us."

"True, true. Wise for one so young."

"I would have what little monies I have accrued to be safe and my uncle assures me that you have always looked after his money wisely and securely. I would you do the same for me."

"Even if you were not the nephew of Lord Aethelward I would agree for I know from your deeds that you are honourable and I am touched that you would honour me so." He looked at me shrewdly. "Perhaps you would like this money to be available to you in places other than in England?" I smiled. He was a clever man. "I would not need to know where you were thinking of but you would need to inform me before you depart so that I could furnish you with the script which would unlock your money abroad."

"As soon as I know Reuben then so shall you. I will return on the morrow with my money."

He bowed slightly. "I am pleased to be of service." He beckoned to Aethelward to close with him. "I would not like to speak disparagingly of the Earls but I have heard rumours from my brethren in London that they are about to submit to Duke William." He spread his arms and shrugged. "Just a rumour."

"Thank you, Reuben, for trusting us so. I will not forget this and should you or your family require my help then just ask."

We made our way back to the Queen's quarters where we were told that she had left for her brother's home in Coventry. Aethelward feigned annoyance that he had missed her and we headed north out of the city. Once we had left the walls behind us we headed north-west and when we reached the river we swam our horses across. Although we were wet we knew that we had shaken off any followers and we could make better time to follow the Queen and her retinue as they headed up the Roman road to my home. We spotted them ahead and Aethelward reined in his mount. "Now we trail slowly. Remember our task is to make sure that no one follows her." We went at what I considered a snail's pace but as my uncle told said, the Queen and her baggage would move very slowly. Suddenly we heard hooves behind us and Aethelward slipped from his mount quickly and began to examine the bottom of the horse's shoe.

Four armed warriors rode up with a clergyman at the fore. I recognised him as one of the priests from the cathedral and the warriors were in the pay of the Archbishop. I remembered how close the church had been with Tostig and did not trust them. When they rode up Aethelward made sure they could not pass his horse.

"Hello, father. What brings you to this empty place?"

I could see that the churchman was not happy about meeting us nor was he happy with the questioning. "We have business at Ripon."

"Ah, well as our paths will be the same for a while we will ride with you." As he mounted he leaned in conspiratorially, "There are many Norse deserters and bandits on this road. I am glad for your warriors." I almost fell from my horse laughing. The two of us could easily have disposed of these finely dressed but inexperienced men. I had to admire Aethelward. He had made the churchman believe that they were helping us while slowing them down so that the Queen could reach Topcliffe unseen. Aethelward was normally a silent man but he chattered away like a village gossip. Although many of his questions and comments seemed inane I later found out that he was finding out about the Archbishop and the two Earls. When we came to the fork in the road I could see that they wished to carry on the Roman road north but they had said Ripon and that was to the west. As Topcliffe was but a couple of miles up the road then I knew that the Queen's destination would remain a mystery, at least for a short time.

We continued to ride slowly as we watched them disappear west. Uncle laughed, "I would bet your axe against a dagger that they will turn around as soon as they can and head back to Jorvik."

"But why did they come north?"

"The Archbishop needs to know where she is. She and the two princes are now a bargaining chip. He can offer them to the Duke in return for retaining his power. I daresay he sent men east, south and west to find her. He will be perplexed when he discovers that she had disappeared without a trace."

Chapter 2

We waited at the road junction until it began to go dark and then headed for home. My back was aching although not as badly as a week ago. I was on the mend. The hall was though someone had emptied a box of newly born chicks onto the floor as all the female servants and poor Thomas, flew around the yard trying to organise things. Amidst it all sat calmly by the fire, was Ealdgyth. Sarah and Gytha both threw a dirty look at me as I smiled my way through them to the Queen. "I appear to have caused something of a stir Aelfraed."

"Do not worry majesty. I normally manage to upset those two." She gestured for me to join her. "You were followed."

"So. Did you see who it was?"

"Better. We spoke with them. It was a priest and four guards sent by the Archbishop."

Her eyes became angry. "I knew that reptile was up to something. It seems that I have come to the right place but I hope that I am not inconveniencing you too much."

"Do not worry for soon I will have to begin training my new men for war will come."

She looked sad and nodded as my uncle joined us. "I know."

"I am sorry to have to be the one to bring it up but what are your plans?"

She looked suddenly like a lost child and her eyes filled with tears. "I know not. I must protect my children. What if I submit to William?"

"You would still be a threat and besides there is always Edith and as long as Edgar has a chance at the throne then she will do all in her power to rid the world of your children and Aelfraed and Aelfraed's unborn child. But Aelfraed is right. We need to build an army to resist any who try to harm you. I will leave in the morning to visit the local Thegns and gather support. I will not say that you are here but that we are raising local forces and then Aeltraed, I think that we need to visit north of the border and speak with Malcolm."

"Can we trust him?"

"Not to take advantage of the state of England? Of course not but can we trust him to protect the Queen and her children then yes."

The Queen looked intrigued. "Why should he do that?"

"Because it will make you indebted to him and more importantly give him something to bargain with if he helped you regain your throne."

I was not certain but I trusted Aethelward and so did the Queen. My problem was I was too used to warriors and the warrior code. Kings and politicians were not bound by such codes and looked after their own interests first. But I was learning. I went outside to speak with Aethelward. There were still worries about leaving my manor at this dangerous time. "Uncle, do I need to go?"

He looked at me strangely. "You do not wish to accompany me?"

"It is not that. Of course, I wish to accompany you but I worry about leaving the Queen and my wife alone when their lives are in danger."

"Aah. I see. Firstly I believe that Osbert and Ridley could easily defend the Queen and your wife as effectively as you or I. Secondly, we will be gone but eight days at the most for the King is in the south of his land, close to Berwick but lastly and most importantly." He suddenly looked old and sad. "I am no longer a young man. I am approaching the age of Nanna was when she died. I am the last of the Thingmen and the last of the warriors who fought for England as young men. Only Sweyn was older and he, like Ulf, my oath brother, are both dead. I still have much to teach you and, just as necessary, I need to introduce you to others who can help you when I am gone. Malcolm, I know. He will remember me but you, he does not. I wish to show you to him for the dark days are coming and a storm is brewing. We need somewhere safe for your chicks and that place is Scotland."

I was shocked. Aethelward had always been there since I was a small child. I had hoped he would be there for my son but, as I looked at him, I could see that his hair now had more white than black and that he was thinner and gaunter than he had been. I had been so used to him that I had not seen him grow old. "Of course I

Outlaw

will come with you and you are right Ridley and Osbert will be the guardians of my Manor."

Grasping my shoulders he embraced me and, after mounting his horse, he rode to visit the other lords. "Branton!"

My faithful archer came over. "Yes my lord?"

"Send your brother to me and then ride to Lord Ridley and ask him to visit."

I was now resolved to head north but I knew that Gytha would not be happy at my departure. I was not a common soldier I was a lord, she would have been better off had I been a lowly Housecarl and I wondered at the wisdom of marrying her. As soon as the thought came I laughed it out- wisdom has nought to do with the heart.

Osbert strode over. He was, like my old friend Ridley, a rock upon which I could always depend. He had never let me down and had saved me on more than one occasion. I wondered why he did not seek service elsewhere for he could have named his price. I was just grateful that he remained. "Osbert, Lord Aethelward and I are leaving in the morning for Scotland." He looked surprised. "Keep that news to yourself. We are asking Lord Ridley to bring his men here to help you and the Queen's guards to protect the two ladies." I lowered my voice. "Their lives are in danger for someone tried to poison the Queen in Jorvik." A mixture of shock and anger filled his face. "I know that you wonder why we have to go to Scotland but I cannot tell you. Believe me, it is necessary or I would not go. I will just take Branton and four of his archers with me. You will need to keep scouts out to watch the roads. No one must know that the Queen is here."

The good thing about Osbert was that once you had explained something to him you did not need to elaborate or ask stupid questions. Any questions he did ask were pertinent. "And the Normans my lord?"

"An excellent question. At the moment they are still in the south but there will come a time when they head north. That is certain. I will be back before then. I cannot see him travelling over Yuletide. But when he does come we will have to fight. Get as many men as you can but they must be trustworthy and they must be good. We will spend any money we have to guarantee that."

Outlaw

Ridley rode in and while Osbert went to deploy his scouts I asked Ridley to watch over my manor. "I know it is asking much of you old friend but I fear for the Queen's life."

"I am honoured that you trust me with such precious jewels. I will return to Coxold and bring my men back."

"Good for I have business in Jorvik and I may be able to gather intelligence."

"Be careful Aelfraed. There are daggers in men's hearts now."

"I will take Branton with me. I trust only those people who will be here in Topcliffe and Coxold. As for the rest…."

When I went to take my leave of Gytha she and the Queen were busy with the twins. I decided to leave before they had noticed I was not there. My money and valuables were in two saddlebags on my horse. Strangely I was not afraid of bandits or robbers. As the two of them rode quickly south I knew why. When you have faced fearsome opponents in a shield wall then all else becomes mundane and almost harmless. "We will be leaving on the morrow for Scotland, Branton. Pick four of your archers to accompany us."

"Scotland, my lord? I have not been there since our old lord was killed. Is there peace between us now?"

"Lord Aethelward believes so but we shall see. We will only be travelling to Berwick and we will need to be swift for I do not want to leave the Lady Gytha alone too long."

Jorvik, again, seemed sinister and threatening. There appeared to be few friendly faces and people had that hunted look I had seen before. When we reached Reuben's home I left Branton on guard with the horses whilst I entered with the bags.

Rueben carefully counted all the money and valuables and wrote the quantities and values on a sheet of parchment. That in itself was unusual for parchment was expensive. He saw my expression and spreading his hands shrugged. "The parchment is worth the expense for it prevents arguments at a later date. Not that I think you would quibble my lord but it is my practice."

"Do not apologise Reuben. I am just grateful for your security."

When it had been tallied he asked almost apologetically, "Would you care to check my figures?"

Outlaw

I smiled, most lords could not read, my dead brothers could not but my grandmother had taught me when I was a child. "Yes, I can read it, Reuben." I scanned the lists and nodded.

He melted some wax, impressed his ring upon it and then wrote his name next to it. I was grateful that I had had a ring made by Ralph my smith. It was a little crudely fashioned but I liked the horse symbol upon it as that had been Harold's sign. When Reuben had melted the wax I made my mark and then wrote my name next to it. Reuben beamed when that was completed and he poured us a drink. That was the first time I had drunk from a glass vessel and it made the drink taste like nectar. Nor had I ever drunk such a fine drink. "This is delightful. What do you call it?"

He shrugged, "It is a wine fortified with spirits. One of my kin brings it from the Country of Portugal in Leon. It is only since the Moors were expelled that we have been able to import it. It is fine is it not?"

I smacked my lips. "It is indeed. So your people are all over the world then?"

"We are a people who lost our homeland many years ago and were doomed to travel but we still keep contact with each other. Wherever you wish to go, Byzantium, Normandy, anywhere, you can access your money."

I was more intrigued than anything, "How does that work?"

"I will give you a piece of paper which you can exchange with any of my brethren and they will give you that amount in the coin of the land." I must have looked dubious for he smiled. "Ask your uncle for he brought just such a document from Constantinople and I gave him the money myself."

"How do I know who to ask?"

"My people live in small areas, we call them ghettoes. You say you are a client of Reuben of Jorvik and they will direct you." It seemed such a simple system and yet I still worried. However, if Aethelward vouched for him I would continue to trust him. After I had said goodbye I left with Branton. "Is there aught we require from the city Branton? I am not sure when we will return."

He laughed, "Before I came to Topcliffe I would have said ale but Goody Sarah makes the best ale I have ever drunk so there is nought. As long as Ralph had the metal for my new arrows I will be happy."

The ride home was pleasant as Branton animatedly described his new arrows. Ralph had made him six to practise with and the results had been excellent. They were still refining and improving but, Branton was certain that when the Normans did arrive they would have a shock coming in the form of a slim but deadly missile.

Gytha took the news of my departure remarkably well. The baby was becoming larger and she was preoccupied with herself and the Queen. The Queen, for her part, enjoyed mothering my wife and Sarah, of course, delighted in waiting on them both. We left before dawn just in case anyone was watching the manor. Ridley and his men had augmented the garrison and Osbert would set them to work improving my defences. It seemed a long time since I had ridden with my uncle but old memories flooded back as well as the knowledge that this might be our last trip together. All of that put my injured back into perspective and I was able to ignore the pain as I talked with Aethelward and Branton about warriors, armour and what the future held. My competent sergeant of archers had two of his men half a mile ahead of us to warn of danger whilst the other two were half a mile behind. It made for a most enjoyable ride.

We halted, the first night at Dunelm which had accommodation, and protection for the Cathedral there attracted many pilgrims who wished to visit the shrine of Saint Cuthbert. "This would make a fine castle nephew."

I had to admit that he was right for the steep hill was surrounded, almost completely by a river. I idly wondered why no one had done so before but then the Scots had always raided down this valley and I wondered if that was the reason. Certainly, this would be our last night in England for on the morrow we would be in the borderlands and we would need our wits about us.

We met our first Scotsman the next day when we were close to the Holy Island of Lindisfarne. He was a herder and, with his son was driving a small herd of shaggy beasts with wicked looking horns to Dunelm. He looked at us suspiciously, especially as we wore helms and carried swords. Had we been rustlers we could

Outlaw

easily have killed the two of them and taken their cattle but Aethelward smiled and put them at their ease.

"Good day to you. Heading south are you?"

We could understand his words as they sounded a little similar but we had to work at it. "Aye, sir. Down to Dunelm." He tapped his nose. "Get a wee bit more for them there. The pilgrims and the churchmen ye nah."

We laughed. "Wise man. We are seeking Berwick. Can we get there today or should we stay at the Holy Island."

He looked at the sky and then our horses. "Aye, ye could, mind ye'll have to get a move on."

"Thank you for that."

We were about to go when he suddenly said, "I'd gan canny bonnie lads for the King is there and his men may tek exception to yon swords and helms."

Aethelward smiled. "Thanks for the warning but I know the King and I think he will make us welcome."

As we kicked on I thought about Aethelward. He had been a friend of the King of England. He had served the only King of Wales and now he knew the King of Scotland. I asked him about this Malcolm Canmore.

"When I was a Thingman he was at Edward's court for he was driven from his land after his father's death."

"Some say that he betrayed the loyalty he owed England when he invaded the north and supported Tostig."

Aethelward nodded. "Yes there were some but remember a king is not as ordinary men. He lived in a difficult time with Macbeth claiming his land and Macbeth was a good king, at least for a while. I do not blame Malcolm for claiming the land north of Berwick; he owed his people that security and I do not blame him for trying to capture the land to the Tees. It is what I would do if I were king."

"But Harold did not try to take Wales when we defeated Gryffydd?"

He smiled, "No for he was not yet king. But believe me, if the Normans had not come and he was secure then Wales would have been added to England." He shrugged. "It is power, it breeds the need for more power and in the language of kings that means more land."

"Edward did not seek more land."

"No, and that is why, although he was a kindly king he was not a good king. You need a king who can be ruthless and single-minded. I fancy Duke William to be such a man."

I gave him what I thought of as my shrewd look. "Don't tell me you knew him too?"

He laughed and he was the easy-going uncle who had first taken me in hand. "No, but I met him."

"What is he like?"

"He looks more like a brawler than a warrior. He is not tall but he is broad and he follows no rules of honour. He is, however, a strategos which is how he beat Harold at Senlac for he saw the weakness, the fyrd, and exploited it." He suddenly stiffened. "We are being watched."

Branton whistled and the four archers rejoined us. "Where my lord?" Even though Branton could not see the watchers he had served with Aethelward enough to respect his senses.

Aethelward looked to the hillside to our left where there was a stand of trees. "There on the hillside."

I stared as did Branton and at first could see nothing and then I saw a flash of flesh which indicated a hand. "I see them, uncle."

"Keep your hands from your weapons. Had they wished it they could have taken us any time. For the moment keep an eye on them but do not do anything. This means that we are close to the Scottish camp."

I suddenly realised that we must have crossed the border and we were in Scotland. I hoped that my uncle was right and Malcolm would remember us or my money would have to be spent on my ransom! It was a nerve-wracking ride as we headed north and the sunset slowly to our left. The short winter days mean that it would soon be icy cold and I wondered how we would fare when we reached their camp. We came around a sharp corner in the rough road and there was a party of warriors with spears levelled. Aethelward spread his arms in a sign of peace and we all did the same. Although the spears remained pointed at us they were lowered.

Outlaw

A huge warrior, dressed like a Housecarl came towards us. "I am Ross, what is your business Englishman in this land of Scotland."

"I come from Ealdgyth, the Queen of England, with a message for King Malcolm."

With a nod, Ross ordered his men to lower their weapons and led us down the track to the walled enclosure that was some way off. "You were lucky you did not arrive after dark for then my men would have attacked first and asked questions later."

"Aye, I know but our mission is urgent and we have had to take risks. These are parlous times."

"Aye, they are that." He looked up at my uncle. "You are Aethelward are you not? The Varangian?"

"I was a Varangian Guard but now I serve the Queen. And this is Aelfraed. Lord of Topcliffe."

He looked at me with new respect. "The hero of Fulford I hear and the man who killed the Welsh champion." I nodded, "Tell me, my lord, why you were not at Senlac with the other Housecarls?"

I forced myself to keep calm for I knew my temper and I suspected that Ross meant no insult but I was insulted. "I received a bad wound at Stamford and I could not move or else I would have died with my oath brothers."

"I meant no offence and I did not know of your wound. We just heard that you and your army slew the Vikings."

"We did."

"And for that, we thank you for they are a curse."

We had reached the camp of King Malcolm of Scotland. We were watched and guarded as we entered his fortified town and the gates slammed ominously shut behind us. I noticed that Branton and the archers looked quite nervous and, perversely, that made me feel better for Aethelward looked like calmness personified.

We dismounted. Ross pointed to a rough building some way off. "Your men can stable their horses and sleep there."

Branton looked at me and I nodded, I hoped they would be fed but Branton was resourceful enough and charming enough to be able to get food for him and his men. I could see a devious mind at work here for my uncle and myself were separated from our men. Should they wish harm to befall us we would not represent too much of a problem. I had learned that the laws of hospitality did not always apply to kings. As we were led to the main hall I suddenly remembered the two Scottish killers who had tried to kill King Edward. How much of that did King Malcolm know? We laid our weapons on a table at the entrance to the hall. I had only brought a sword leaving Boar Splitter and Death Bringer at my hall-I could not see me standing in a shield wall up here in Scotland.

The King was seated on a modest throne on a raised dais. He had four burly bodyguards, armed with axes around him and he watched us warily. He had eyes that seemed to bore into you. He was far more silent than either of the other kings I had met and he seemed to be weighing you up and assessing you. We both bowed and Aethelward began, "Your majesty I come bearing messages from the widow of the King of England, Queen Ealdgyth."

"Rise Lord Aethelward for I remember you and your kindness when we were at Winchester." He suddenly turned to me. "And this is Harold's bastard is it, Aelfraed? And would you be king?"

I was shocked at the abrupt nature of the comment. It had never occurred to me that I might become king. I raised my head and met his stare. "My only wish, your majesty, is to serve my Queen and defend my land from invaders."

He laughed and it took me by surprise. "I can see Aethelward that you have raised your nephew to be like you. He has a quick mind and an even quicker tongue. For tonight we will eat and feast and you can talk of your embassy on the morrow. Come, Aethelward sit on my right and Aelfraed on my left."

He led us to the table and I felt the stares of the warriors around me but even more acutely I could feel Aethelward's stare for we had not had time to talk about this situation. We had assumed that we would make our plea and have an answer. This Malcolm was clever and devious and I resolved to drink little. The King sat and we followed. He leaned over to me. "Excuse the stares of my men Aelfraed but your reputation precedes you. They see in you a little of my predecessor, Macbeth, who like you was a formidable warrior. I think some of them would like to try your skills."

"I came unprepared for combat your majesty for this is a peaceful embassy but I am sure that if your majesty invites me back and I am not fighting Normans then I could oblige them."

Outlaw

He slapped my back. "Excellent. If we have time we shall do so at Midsummer."

I saw my uncle's eyes pleading with me to be silent and listen and I nodded. He immediately engaged the King in conversation and I resolved to listen more than I would speak. The man opposite kept staring at me, even more than the others. It began to put me off my food for he ate little and kept staring. Did he wish to fight with me? I could see now that a warrior's reputation could be something to regret rather than celebrate if every warrior thought he could defeat you. Eventually, I put down my knife and stared back at him.

He must have realised that he had been staring for he suddenly grinned and said, "I am sorry my lord for staring. It was rude of me."

I relaxed a little, his smile had disarmed me. "I was beginning to worry that I had grown horns."

"No my lord it is just that I owe you a debt."

I was puzzled. I had never seen this young man before. "Me? But I have never met you before."

"I am sorry my lord, I am being rude and ill-mannered tonight. I am Calum, Thegn of Fife and you are right we have never met but you killed my father's murderers." I must have shown the confusion in my face for he went on, "The two men who tried to kill your king had murdered my father and were outlaws. It is why they were hired for had they been in Scotland we would have killed them but you did what we could not and for that, I am in your debt and if there is anything I can ever do for you, then just ask."

"I killed them because they were trying to kill my king but I am pleased for the information you have given me for it puts my mind at rest." I could see that he did not know to what I was referring but I now knew that Malcolm had had nothing to do with the attempt and I began to relax more. "Why did they kill your father?"

"They had been his warriors and when he punished them for raping some women on the estate they killed him and fled."

I was silent. That said much for the young man's father for you had to know your men well if you were to fight with them in a shield wall. He had obviously made bad choices. "Tell me, my lord, do you fight and train with your men?"

He looked puzzled. "Why would I do that?"

"When you lead your men into battle you need to know that they will protect your back and the only way to do that is to train with them and fight with them so that you know their strength and weaknesses."

"I had not thought of that but here we have had no major wars and battles since Macbeth was deposed." He looked a little embarrassed. "I am experienced at border raids."

I laughed. "Do not despise that for it is good training. But if I may give you some advice Calum I would spend a couple of hours each day with your men at arms. When the day comes for you to fight with them you will see the difference and you will have more chance of surviving."

I suddenly noticed that the table was silent and all, including the king, were listening to me. King Malcolm nodded, "I can see now Aelfraed the Bastard that your reputation is deserved. I wondered how one so young could have achieved such fame. Those are good ideas and from the silence around the table I can see that many of my lords are listening." The rest of the evening was spent with me answering questions about the battles in which I had fought and my men. I could feel my uncle's stare and I was glad that I had taken no ale for I thought about each word before it slipped from my tongue.

At the end of the feast, Ross escorted us to a small chamber at the end of the hall, close to the guard room. It showed that whilst we were being honoured, we were being watched. Once in the room, my uncle spoke quietly to me. "That was well done Aelfraed. The King is a careful man. He wished to hear us make a slip in our cups and divulge information that he could use. You did well and I am pleased that you have impressed them for that may help us in the future. This may end the way we wish it to."

The next day we were taken to meet the King along with Ross who was obviously his lieutenant. "Firstly Lord Aethelward I have to tell you that I have no intention of fighting the Normans. If that is your embassy then this will be a short meeting."

"No your majesty, we will fight our own battles. There was an attempt on the life of the Queen and she fears that with the unrest in the country, she and her children are at risk. She would seek sanctuary with you much as you sought it with the Confessor."

Malcolm rarely showed what he was thinking but I detected relief upon his face. "It is our Christian duty to aid our sister. Is that it? Is that all that she requests?"

"It is…"

"Except," Aethelward shot me an irritated look, "I would ask, your majesty, if my wife and unborn child could also be housed with the Queen for I fear for her safety too."

"That will be an honour Lord Aelfraed if only for your illuminating lecture last night." In honour of our visit, the king presented us both with a pair of daggers. The steel was from Toledo and the handles were carved from bone and inlaid with silver. "Take these as a symbol of the love and respect we have for two warriors but this is the only armed aid we can provide."

"Your majesty, this is more than enough."

As we headed south Aethelward called Branton over. "Well Branton, what did you discover?"

"They are waiting to see what happens with the Normans, my lord. There are armed camps all along the border. If Duke William succeeds in England and tries to come North they will repel him and if not then their king will see what he can steal from England."

Aethelward had obviously briefed Branton to be a spy. "Well, uncle it confirms what you said, with the Queen in his court he has a hostage."

"Hostage, guest, the terms are interchangeable. It is what we do in the field which will determine the outcome of this war not where the Queen is. I would rather her in Scotland and safe than in England and at risk. This way we will not worry about our women and we can fight harder."

Chapter 3

March 1067 Topcliffe

Christmas had not been the joyous time we had hoped. William was crowned and he showed his political acumen by restoring the lands of Edwin and Morcar to those two earls and giving Edgar the Aetheling large tracts of land in the south. If it had not been for the indefatigable Queen then we would have all been down at heart but the news from Scotland had heartened her as she now had a sanctuary and she was the reason we survived the dark times of midwinter. Gytha's pregnancy was not going well and it took all my patience to control my tongue as she lambasted all bar the Queen. Poor Sarah could not do right and I for one was glad when, as the first flowers of spring thrust their heads through the icy ground my son began his journey of life. The Queen and Sarah dismissed me, along with the other men so that they could concentrate upon the task in hand. Ridley came over as soon as he knew and it felt good to have my oldest friend with me on that momentous day.

When Harold was born I finally realised that my responsibilities had doubled. I now had a wife and two estates to care for in addition to all my warriors. The child was my future and he suddenly dominated my life. The walls of my castle which had seemed so secure now felt perilously thin and the news of their uncle's submission to the Normans made our place in the land even more perilous.

Aethelward and my men insisted on the ceremony of wetting the baby's head. This was a simple enough process, it meant drinking as much ale and wine as we had and telling each other how great we were as warriors and how powerful Harold would be. Before I became totally inebriated we managed to have a serious conversation about the future.

"We could fight for this land!"

"Yes Aelfraed, if we had the support of all the lords but the Earl's defection has thwarted us. I have spoken with the lords hereabouts and we can only count on a thousand men at most and of those, it is your men and Ridley's who would be the shield wall. Less than one hundred could not stand up to the Normans when they come. We will have to hope that the Earls change their mind. Now that William has returned to Normandy there may be some hope." None of us could actually call the Norman, King as though by not naming him it would make his state untrue.

"So you would have us submit to William?"

Aethelward had looked at me sadly. "It is not even as easy as that. Ridley could submit but you are the bastard son of Harold. You are the hero of Fulford and Rhuddlan. You are a threat to William. Add to that the strategic nature of this place and you can see that William would have to put one of his own men in place here."

At that point, Ridley had looked appalled. "If Aelfraed is thrown off his land I would join him."

"Think about your people both of you. If you fight then your people would suffer. Do you want that Ridley?"

He was silent; torn between his duty as a lord and his duty as a friend. Osbert swallowed off his ale and said flatly. "I care not, I will follow my lord to the gates of hell if needs be. I am his man and I think most of the others would feel the same too." Branton and the others had banged their beakers in agreement and as tears filled my eyes we had drunk ourselves into oblivion.

By the time that summer arrived the three children of the house were a noisy distraction. The twins, Harold and Ulf had begun toddling and managed to find every nook and cranny which they could. They were both fascinated by my Harold who seemed a placid enough baby. He looked to have more of his mother about him than of me and I did not mind for I had always thought of myself as unattractive. I had never seen my face save reflected in someone's shiny shield but it was an impression I had of myself. I was content with the way things were. The early summer was, however, spoiled by Aethelward's illness. He began coughing, not uncommon in the wet spring but Sarah confided in me that she had seen blood mixed with the sputum. My uncle laughed it off and he recovered but it was the first sign of his decline.

When we heard that Edwin, Earl of Mercia was to marry one of William's daughters then we knew that there would be no revolt. Despite the unrest in Hereford and Exeter the Normans had just taken over. We knew that was largely because there were no leaders south of Mercia, they had all died at Senlac Hill and we deluded ourselves that William had not come north because there were leaders and he feared them. That was arrogant and we were wrong. It did, however, make the Queen's mind up. Word had got out that she was in Topcliffe and Branton's scouts had reported many spies in the hills.

One morning she came to speak with Aethelward and me. "I will take Malcolm up on his offer of sanctuary. You are sure you can trust him?"

"I believe he is an honourable man and it is in his interests to keep you safe."

"Then I will go in high summer." She turned to me. "I will miss Gytha and yourself Aelfraed; you have shown true generosity and I can see your father's nobility in every inch of you. I hope that my sons turn out as fine as you."

I was touched. "Majesty I would not separate Gytha from your side. The King has said that he will shelter my lady and I will feel happier if she is there when the storm breaks."

"You believe that the storm will break?"

"My uncle does and he is rarely wrong. I believe it too and this land will not be safe when William does come north."

"Does Gytha know of this?"

"Not yet." I hung my head. "I fear no man in battle but I dare not broach this with my wife. Does that make me weak?"

"No Aelfraed, that makes you a man. I will speak with her."

I thank the lord for the Queen. She had a charm about her that took one's breath away. Gytha could not say no and by midsummer, we set off north. I took Branton again for Osbert would be needed to defend the manor. Ridley promised to watch over my estates as well. In truth, we were doing well. The crops and animals had done well and I had taken a great deal of coin to Reuben the Jew. If it was not for the spectre of William looming over us life would have been good. I now had forty men at arms and I took five of them with us for we had the Queen. Our progress was slower than it had been and it took us six days to reach Eidyn Dun where the King was spending the summer. This time we had no trouble for his lords were expecting us and they cheerfully escorted us the last few miles to the new hall the king was having built on top of Arthur's seat.

When he met the Queen he was as gallant as any man wooing a woman. He had no wife and I idly wondered if this could be a union that might turn out well for England. If the King of Scotland married the Queen of England then they would be a powerful force to face the Normans. There may have been political will for such a union but there was neither spark nor emotion and they just became good friends. Aethelward and I had intended to return swiftly south but Ross and the King reminded me that I had promised I would try out a few bouts with some of his eager warriors. I regretted that promise but I could not renege and we stayed for a month. Luckily this allowed me to prepare for combat. I had not fought for almost a year since I had been wounded and training was not the same as a bout. I wished that Ridley was there for I had always trained with him. Nor was Osbert available and I had to use my men at arms. They meant well but they were, in truth, in awe of me firstly as their lord and secondly as a renowned warrior. I did not improve my skills but I did manage to become fitter. I just hoped that the muscles would remember what they ought to do when I faced one of these Scotsmen, all of whom looked like giants.

I had never fought for exhibition and I asked Aethelward about it. "You use swords and shields but the swords are blunted. There is a master of ceremonies who determines when to stop the combat for no-one is supposed to die."

I became worried. "Do they die?"

A cloud appeared over his face. "Men have been wounded in these combats when the combatants become too excited. I would finish it early if you can."

As Branton helped me to dress I confess that I was feeling quite nervous. I should have remembered my promised and tried my arm against Osbert who would have given me a better assessment of my fitness for combat. Now it was too late. What exacerbated the situation was the fact that Malcolm had deemed our combat to be the highlight of the games and I had to sit, along with the King, Ealdgyth and Gytha to watch the other events. I had no opportunity to practise. The games themselves would have been interesting had

Outlaw

I not had this gnawing feeling in the pit of my stomach and a sudden ached down the scar which ran along my back. There were wrestling bouts, warriors threw hammers, warriors danced across razor sharp swords and two teams of warriors engaged in a tug of war across a pit of fire. All of it passed before me in an annoying blur as I wondered who I would fight.

As the last of the defeated tug of war team rid themselves of the last sparks from the fire Malcolm turned to me. "Now my Saxon friend, it is time for you to finish the show."

"And whom do I fight?"

The grin he gave me was that of the wolf. "It is Duff; a warrior from the highlands. He is the chief of a tribe and he has fought many Vikings from Orkney. He is a fierce warrior."

As I stepped down I saw Aethelward give me a confident nod. He did not look worried but then he did not have to face this warrior who had never been defeated. Branton was waiting with my shield and the sword I was to use. It was not as balanced as mine own but it was not as heavy as I had expected. At least I had my own shield and I knew that to be strong. Branton had my cap which went beneath my helmet and he made sure that it fitted snugly before encasing my head in the helmet Ralph had made for me. I had never seen such a fine helmet on any field of battle and he had added a small spike at the top in which we could place a feather to mark me in battle. We had done so after Stamford but I had yet to fight a battle using the identifying feather. Finally, he held my gauntlets and I was ready.

The sound of horns told us that it was time to enter the arena. "Good luck my lord but you do not need luck for you will beat him."

He like Aethelward looked confident but I was not. When I stood before the King and the other lords I glanced to my right and saw that the warrior I was to fight was a whole head taller than me and I am not a small man. He had the shoulders of Ridley and I felt a sickening feeling in the pit of my stomach. The King just said, "Finally we have a contest between a champion of the Saxons and one from the Highlands. May the better warrior win."

I turned to face Duff. He had teeth missing so that when he grinned at me it was like looking into a rock-filled cave. "And

Outlaw

dinna fret wee man, the better man will win and you'll be on your arse before too long."

It seems strange now but it was in that moment of arrogance and pride from Duff that I knew I would win for he was one man and I knew that I could beat any warrior one on one, the secret was finding his weakness. He swung his sword above his head and I could see that he had a longer reach than me which meant I had to get in close. I remembered the words of Aethelward, finish it quickly and I determined to do just that. Suddenly he swung his sword all the way from his back to crash down on my shield. Had it been another shield it would have shattered and I think he thought so too for, as the sword slid off the metal discs, he looked surprised and then annoyed. I wondered how strong his shield was if he had won his other combats by breaking his opponent's shields with his first blow? I swung my sword sideways at his shield for his move had been risky. I connected well and saw a sliver of wood slice off and he stepped back a little. With a roar, he swung overhand again and this time I stepped inside his swing and punched upwards catching his sword hand with the boss of my shield. The blow did not connect and he stepped backwards, warier now. His eyes narrowed and I could see him assessing my strengths and weaknesses. The crowd, too, had quietened and I suspect that many of the Scots had seen him fight before and had expected an easy, early victory.

He circled me and began to use his longer reach. The problem was he could not strike me hard enough at that range but I too was feeling the effects of my first combat as muscles began to ache as did the wound on my back. As he swung at me I stepped inside and hit against his knee; his extra height made it easier for me to strike below his shield and he roared back in anger. The sword was not edged but he had been hit by an iron bar and it had hurt. He now swung, in a fit of anger fuelled by rage, at my head. I just ducked and punched again with the boss of my shield. As he stepped back I punched at his shield with the fist, wrapped around the pommel of my sword. The two blows took him by surprise and he fell backwards. As he tumbled I pulled my sword back and smashed down at his head. He was good and, for a big man, had quick reactions; he protected himself with his shield. This time it was a sliver of wood which fell from it but a chip and a crack appeared. He rolled to the side and leapt to his feet. He now knew he had a contest and I could see that he was going to finish it quickly. His eyes narrowed and he grinned; once more I looked into the rocky cave. He pulled his sword back to swing for my head and once again I stepped inside with my shield to punch him but it was a trap. The sword did not come down but he enfolded me with his arms.

"Got you now you scraggy wee shit!"

He pulled his head back and I knew he was going to head butt me, I had used the tactic myself but what he had forgotten was his height and I put my head forwards so that he connected not with my nose but the top of my helmet. The spike Ralph had fitted on the top was no bigger than a thumbnail but it was enough to pierce his eye socket and as he roared back screaming, with blood pouring from his wound I saw the remains of his eye drip to the ground. The warrior charged with supervising the contest raced in to prevent me from continuing, not that I would have done so and the crowd remained silent. Suddenly I heard clapping, a single pair of hands and saw the King, on his feet applauding. Next to him with shocked expressions were my wife and the Queen while Aethelward and Branton smiled and nodded. The King's applause signalled the crowd that they too could show their feelings and they began to shout and cheer, the warriors banging their shields.

I felt a movement behind me and turned to see Duff lurch towards me his hand covering the mess which had been his eye. I was on guard for I knew not what he intended. To my immense relief, I saw him grin and hold out his right hand. "Not such a scraggy wee shit eh wee man? I can see that your reputation is deserved and I will have to ask you about your weapons when we have the chance."

"You are a brave and fearsome warrior. I was lucky."

He shook his head. "No, for if we had had blades with edges I would have been dead long before the end."

As he was led away Gytha and Branton raced over. "Aelfraed I was so scared. I thought he was going to kill you." As Gytha hugged and kissed me I felt her body shake with emotion. "Had I know that this was what combat was like I would never let you go to war."

Branton removed my helmet. "Nice move my lord, I will get Ralph to put one of these on my helmet eh?"

When Malcolm arrived I bowed my head slightly and said, "I am sorry your majesty, I did not mean to wound your warrior."

He looked puzzled. "He was engaged in combat as you were; he will not mind and he will bear his scars with honour and tell the tale of his combat with the English hero."

I suppose that was the difference between me and Duff for I would have been annoyed to be wounded in an exhibition; combat is a serious business. I was, at least, happy that I had not lost the ability to fight. Gytha led me to our quarters with a protective arm around my shoulders and tears of relief still coursed down her cheeks. I was glad that she had not seen a real battle that would have reduced her to a quivering wreck. She continued to fuss and mother me as she dressed me for the feast. "You must look your best tonight for everyone wishes to speak with you." I say dressed me but it was more a case of her choosing my clothes and then adjusting them to create the best effect. For me, I could have worn anything so long as it was comfortable.

The feast was magnificent as it marked the end of the summer games and also the arrival of the Queen of England. It was not only the lords who were intrigued and fascinated by their English visitors but the lord's ladies were keen to speak with the woman who had been married to two kings. I was on the King's left side with Gytha between us whilst the Queen and Aethelward were to his right. It meant that I had no opportunity to speak with my uncle but in truth, I would have had no opportunity to do so as I was inundated with questions from the other warriors. They were intrigued by my shield and when I told them that it was the first thing I had made when I became a Housecarl they became even more enthusiastic. All of them wished to see my helmet closer up and all of them regretted that I had not brought Boar Splitter, my spear and Death Bringer, my axe. Their eyes lit up when I told them of the forging of the spear and the mixing of the metal with my blood and with the stories of my two weapons. Gytha too was entranced as she had never heard the stories. The evening ended perfectly when a minstrel sang the song of Aelfraed and Duff the one eye. I think Duff was even more pleased with his fame and he stood to take bows at the end, his head and eye still heavily bandaged.

After the feast when we sat before the roaring fire, for the midsummer nights were colder in the north, Calum, Lord of Fife, joined us. His eyes were aglow as he effusively praised me and my skills. Gytha and the Queen were quite taken with the Scottish lord and he told them of our connection. Both women were intrigued by the strange connection. Ealdgyth nodded at the end, "It is *wyrd*. Your life is being shaped, Aelfraed, by powers beyond this world."

"I believe that my mother and grandmother watch over me and protect me."

"No there is more to it than this. You are the thread which joins your uncle to me, to the Lord of Fife and to Harold. The Danes have beings they call the Norns who spin webs around men's lives. I can see their hand in this."

"Is it good or evil your majesty?"

"It is *wyrd* and that can be good and evil at the same time. When my first husband was killed, that was bad for him but good for Harold and for me."

Calum suddenly looked embarrassed. "Your majesty, my lady, I too believe that this is *wyrd* for I have wanted to find a way to repay Lord Aelfraed and now I believe I can. The King has offered you his protection and I would like to do the same. I have spoken with him and my castle, which is across the estuary, is even safer than the half-built castle of the King. I would be honoured if you would allow me to offer you my protection."

Aethelward turned to Malcolm. "How does your majesty view this?"

"It is a good thing Aethelward for I know that the ladies will be safe and I can concentrate upon defending my kingdom for we have heard that the King of the Danes is beginning to look across the waters."

Aethelward became interested. "He claims the English throne through Cnut and he is a powerful King." He looked first at the Queen and then at me. "I believe that it is safer for you to be in

Fife which is further from the Danes and the Normans majesty but it is, of course, not my decision."

"We would always take your advice Aethelward for it is always wise and well thought out."

Gytha looked to me and I nodded. "Thank you, my lord and the debt which I did not think you owed me is now paid." I was pleased for it meant that my wife and child would be safe. I had doubted that the King would be able to give the two women his full attention but the Lord of Fife was keen to build up his lands and would stay closer to home. As it turned out this was *wyrd*, and the Queen was right for both good and evil came from it.

Although I was not eager to leave my wife and the Queen the news of the Danish King worried both of us and we bade farewell to our hosts. Whilst we were sad to be leaving I was happy that we had, at least, made friends. We had somewhere safe should the Normans or the Danes make life unpleasant for us. I suspected that the good times were over and I wanted to be as prepared as we could be.

The return journey was swift without the women and their baggage. Once we reached Topcliffe I could see that they had worked hard during our absence. The men were drilling in the courtyard and there were more towers around the wooden walls. I was also relieved to see no sign of Normans. I had seen some of the early crops being harvested and knew that Thomas, my steward, had also played his part. During the journey back from Scotland we had discussed visiting Edwin and Morcar to determine their plans. I was all in favour but Aethelward was not. Eventually, I persuaded him that we needed firm information for up to now it was hearsay and conjecture. They had both submitted to William but we did not know what pressure had been applied. When we heard that he had returned to Jorvik it made our decision simple and, together with Ridley, Osbert and my men at arms we descended upon the city. Aethelward had insisted upon a show of force and, as we rode south he kept a wary eye out for ambushes. "I know you like Morcar, nephew but he has been under the influence of his brother and Edwin has always been an astute politician. We need to tread warily. I want the Earl to be under no illusion; you and your men at arms are the most formidable force in this part of the world. The Earl cannot muster as many hardened warriors as you possess. I hope that their presence may inject a little iron into his backbone."

He was right of course. I did like Morcar but I had been disappointed when he had deserted us at Fulford and so many men had died needlessly. What depressed me the most was that without a figurehead like Morcar, Earl of Northumbria I could not see how we could fight the invaders. Thankfully we had heard that William was still in Normandy dealing with rebels there and it was Odo who was ruling in his name. The North seemed to have escaped his notice but he would, eventually, realise its potential. The excuse we were going to give for our visit was the news of Sweyn, the King of the Danes and his intentions. We attracted attention as we rode through the gates of the city. The red horse on our shields was recognised and I was pleased with the smiles and the occasional cheers we received. What none of us was happy about was the sight of kite shields for that meant only one thing, Normans. They had reached Jorvik, and all of us kept our hands on our swords as we rode up to Morcar's hall.

We were too many men to be housed safely in the hall and Osbert sent his men at arms along with Ridley's to the warrior hall whilst the four of us went to speak with the Earl. I noticed some embarrassed and some furtive looks from the guards who admitted us. Some of them were known to us from Fulford and Stamford but none of the ones we saw had covered themselves in glory. I had to keep an eye on Osbert for he was itching for one of them to say something so that he could start a fight. The behaviour of the Earl's men at Fulford still rankled with him and the loss of Aedgart at Stamford meant he resented those who had cowered behind Jorvik's walls while brave men had died. I leaned in to speak quietly to him, "Osbert hold that temper of yours in check or you can join the other men at arms."

"Sorry my lord, I forget myself."

Morcar had aged a little in the year since we had seen him. He had put on weight and was developing multiple chins. It showed that he had let himself go and not trained as a warrior. It was a mark of the man, demonstrating his brother's influence. "Lord

Outlaw

Aethelward, Aelfraed, Ridley. It is good to see you. It has been too long." He embraced each of us. "How is my sister?"

"You are now an uncle my lord, Harold."

I detected the hint of a frown but he quickly hid it. "It is good to have old friends to visit us and what brings you here."

It was strange that he should ask that for we were the leading Thegns in the Earldom but I let it pass. Aethelward began to tell him of the danger from King Sweyn whilst I scanned the room. There were too many unfamiliar faces for my liking and the three Normans who hovered behind his chair were distinctly sinister and they eyed us equally suspiciously. When Aethelward had finished I could see that Morcar was worried. His eastern coast was the closest point for the Danes if they chose to invade and he remembered Hadrada and the drubbing he had given them.

"This is serious news." He turned to one of the Normans. "You will need to tell the king this news, Lord William."

The young knight sneered. He spoke English but it was heavily accented. "The King does not fear these Danes. We have beaten them before and we shall beat them again and we would not fear a naked man with an axe."

The smile told us that the insult was intended and a reminder of the brave berserkers who had held us up at the bridge. I felt Osbert and Ridley stiffen and I restrained both of them. "I am sorry my lord you have the advantage of us."

He turned to face me and when I saw his arrogant and superior look I knew that I did not like him. "I am William of Perci."

"Well, William of Perci. I do not consider myself a coward and yet when I faced those berserkers at Stamford Bridge then I feared him as any warrior who faced an enemy that unafraid of dying. Or are you not afraid of death?"

He looked confused. "Why should I die? I am a Norman knight and no man is my equal."

Aethelward spoke. "I heard that Harold's Housecarls slaughtered many Norman knights at Senlac Hill which means they were your equal for they were outnumbered and still held off many charges."

His hand went to his sword and Morcar nervously interrupted. "Come let us not rake over old wounds. Not with Danes on the horizon. Take your hands from your swords I command it."

Outlaw

He sounded like a petulant child and I smiled and spread my arms. "It is not we who have our hands on our weapons, my lord, for we understand the laws of hospitality. Perhaps Norman knights are not taught such manners."

William reddened and, without bowing to the Earl, stormed out, followed by his countrymen. His lack of respect for the Earl worried me as did his presence. Morcar looked at the door ruefully. "Well, that could have gone better."

Aethelward looked at the courtiers and then back at Morcar. Morcar was many things but stupid and slow were not characteristics of that Earl and he waved away his courtiers. "Osbert, guard the door."

Earl Morcar looked worried. I smiled. "Your life is not in danger brother but we would not be surprised or overheard."

Relieved he relaxed in his chair as Aethelward leaned forwards. "Why did you and your brother submit?"

He looked shocked. "A little blunt Aethelward."

"But understandable, yes?"

He inclined his head. "There was no support for a rebellion and we thought to bide our time. You and your Thegns are the only opposition to the Normans."

"I hear Harold's mother in Exeter and the rebels at Hereford would disagree with you."

"They are little more than armed mobs. They cannot stand up to cavalry." Now we had it, they did not fight because they thought they would lose.

I stared into his eyes looking for a lie. "And did you have aught to do with the attempt on the Queen's life?"

As I said Morcar was generally an honest man and the look of surprise and shock on his face convinced me that he was speaking the truth. "Someone tried to kill the Queen? When? Where?"

"Here, last year."

He sagged back into his seat. "I did not know. I had nothing to do with it I promise you."

"I believe you. The question is what can we do now and what are the Normans doing here?"

He looked uncomfortable and squirmed a little in his seat. "The King sent them here to ensure my safety."

Outlaw

Aethelward looked as shocked as I had ever seen him. "Protection? From your own people?"

"I know." He paused and looked at the ceiling. "I think they are my guards. Edwin has some with him and Edgar others. The King does not trust us."

There was an uncomfortable silence in the room. Aethelward sat on the other chair close to Morcar's. "Then my lord you have a choice. Continue to be the prisoner of William and enjoy your empty title or join with us and throw off the shackles."

It was then that I realised that he was afraid. He had not had the success in war and battle that Ridley and I had enjoyed. To him, war meant humiliation and retreat. He did not think we could win and could not be the figurehead we wanted. I suspected that the same was true of his brother and as Edgar was still barely a man we were no better off. I caught my uncle's eye and nodded towards the door.

"Well my lord we will take our leave. What do you intend to do about the Danes?"

His voice sounded dull and without life, as though he knew that he would remain a prisoner, he was a bird in a gilded cage, but a cage nonetheless. "I will have men watch the coast and light beacons."

As we were leaving I turned and said, "Perhaps you might improve the defences of your city my lord eh?" He nodded but I am not certain he heard me.

Chapter 4

When we left the Earl we mounted our horses and rode to join our men. Ridley's sergeant at arms had been watching the gates and he sought out his lord as soon as he could. "My lord, not long after you entered the hall four Norman knights rode out of the gate and headed south."

"Good man. "

"Well, Aelfraed I think that confirms what we are all thinking. If there is to be any opposition to the Normans then it will come from us."

"I know Aethelward but we seem pitifully few in numbers."

He smiled, "Remember how three men held up the whole of Harold's army? An avalanched starts with just one rock, and we have three." He grinned at Ridley, some of them bigger than others."

Ridley took the ribbing in good part and while Aethelward went to speak to some of the older men he knew in Jorvik Ridley and I went to visit Reuben. Ridley had acquired money and wished to engage the services of the Jew. He had always been like that; he was a follower, like a younger brother always copying his sibling.

When we had conducted our business Reuben offered us more of his fortified wine. I looked around the room and noticed that he had invested in some fine furniture and objects. "Things must be going well Reuben. "

He spread his hands. "When there is war then merchants always make money. The crops in the south were poor last year because the men who would have tilled the fields lay dead with Harold. I was able to buy wheat in the north and sell it in the south for a great profit. There were other deals I did that increased not only my fortune my lord but yours. You now have even more gold."

"Gold will do me no good if the Normans return."

Reuben's eyes twinkled and he tapped his nose meaningfully. "Perhaps but with money, you can start again in another country and be a wealthy man."

"But this is my land and I am loath to leave it."

He suddenly became serious. "You may have to leave it, lord."

Outlaw

"Come, Reuben, no more games. Speak plainly and tell me the words that hide behind your dancing."

"People tell me things and I listen. There are six Norman knights in Jorvik.|"

"I saw only three and I thought they had left."

"Trust me my lord there are six. Their leader is William of Perci and I hear that the King has promised him land in the north."

I felt a chill creep down my neck. This was *wyrd*. I had a premonition of what was coming. "Where in the north?"

"Close to here my lord."

I swallowed the fiery yet wonderfully sweet liquor. "Topcliffe."

He nodded, and then looked at Ridley, "And Coxold and Medelai."

That was the first time I have ever seen someone's jaw drop in shock, but Ridley's did and it made me smile. "Thank you for that old friend. Let us say that we do lose our lands, although we would fight hard to retain them, then what would you suggest we do?"

"I am but an old Jew. I am no warrior. My people gave up fighting long ago and turned to trade. You ask, what I would do? I would leave now. I would take my money and find another home where I could buy safety."

"Where is such a place?"

"I believe you have friends in Scotland, my lord?"

I laughed. "Is there anything you do not know you old fox?"

"As I said, people tell me things."

I closed my eyes and tilted my head back. Reuben would make a fine chess player for he was always thinking moves ahead. Perhaps I should do the same. I sat forwards. "Could you arrange for some of my money to be made available in Scotland?"

"I will do so. My brother Jacob lives there close to the shrine of Saint Andrew."

I looked surprised, "A Jew near a Christian shrine?"

He rubbed his thumb and forefinger together. "Pilgrims have money…"

"Excellent then make it so."

"I would also suggest money in Constantinople and Paris. It will not affect how much you can have in Scotland but it means that you have more choices."

Later that evening, as we rode home, I compared notes with Aethelward and Osbert who had listened in the taverns and the alehouses. "Morcar will not fight until Edwin does and the Normans are coming north."

"Should we do as Reuben says and flee?"

Aethelward looked at me and I could hear Osbert and Ridley, holding their breath and listening for the answer. "If you flee you will not return."

"But why stay? There is no figurehead."

Aethelward halted his horse and stared at me. "Sometimes Aelfraed you surprise me with your naivety. You are the figurehead. You are the one who could unite the warriors."

"Me?" I turned to see Ridley and Osbert grinning and nodding. "I cannot see that."

"You are Harold's son. You are the only undefeated Saxon left alive and you have a reputation as a warrior. Men will follow you wherever you go."

I thought about his words and saw that they did make some sort of sense, no matter how incredible. "But Edgar, he is Harold's son too."

"He is no warrior and he has no reputation and besides that no-one knows him. When people mention your name then a host of stories flood out."

"Aye my lord. When I was in the tavern I heard how you defeated and blinded the Scottish champion Duff and five other warriors in single combat."

"But that is not true! Well, not all of it."

"We know that Aelfraed but they are desperate for a hero and, at the moment, you are he."

Over the next few weeks as we built up our pathetically small army I reflected on those words. My life had changed beyond all recognition in the last three years and I was not certain that I liked it. I yearned for those days before I had foiled an attempt on the King's life when Ridley and I were just Housecarls. Of course, I would be dead along with Wolf, Ulf and Osgar but now I had the weight of the world upon my shoulders, or at least, the weight of England. To take my mind off that I worked as hard as I had ever worked; either I was training with Osbert and my men at arms or I

Outlaw

was planning with Aethelward. Branton's arrows were now ready in large numbers and we had tried them out on dead pigs covered in mail- they worked! We had also recruited and trained more archers; Branton ensured that they could all ride. We would not be a static force facing the fearsome Normans – we too would be mobile. We still could not fight on horses as they did but we could move to and from any battlefield quickly. Gytha had sent a letter to me asking for Sarah. When I told Sarah she was torn between staying with her husband and looking after the child. Thomas persuaded her to go and, as she left with an escort of archers, he thanked me.

"Why are you thanking me old friend? I feel guilty for separating you and your wife."

He shook his head and his eyes filled. "We could not have children, my lord. *Wyrd*. But she dotes on you and the Lady Gytha. When Harold was born she was the happiest woman in the world and she missed them. She can now have the child that was denied her and," he wiped his eyes, "I fear that war will come here and despite all your efforts my lord, I can see a time when these walls will fall and there will death. In Scotland, she will be safe."

I was appalled. "Thomas, if you feel that way, join your wife. You have been a loyal servant and you can serve my wife still."

He stood stiffly. "My lord, I am your Steward and until you dismiss me I will still be your Steward and I will watch over Topcliffe and defend it with my life."

Not daring to speak I patted his arm and he walked back to his lists. This was what my title had brought us to. Doom and destruction; but if Thomas was willing to die for the land then so would I.

It seemed lonely that night as Aethelward and I ate a quiet meal without Sarah fussing over us and I told him what had transpired. He nodded as he gnawed on a pig bone. "It is as I said Aelfraed, you inspire loyalty."

"I will do as Thomas then and die defending Topcliffe."

He slammed the pig bone top the table and shouted. "You will not for this is just land and you are greater than a piece of land. I did not come back to train you just to die on a Norman lance for a few stones and a house."

Outlaw

"But if they come and we lose?"

"Then we move on and regroup and fight again."

"How? Where? With what?"

He smiled, "Ah how I have missed your questions Aelfraed. How? With your mind and with your men. Where? Here. You hide in the forests and strike suddenly. With what? With the weapons you have." He paused and coughed, putting a cloth to his mouth; not soon enough though for I saw the blood. "If Harold had done as I advised then William would have been beaten on the beach. But if Harold had survived then he could have used the land to defeat the enemy. Remember Aelfraed that the Normans use horses. They double their need for food. You remember when we first fought those mounted Welsh knights and you were apprehensive. What happened when the horse fell?"

"The knight died."

"Exactly. The weakness of the horse is that it can be hurt and the rider is hurt too."

The next day I began to prepare our men to face horses. I used Branton and his archers for they were skilful riders. I made my men stand in a line with only a stick for defence. As soon as they realised that the horses would not willingly hit them they gained confidence. I then told them of facing horsemen when in Wales. "This is where your spear comes into play for you can strike the horse before it reaches you. If you have no fear then use your axe or your sword to strike down the horse. If the horse falls then so does the man." They looked at each other and nodded. Branton and his archers stood in a half circle beyond them. "And remember men we have a secret weapon, which is only available to us." This time all but Branton and Osbert looked puzzled. "We have Branton's archers and their new arrows!"

The rest of the autumn and early winter seemed to drag on as we prepared to fight an enemy who didn't come. We heard that William was in the south-west subjugating the forces raised by Harold's mother but we were left alone. For men of action, it was frustrating. Had Edwin or Morcar mobilised their forces then we could have struck south while William was engaged elsewhere. That first autumn, a year after Stamford was the time to strike but it passed and we did nothing.

Outlaw

I had missed Gytha and Harold and I visited them in Fife for the winter solstice. I left early in January and trudged, with faithful Branton and his archers, through snow which was sometimes up to the horse's hocks. Perversely it felt good to be fighting something, even if it was only the elements and as a warrior with a reputation, we found a friendly welcome in the homes and taverns we used heading north. The King was not in the south of the land and had gone north to watch for Orkney raiders and we reached Fife without speaking with him.

The Lord of Fife had had word of us and he rode out to meet us with an armed escort. The escort was more for show than anything. He seemed to like me and embarrassingly seemed to try to copy me so that his men were mailed as mine and rode with his emblem of the Raven on his shield. I suppose I should have been flattered but I was unaccustomed to such attention from another man. He gushed about how much Harold had grown and what cheeky boys the twins were and I let it all flow over me. I did not want second-hand accounts of my son I wanted to hold him and bounce him on my knee and most of all I wanted to hold Gytha.

His castle was close to the shoreline and had a commanding view towards the northeast. I suspected it had been built to counter the raids of the Norsemen and, as such, it would have been effective. It did not have a ditch but it was built of stone and had an inner bailey and a keep in the Norman style. It impressed me and I thought then about changes I could make at Topcliffe. The advantage he had with the keep was that he could protect all of his family and his animals should his walls fall. As long as there was a well in the castle they could keep out an enemy.

He saw my scrutiny. "Do you like it, my lord?"

"It has a pleasant aspect and yet it is defensible. Does it have a name?"

He beamed happily, "It did not until my visitors arrived and now it is Queen's Haven."

I thought at first that it did not sound military until I remembered that the name of my manor at Topcliffe was Maiden Bower. "Good name and appropriate. How is the Queen?"

Outlaw

For the first time, his face became serious. "She still frets about the safety of the boys and yet she misses being at the heart of intrigue and power."

I nodded; she had not had an easy life with two husbands killed but she had had a busy life. I could understand her frustration at being stuck in the lovely but lonely part of a land in which she was a foreigner. I hoped that I could, in some way cheer her up, but I thought it unlikely.

As we rode through the gates the two princes raced across the snow giggling and throwing balls of snow at each other. I saw their nurse trying to catch them and I spied, in a window in the keep, the face of Ealdgyth watching with a smile on her face. The boys, at least, were content. Even as I dismounted Gytha had raced out and thrown her arms around me, I could hear Sarah's voice in the background, "My lady! Your wrap!"

"I have missed you, wife."

"And I, you, husband." That was a perfect moment when time seemed to stand still as we gazed into each other's eyes. She was even more beautiful than she had been and I was amazed, again, that she should have chosen a rough-hewn warrior like me to be her husband. "Wait until you see young Harold, he can almost walk. Well, he grabs things, staggers and falls over, but he will walk soon believe me."

Sarah waved an admonishing finger at Gytha and then wrapped a wolf skin about her shoulders. "Good to see you Sarah, Thomas send his love."

Her stern face suddenly broke into a smile and I wondered at her loyalty to Gytha and myself which had transcended her love for her husband. "Is he well?"

"He is. He misses you, as we all do but we survive."

You would have thought I had given her terrible news for she suddenly burst into tears and ran back inside. As we followed her Gytha said, "She misses him terribly as I miss you. Could we not return home? Nought has happened; it must be safe."

"We will talk later." I was coming around to the thought that they could return. It seemed unlikely that anything would happen for a while. "Where is my son?"

Outlaw

She led me to the main hall where there was a roaring fire and a young girl played with Harold. He looked a healthy enough child, not that I know much of such things and he giggled much. I was pleased that when he fell he did not cry but stood again. He would be a good warrior who did not submit to setbacks. "Harold, come to your father." I did not think he would remember me but I crouched down and held my arms wide. He turned to face the sound of my voice and a puzzled look came over his face. The girl supported him with her arms. "Come on Harold, let us see you walk." I grinned as I said it for I was happy and I had missed many days with my son. My joy was complete when he grinned back at me and launched himself forward. He was but two of my paces away from me but with his small legs that was a huge distance. Never taking his eyes from mine he lurched forwards, his arms held out and he waddled into my open arms. It was a moment I have had never enjoyed before and later, when I shivered in hiding, pursued and surrounded, it was the one thought which gave me heart and filled me with hope.

That evening Calum had laid on a magnificent feast with game and sweetmeats. He served the fiery spirit they drink in the highlands but I was always careful when drinking in company and while the other lords became inebriated I just felt warm inside. Gytha retired early with Harold and I was about to join her when Ealdgyth restrained me. "Before you follow your lady, a word Lord Aelfraed."

I could not refuse her for I served as I had served her husband. "Whatever your majesty desires."

She gave me a rueful look. "Queen of what? "

"You will always be the Queen to me, majesty."

She touched my hand, "Dear loyal Aelfraed. If only my treacherous brothers had shown such loyalty."

I felt uncomfortable for I still liked Morcar. "Your brother, Earl Morcar, would have done more I am sure…"

"If he were not under the influence of that viper Edwin. You are a fine warrior Aelfraed but you are naïve when it comes to politics." She held my hand in hers and I was amazed at the softness of the skin and the delicate touch. It was uncomfortable

Outlaw

for I felt myself becoming aroused and I had to concentrate on her words. "Will my people rise against the Norman invader?"

It was a blunt question and required an equally blunt answer. "Your mother in law has raised a revolt in the south and Eadric has attacked Hereford."

"And what of the north?"

"Aethelward has promises from many lords but the total force would be a thousand men and then the fyrd."

"The fyrd!" She almost spat the word out. "They are the reason my husband is dead and I am in exile."

"They all died majesty and they were not warriors."

She smiled. "I am sorry Aelfraed. You are right and it is the words you do not say which speaks volumes. Unless my brothers rise then there will be no rebellion." I nodded, I could not lie. "Thank you for your honesty. When you return home I shall give you a letter for my brother Morcar. You are the only man I trust to deliver it."

"Whatever you command your majesty."

She then did something totally unexpected; she rose and came over to me. She placed her hands on my cheeks and kissed me full on the lips. "Now go to your lady's bed before I do something I will regret and take you to mine."

Gytha was asleep when I entered our chamber and that was a relief for I felt that I had betrayed her in some way for I had wanted to bed the Queen which would have betrayed not only my wife but my dead father. I had not known then she was attracted to me but I suppose the signs had been there as far back as the journey from Rhuddlan all those years ago. This was the start of the torment I felt. Each time I saw her I desired her more and more and Gytha became less desirable. It was like the story my uncle had told me of Pandora and her box. The Queen had opened it but I was the one who had to face the consequences. I did lie with my lady each night but it did not feel as it had before. As she lay beneath me I pictured the Queen.

Oidhche na Bliadhn Ùir is the Scottish festival of the new year and I found that they celebrated it more than Yuletide or Christmas. I would have left earlier but Calum insisted that I stay for the celebrations. I wanted to leave for I found each day increasingly uncomfortable. I think that I was the only person not inebriated. It is hard to watch those you like behaving in an excessive fashion when their inhibitions are down. There was wild dancing and flings. Many of the lords present passed out in a drunken stupor and even the Queen and my wife were a little drunk. Calum had a perpetual grin on his face and he travelled around the room kissing all the ladies; apparently, it was a Scottish custom. He even kissed Gytha and the worrying thing was I felt no jealousy. He staggered off to bed and Gytha fell asleep in her chair. I was about to take her to bed when I realised that the Queen still remained.

"Your majesty, can I escort you to your chamber?"

She stood a little unsteadily. "It appears Lord Aelfraed that I am the only lady not to be kissed tonight." She lurched toward me. I felt dishonourable for I knew what she intended and did nothing to stop it. A part of me wanted it to happen and when our lips met I held her as tightly as she held me. When we pulled away there was a wild look in her eyes which I knew was also in mine. She took my hand and led me to her chamber.

When we had finished and she lay back, her eyes sleepy but content, she murmured. "It was worth waiting for and was everything I had hoped."

I believed I was the worst kind of traitor as I trudged back to the hall. I too had enjoyed the moment but now, the moment it was over, I had felt so guilty that I almost fled the chamber. When I reached the hall Gytha was still asleep and I picked her up in my arms and carried her to our chamber. I deposited her on the bed and then sat in the chair. How could I lie next to her when I had been unfaithful? When it came to fellow warriors I would never break my word but with the mother of my child…

The next day I resolved to leave if only to avoid a further moment of indiscretion. The Queen acted as though nothing untoward had occurred while Gytha was just embarrassed about passing out and kept apologising to me; that made the whole thing seem much worse. Calum, Thegn of Fife pleaded with me to stay but I was able to use the excuse of the Queen's missive and I rode through his gates desperate to be back in Topcliffe where I would not have to view the scene of my shame.

Outlaw

Branton was quite chatty on the way home. It seems the serving girls had taken a fancy to him and he had enjoyed the company of a different woman each night. I admired the fact that he had the freedom to do so and to be free from guilt. He had also picked up some gossip which I found interesting. "One of the servant girls overheard a conversation between the King when he made a visit and the Thegn of Fife. It seems that one of the Aetheling's visited Sweyn in Denmark."

"Does that not seem strange Branton? That a servant girl should be privy to such information and then pass it on to you?"

He grinned. "Oh, there was a reason, my lord. She was telling me because she said that when the Danes invaded I could run north and set up the house with her."

I rode in silence as I weighed up that piece of information. It sounded true and I could not see what the girl could gain from a lie. What was more worrying was that the Thegn of Fife had not told me that information. It called into question our friendship. Why had he offered to look after the Queen and Gytha? Was he a gaoler? For, unlike the other lords, he did not seem to join the King on his journeys through his land. It was a Gordian knot and it would need Aethelward and me to untangle it. The rest of the journey was a pure horror of snow, ice and driving wind which ripped sleet and snow through every minuscule gap in our clothes. Even the hardy horses struggled to make it through some of the snow drifts and we were glad to see the familiar walls of home loom large in the distance.

Thomas banked the fire up and had the servants bring us ale heated with a red hot poker. It felt good to have warm veins once more. Branton left to see to the horses and I sat with Aethelward and Osbert to tell them of our news. Aethelward agreed with me that the girl had had no reason to lie to Branton. "But my lord, where would that put us? Would we fight for the King's son and this Dane? It does not sit right with me."

We all stared into the fire for I had had the same dilemma. Aethelward looked over at me and then nodded to Osbert. "There is one solution to this, Osbert. We support the eldest son of Harold."

Osbert looked puzzled, "You mean support the Danes and Edgar?"

"No Osbert, I mean throw our weight behind Harold's eldest son, Aelfraed."

A huge grin erupted across the sergeant's face. "Now that I could do."

"Tell me nephew do you know what was in the Queen's letter?"

It was on the tip of my tongue to say no but I do know what is between her legs but thought better of it. "No uncle but it is addressed to Morcar and not Edwin."

"You see if we could persuade Morcar to support you as regent for Harold and Ulf then that might unite everyone."

"Everyone apart from Edgar and the Danes, my lord."

Aethelward waved the argument away as he would a summer bluebottle. "If he is talking with Edgar's representative now then we will not see him before the end of summer; if we have not struck by late spring then nothing will come of this."

"It is a risk. Perhaps William will turn out to be a generous leader, someone we can follow."

"Submit?" He looked puzzled. "That does not seem like you Aelfraed. Did anything untoward occur in Fife?"

Hurriedly I added, "No uncle it is just that we have not even met William yet and we are making judgements about him."

Aethelward relaxed a little. "Ah, I can see wisdom has crept into you over the winter. You are right in that we should avoid making judgements but so far we have seen a vindictive winner who took the land from all whom he fought, including their wives and children. We have seen him place guards around the Earls to control them. So I would not get my hopes up about him being another Confessor."

"I will ride tomorrow to Jorvik and deliver the letter and perhaps try to have a talk with Morcar."

"I will come with you but come what may we might as well prepare for war. If we do not fight the Normans we will certainly have to fight the Danes for remember, both of you, the Danes regard Northumbria as their land which we stole from them. If Edgar is plotting then it will be for joint action against us. Osbert, get Ralph to begin weapon making again and then train the fyrd.

We need to have as many armed men as we can if we are to fight off either of these invaders. Tell Branton I need a small escort of archers."

As we rode through the melting snow the next day I was desperate to tell Aethelward of my dilemma but it was not the sort of thing you discussed with your uncle. The only person I could have spoken with was Ridley but he had no experience, at all, with women and I knew that he would have hated to be put in that position. No, this was one problem I would have to wrestle alone. "How are Gytha and Harold?"

I jerked my head around. Was Aethelward reading my mind? Did he know something? I was relieved when I saw that he was gazing to the south and rubbing his leg. "Gytha is fine and Harold is growing so much. He learned to walk when I was there."

"I suppose that is my one regret Aelfraed. That I had no son." He smiled at me. "I know I regard you as the nearest thing I have to a son but I did not see you toddle, nor hear you cry like a child nor hear your first words. Ah well too late now. At least I can play at being a grandfather."

The only sound, for a while, was the sound of hooves in slushy snow. "Did you never have a woman?" I hurriedly added, "I know you have not talked of such things and if you do not wish to...."

He held his hand to silence me. "Do not worry Aelfraed, your words do not embarrass me and I feel remiss for I should have spoken of such things when you were growing up for that is what fathers," he smiled wryly, "even pretend fathers do. They pass on their experience. Yes, I have had women. Many women." He looked earnestly at me, "That is where you are lucky, you found Gytha when you were both young and you did not make the mistakes I did."

"Mistakes?"

"Aye. When you are a famous warrior then women want to bed you to brag to their friends or to carry a child with your power. I read in Constantinople, of high born ladies who would lie with gladiators. It may seem strange to you but when that happened to me, I felt used. In Constantinople, there were many such women." He shrugged and spread his hands. "They were generous with their gifts. But none of them, as far as I know, resulted in a child. I think they were too careful for that."

The rest of the ride was conducted in silence. I think my uncle was remembering his youth and I was thinking of the Queen. Had I been used? I thought back to the events leading up to that liaison. It was not the drink, I believe that was the excuse, and she had been building up to it. I suddenly thought back to the accidental touching of hands the quiet, intimate conversations, the looks beneath hooded eyes. No, I was not a trophy and there had been tenderness as well as a fiery passion that was missing in Gytha. It was like the difference between a training combat and a fight to the death. Neither Ealdgyth nor myself had held back and I still bore the scratch marks down my back to prove it. Then why? Perhaps she was lonely but then the Lord of Fife was a fine looking and available suitor. It came back to me, she was attracted to me and the insidious thought crept into my mind. I was attracted to her; I wanted her again.

Chapter 5

"So you saw my sister?"

Morcar became quite animated when I handed him the letter. "I have my lord."

"And where is she? The rumour is that she resides with Malcolm in Scotland. Is it true?"

I shook my head. "If the Queen chooses to tell you where she resides then so be it otherwise I could not in all honour betray the trust of my Queen whom I serve still." I caught the flick of my uncle's head indicating his approval.

"I am sorry Aelfraed. I do not mean you to betray her." He looked a little shamefaced. "In truth, I feel I have let her down but Edwin told me that we had to distance ourselves." It was always the case with Morcar, when he thought for himself then he was the finest friend a man could have and a sound leader but when he listened to his self serving brother, the man who had betrayed their father then he made poor decisions and became a shadow of his former self. Whatever Ealdgyth had asked of him would only come to fruition if Edwin approved. I knew the Queen well, and cunning and subtle planning were two of her strengths, perhaps she too was playing games.

He read the letter in silence. "She is in Scotland then but she says not where." So she did not trust her brother; wise woman. He looked at me curiously. "I know my sister is fond of you; did she divulge to you the contents of this missive?"

Fond! It was a little stronger than that but I kept my face impassive. "No, my lord." Perhaps she did not trust me either but then I dismissed the thought. My face was as a book for men to read and she knew that I would have had to lie and I did that so badly.

"It seems that King Malcolm has heard that William's daughter, the one who should have married my brother, will, instead be marrying someone from Burgundy. Edwin will not be pleased."

I glanced at Aethelward who raised his eyebrows. Like me, he wondered about all this sudden intelligence from north of the border. We maintained our silence for there was little we could say. He carefully folded the letter and put it in his tunic. He walked

Outlaw

to the window which looked out on the cathedral. "I think she wants us to fight the Normans."

My face showed my joy but when I glanced at Aethelward he angrily shook his head and my face, once more became like the gargoyles on the church, made of stone. "And you, my lord. What would you have?"

His face was almost tearful as he looked around. "Aethelward you do not know the half of it, King William keeps his men constantly around me, watching my every move, and he trusts me not. You are just fortunate that his men are out hunting today or this would not have been a private interview. I know I can trust you but who else is there?"

"Earl Morcar, there are many men in the north who would fight for you. Remember that Harold's mother is leading a fight in Exeter and the men of Hereford are fighting too."

"I am not sure. My brother...."

"Invite your brother up here and show him the letter. Let him make that decision with you." I could see that Aethelward had given Morcar a solution. It would not be his decision to go to war, but, like his brothers, Ealdgyth was clever.

"That is a fine idea. Thank you. You two have always been my best advisers and I will not forget it." He looked around as though someone might be listening. "Did she tell you of Edgar and King Sweyn?"

"No, my lord." I knew that he had but it had been Branton who had told me not the Queen.

"That may decide my brother for the last thing I need, that is we need, is a Danish army close to Jorvik again."

"Come we will eat. You have given me an appetite."

We too had an appetite, an appetite which was taken away when the Normans swaggered into the eating hall. The first two were big burly men I did not recognise but the taller one I did, it was Guy of Evreux; an arrogant Norman knight whose horse I had struck knocking him to the ground. It had been some years ago when King Edward still ruled but I knew that he would remember for he had wanted to fight me that day. As soon as he entered he recognised me. His eyes narrowed and his hand went to his sword. Aethelward put his hand on mine to restrain me.

"So you Saxon cur. I have found you at last!"

Aethelward affected a puzzled look and glanced around the table. "You will have to be a little more specific young knight of Normandy for, as you can plainly see, there are many Saxons around the table and whilst we would not call ourselves dogs. There are many qualities of the dog which are to be admired." I almost laughed aloud for Guy of Evreux had a confused look on his face and my uncle took advantage of it and stood. "They are loyal, faithful, they will defend their master to the death and they only make a noise when an enemy is near. As you can see, we are silent which means these dogs do not recognise an enemy. To which of us do you refer?"

Just then another Norman entered and him too I recognised, William of Perci. He took in the situation and strode quickly to Guy, pushing his sword back into the scabbard. "This is no place for swords Guy. What is the problem?"

I could see that Guy felt foolish, just as he had in Winchester all those years ago. His bluster was gone. If I ever had to fight him all that I would need would be patience for he would rush in and leave himself wide open for a counter attack. "It is him, this Aelfraed. He hit my horse."

At this point, even the Norman knights laughed and they sat at the table the situation defused. William tried to help out his young friend. "He hit your horse?"

"Yes I was galloping in Winchester's streets and he punched my horse and knocked it over."

Rather than getting the others on his side, it made them look at me with new respect. Even William knew when a cause was lost and he put his arm around Guy and led him to the far end of the table. "I think we steer clear of any warrior who can knock a horse to the ground with his fist alone. Gentlemen my apologies for the outburst and enjoy your meal."

I had to spend the next few minutes telling the story to the Saxons around me. I was amazed when I observed a couple of Normans listening. Aethelward, however, was worried. "It is not your fault that he is here but this complicates things. He will try to get revenge."

Outlaw

Morcar had heard our conversation and leaned over. "He is a headstrong youth. Apparently, he killed a thrall in their service who did not groom his horse well enough."

Aethelward looked over, "Perhaps he is like Caligula and loves his horse just a little too much!" Our end of the table laughed at the lewd comment and I saw Guy redden. My uncle was not doing anything to help me.

"If he tries to fight me, my lord, what should I do?"

Although I said it quietly, the other Thegns heard it and became silent. Morcar looked at me and said quietly. "Defend yourself. It is the only honourable thing to do."

Aethelward asked, "Who is the leader of the conroi?"

"The one who took him to one side, William of Perci. He is a powerful friend of William. I have been told that he is to be given lands in the north."

The only estates I knew of, which had no Thegns, were Skipton and Scarborough and I did not think either would suit him. "The sooner you send for your brother, the better."

I did not fear a meeting with the arrogant Norman, in fact, I relished it but Aethelward took me to one side and warned me of the dangers of such a confrontation. "At the moment Duke William," he still could not name him king, "is far from here but an incident between one of the most notorious Saxon lords and one of his knights might make him decide to pay a visit and, until Morcar has spoken with Edwin we need the Norman's interest to be elsewhere. It would be better if we remained in the hall tonight and travel back tomorrow in daylight. It would avoid a regrettable incident."

"I am not afraid of this Guy of Evreux but, as always, uncle, I listen to and take your advice."

We remained in the hall and I envied my men staying in one of the lively taverns in the city. I preferred the company of Branton and his archers to that of other lords, for many of the ones in the hall had not stood in the shield wall at Stamford and had cowered behind the walls. That still rankled.

As soon as we left the hall, the next day, and met with Branton I knew that there was trouble. My sergeant of archers normally had a

Outlaw

smiling and open disposition but his face was dark and angry when he met us at the stables. "What is amiss Branton?"

"It is Edward, my lord." Edward was one of my young archers, a cheerful young man and a good archer. "He has been killed."

Aethelward took us both to one side. "Tell us quickly and quietly Branton."

"Last night we were at The Saddle enjoying a beaker of ale and some Norman lords came in. They were looking for trouble but I warned the men to bite their tongues and take their insults. After they had knocked over a few beakers they left. Later Edward went to take a piss and did not return. We went to look for him and found him run through," he paused, "with a sword."

A sword meant a knight or a Housecarl. "Where is the body?"

"We have wrapped him in a cloak and placed him on his horse. His mother will wish to bury him."

His poor mother! He was an only child, the others having died young and her husband had fallen in the fyrd at Fulford. My hand, involuntarily, went to my sword. Aethelward restrained me. "You go with your men and I will tell Earl Morcar. We need the law to deal with this."

I did not care what my uncle said, I would have revenge on this Norman for I knew who it was. A short conversation with Branton confirmed it. "Did I do right, my lord?"

"You did Branton and this is my fault for I should have stayed with you and this might not have happened. The man who committed this crime has no nobility and if the other Normans are like him then England is in a poor place."

When Aethelward joined us he seemed satisfied. "Morcar has issued a warrant for the Normans. He will ask them to explain themselves."

"That will not bring Edward back."

"Nothing will bring Edward back. You are no longer a boy. You are a man and more than that a Thegn with responsibilities."

"Yes to my men."

"Your men serve you and would give their lives for you. Is that not true Branton?"

Branton was just behind us and within earshot. "Yes my lord, it goes without saying."

Outlaw

I was angry and, for once, would not accept my uncle's advice without thought. "Uncle I respect you and admire you but know this, the next time I see that arrogant Norman, he dies."

We rode in silence and I knew that Aethelward was angry. He seemed to struggle to regain control of himself and when he spoke his voice was cold and commanding. "Your father would have been proud of all you have done up to this point in your life Aelfraed but this he would not understand. You would throw away England's only chance of freedom from a tyrant to avenge one archer?"

I had no answer and we rode along in an uncomfortable atmosphere until Branton said, in a quiet voice, "Edward loved you my lord and he loved England. Standing with you at Stamford was the proudest moment in his life and when he knew that you were Harold's son he felt even prouder. He would not wish you to throw away a chance of a free England to avenge him." He nudged his horse forward and lowered his voice so that only Aethelward and I could hear, "And unless I am wrong we will have a chance to revenge Edward on the field of battle."

As his horse slipped back my uncle turned to me. "Branton is showing wisdom Aelfraed and he is right. Wait until this Norman faces you with a lance and then Edward will have his revenge and England will have a leader that they can be proud of."

As we entered the yard at Maiden Bower I decided to do as Aethelward asked but it was because of Branton's words, not my uncle's and I would train and prepare even harder for the day when I would face Guy of Evreux on the field of battle.

It was a month or so later, not long before Easter when we received word that the Normans who had been in Jorvik had left after questioning by Morcar. We heard this from Ridley who had visited Jorvik to deposit monies with Reuben. He rode into the castle with his men at arms one April morning. He embraced me as though he had not seen me for years when it was only months that had elapsed.

"It is good to see you, my... Aelfraed. How is Harold? Gytha?"

"They are both well. And have you not taken a wife yet?"

He blushed. "Not yet, but there is still time. We are both young men."

Outlaw

"So you have been in Jorvik?"

"Aye, and the city was a buzz with the murder of your archer. Morcar showed himself to be cleverer and wiser than we thought for he interviewed the landlord of The Saddle and other drinkers. They confirmed the behaviour of the knights. When he interviewed the knights they were belligerent until the Earl produced the evidence. Apparently, William of Perci knew nothing of this. The next day Guy of Evreux and five other knights were sent to London, apparently on a mission for their lord but really they left in disgrace."

I think that Ridley expected me to be pleased but I was not. I cared not for his disgrace, I wanted his blood but there was little point in showing such poor grace before my old friend. "Thank you for that and the Earl did he say aught about his brother?"

"He said that he had sent a letter to Edwin but that was all. Why?"

I knew that I could trust Ridley and I beckoned him closer. "We have spoken with the Earl and warned him of possible treachery." I explained about Sweyn and Edgar. "Perhaps Edwin will join with us in resisting these Normans."

He looked at me long and hard; the thing about Ridley was that you could see the thought processes at work. Suddenly his face broke into a half smile. "With you as the leader?"

"Perhaps but I would only be standing in for Harold's sons, Ulf and Harold. I have no desire to be king. I am not even sure I wish to be a lord."

Ridley shook his head. "You do not know yourself. Men would follow you to hell and beyond if you asked them. You are the best leader I know for you are trustworthy. You would be a fine king."

"Thank you for that thought and I will allow Aethelward, Edwin and Morcar use me as such but I want all to know I would be a regent rather than a ruler."

Although he did not look convinced he nodded. "How does Edwin feel about this?"

"I know not and I suppose we will have to wait until he travels north to discover that."

Edwin did not visit Jorvik until after midsummer. Aethelward had picked up a little over the summer and looked healthier than he

Outlaw

had in the winter but he now had an urgent air about him as though he wanted things to happen quickly. It was so unlike the calculating strategos we had known. Osbert too wanted action. His men were well trained and prepared and now they wanted more than just practice swords and tourneys. I was happy that nothing had happened swiftly as I wanted as many warriors and men available as I could get. Ralph had worked wonders and we had a fine store of weapons; when my fyrd went to war they would be as well equipped as any man at arms. Their Sunday training was the highlight of Osbert's week as he saw them gradually change into a reliable force.

Edwin did not ask us to go to Jorvik, instead, he and Morcar visited us at Maiden Bower. He and the Thegns with him were dressed for hunting. He and Morcar dismounted while his lords stayed with the horses. Aethelward had seen them coming and had joined me. "Shall we go to my hall, my lord?"

I led the way and noticed that Edwin, like his brother, had the comfortable look of someone who dines well. He had no lean and hungry look. When I had seen them both at Fulford it had struck me then that they preferred to watch rather than fight. I was never a watcher.

Edwin came directly to the point. "It seems my sister has information and knowledge which I have not. She believes that Edgar is enlisting the aid of Sweyn, the Dane."

"We have heard that as well. Have you spoken with the Aetheling?"

Edwin looked troubled. "He is abroad, apparently."

Aethelward nodded, "I would hazard a guess that he is with Sweyn. Is his mother with him?"

Edwin's eyes narrowed. "She is but how did you know?"

"I didn't. It was a guess but if she is then it means she is the one who is working to make him king. Did you know that she tried to kill the Queen?"

"Aye, Morcar told me. What concerns me more is this news from Ealdgyth that William has promised my bride to be to another."

We both shook our heads. "We had not heard that my lord," I added, "but Malcolm Canmore appears to have spies everywhere and if the knowledge came from him then there is a chance it may be true."

I saw Edwin biting his lip. He was worried, that was obvious. "What we need is a spy in William's court." He looked at me.

"I am the last person who could be a spy. The Normans know me and do not like me. Ask your brother."

He glanced at Morcar. "It is true. There are a number of Normans who would like his head on top of their lance."

"Then who is there?"

"Surely there must be one of your lords who could do the job." I had to bite back the end of the sentence for, as Edwin and Morcar's men had not fought the Normans they would be perfect choices.

"They are not suitable."

"You do not trust them." Aethelward did not care for reputations any more and he did not care who he offended.

"Of course I…"

"No, with respect my lord, you do not otherwise you would have planted one at court already."

His shoulders sagged in silent acceptance of the truth. "So, there is no one."

"I will go." All of us stared at the oldest man we now knew who was volunteering for a dangerous and risky enterprise with no certainty of success. "But there are conditions."

"Conditions?" Edwin began chewing his lip again but I could see the relief on Morcar's face.

"Aye. If I discover that the Queen's intelligence is true then you and your brother will join with us and rebel against the Normans."

"And?"

"And we will use Aelfraed here as the figurehead. But we do this for the Queen and Harold's children."

Edwin sneered. "Make this Housecarl a king?"

"You were not listening, Earl Edwin. He would be the figurehead and a council would rule until the boys were of an age."

Edwin turned to stare at me. "And you Aelfraed. What do you say?"

"I am a reluctant figurehead my lord but if it means we rid this land of the Normans then so be it."

"I think it is a good idea." Edwin shot a look of pure disdain at his brother.

"Well my lord. Do you want me as a spy or not?"

"Would William not be suspicious of you? You are related to Aelfraed."

"I would use my friendship with the Queen as a lure. I would go as her envoy. I believe that she would agree to that but Aelfraed can go to visit her to get confirmation."

"That would delay your departure."

"Only by a day or two. If Aelfraed left now then he could send a rider south with the news and they could be back here four days from now." Aethelward was, of course, being highly optimistic. I would have to ride hard to make Fife in two days. Fortunately, the days were longer than the last time we had travelled and the roads would be better. I nodded my acceptance.

I could see Edwin mentally persuading himself that this was the best solution. He had deniability. If William found out he could say he knew nothing about it and he would be back in Mercia by the time Aethelward left.

"Under those conditions, then I accept."

"You swear a binding oath?"

Edwin reddened, "If it is necessary then I do."

Bluntly Aethelward said, "I swear."

Aethelward looked at Morcar who quickly said, "I swear."

"Good." He turned to me. "You had better prepare Branton and his men again. If you leave now then you could be there the day after tomorrow."

I bowed my goodbyes and went to get my men. This was all a little sudden but then I brightened. I would be seeing the Queen again. It was only after I had spoken with Branton that I realised I had not even thought of Gytha and my son!

I watched the Earls leave. Aethelward limped over. "Make sure you tell the Queen all that I have told you. If she agrees I will leave immediately."

"Will you take anyone with you?"

"With your permission, I will take a couple of your newer men at arms; ones who did not fight at Stamford Bridge."

I waved away the request. "You do not have to ask. How safe do you think you will be?"

He shrugged. "I have met William before and he is a cautious man. He will want to know the Queen's thoughts first but it matters not. So long as I can get the information which Edwin needs then we will have our revolt and, perhaps, the tragedy of Senlac Hill might be forgotten."

I rode away north, not knowing if I would ever see my uncle again. I took four spare mounts for Branton and the other two riders for we would need to ride hard. We stayed at Berwick on the first night and then, as we struck the estuary we found some good fortune; there was a ferry. I would not have liked to travel it during rough weather for it seemed to be merely a big raft with a rail around it and a small sail but, as it saved us almost a whole day it was worth it. Branton was unhappy for he felt that the ferryman robbed us but as I told him time was the one commodity you could not buy. We rode into the Thegn of Fife's castle shortly before sunset. Weary but pleased with our progress. "Branton I will see the Queen immediately. You will need to travel south in the morning. You can take two spare mounts each and we will travel back in a more leisurely fashion." There was no need for me to rush back and I was keen to find out as much as I could from this nest of spies and if I am being truthful, I wanted to see the Queen again. The guilt I had felt on the journey back had been replaced by a curiosity about the Queen's attitude towards me.

Calum appeared surprised to see us which, I suppose, explains why he seemed less enthusiastic in his welcome. I suppose it was understandable. I had not told him I was arriving and he would have to make arrangements for my men. I apologised. "I am sorry to drop in unexpectedly but it is important that I speak with the Queen and I have not seen my wife and child for a long time."

His demeanour changed immediately, "I understand and forgive me for my lack of grace. You are always welcome here in my home."

When Gytha came into the hall to greet me she looked a little flustered. "Why did you not tell me you were coming? I could have prepared…"

Outlaw

"You look lovely as you always do, dear wife and my visit is sudden as I bring a message to the Queen from her brother. She wrote him a letter you see and…"

She hugged me. "You do not need to explain. I am glad to see you but you must let me prepare the chamber, it is a mess."

I was puzzled. "You tidy a room for me, dear wife? You know I am the messiest man in England. I care not if the room is a mess."

She reddened. "Well, I care!"

I kissed her. "Well I have to see the Queen first and then I can spend as much time with you and my son as you like."

It actually suited me for I did not know how I could face my wife. The guilt I thought had disappeared rushed back into my head. Damn the Queen and damn my lust! A servant had obviously gone to the Queen to warn her of my arrival for she entered the hall just as Gytha left. Calum nodded, "I will arrange for your men and horses to be accommodated while you converse with her majesty."

We were suddenly alone and I bowed. She held out her hand and I kissed the back of it. When I looked up she was staring at me with hooded eyes, her lips dancing in a half smile. "I do not know whether or not to be disappointed that you have taken so long to return my lord. Did I so disappoint you?"

I quickly looked around in case anyone had overheard. So much for her being inebriated and not remembering. I stammered my reply with a pathetic grin on my face. "I did not know your majesty. What I mean is I worried that I had, in some way offended you and…" My voice trailed off and she looked at me in a sultry manner, or what I imagined was a sultry manner but my limited experience with women had not prepared me for this.

She too looked around and spoke quietly. "You are right we cannot talk here." She took my arm and began to walk with me across the hall, "You say that you have a private message from my brother?"

"Yes Edwin."

Her voice suddenly became unnaturally loud, "Then we must speak in private."

She led me to her chamber. As soon as we were in she slammed the door shut and then throwing her arms around me, began to kiss me passionately. Her hands began to pull at the ties which held my tunic. I found myself propelled towards the bed. We tumbled upon it and she was lying on top of me. Despite myself, I found that I was becoming aroused. In spite of my determination not to pleasure myself again, I began to respond to her kisses. My hands pulled her dress over her head and she was suddenly naked, as was I. There was a certain vicarious pleasure knowing that, but a few paces away, my wife was tidying our room and I was here with the Queen making love. Gytha was gentle and shy in the bedroom but Ealdgyth was like a wild untamed animal. Gytha was gentle, barely touching me but Ealdgyth tore at me with her hands and teeth. We lay, after the first time, in a sweaty heap gathering our breath. I was about to speak when she began to devour me. Her touch aroused me again and once more we became one.

Finally, she stood and looked down at me. "So my lord, the first time was not a happy accident."

"This is wrong your majesty. I am married and you are the Queen."

"And a Queen cannot love? And as for being married! Tell me my lord who makes your blood race is it Gytha or is it me. Who do you want to wake up next to in the morning, Gytha or me?"

"But I have a son."

"I have two. Is this a bragging contest?" She took me in her hands. "Tell me truthfully Aelfraed; do you wish this to end? Do you wish never to make love to me again? If you say yes then it ends now."

The silence was eloquent and she laughed as she lay back on the bed. "But this is impossible. How can I wake next to you? Gytha…"

"I did not say we could wake together, at least not yet but… Now we have been alone long enough. What is the message from my brother?"

"It is a message from Aethelward." I told her the plan which Aethelward had concocted.

"I knew that my brothers would not be able to handle the information I gave them. I hope that Aethelward is not being foolish for William is a dangerous man. He has had some men visit Malcolm and I fear that he aims to ally with him. That would place me in an impossible position."

"And his proposal?"

She waved a hand dismissively, "Of course. That goes without saying." She lay her naked body across mine and, looking up into my eyes said, "But you Aelfraed, you are putting yourself in a dangerous position. You would guarantee the throne for others and yet you would be the target for not only William's enmity but also Edith and Edgar. It would make my life safer and I am not sure that I want you in so much danger."

"But what is the alternative? If we do nothing then you lose and I lose. This is our one and only chance to free England. We have one throw of the dice."

"But if we fail?"

I shrugged. "Then we fail but we will be no worse off than now."

"I can see much of your father in you." She looked down at me and giggled. "In fact, some parts are identical."

I laughed. God, but she was an easy woman to love. "You are incorrigible and now we had better go down in a presentable fashion, having delivered my message and received a reply then Branton can ride in the morning."

"And tonight…...?"

Chapter 6

When we returned to the main hall it was still empty. My wife's room must have been really untidy. "I will go and give Branton the message. He will need to leave before dawn."

"You do not leave with him?" The smile in her eyes spoke volumes.

"No your majesty, I will remain a few more days for Branton will need to be quick."

"Good then I will ask the Thegn to hold a feast for you; a midsummer festival." She squeezed my hand as she parted, her nails leaving tiny indentations in my skin. All my resolve had gone and now I was a deceitful, unfaithful husband once more.

I found Branton and told him the message for Aethelward. "Get back to Maiden Bower as quickly as you can for Aethelward has much to do." I handed him a purse with money. "Take the ferry. I know we are being robbed but time is a precious commodity."

He smiled, "I will do, my lord. How is Lady Gytha?"

"I have not spoken to her yet. She is busy tidying the room." Branton looked at me as though the idea of tidying was not natural. I smiled and shrugged, "Women!"

"That is why, my lord, I will not be tied down. Love 'em and leave 'em."

I smiled as he left me but I found myself envying him. Gytha was waiting for me in the hall when I returned and she embraced me. "I am sorry about before. It was such a surprise to see you."

Calum entered too. "Have you seen the Queen?"

"Yes my lord, I have given her brother's message." I kissed Gytha, "Now I am all yours."

"Come you will see a real change in Harold."

I was genuinely excited as we went to our chamber. Gytha pushed open the door and stepped inside. Calum and I were framed in the door and Sarah held Harold. His eyes lit up and he shouted, "Dada" and ran to the door.

I felt tears in my eyes and I raced forward to sweep him up in my arms. Suddenly he began crying and I became confused.

Gytha hurriedly took him from me. "Do not worry Aelfraed, he is unused to you. Now that you are here, he will get to know you again." She handed the crying child to Sarah who cooed to him as she held him and, linking the Thegn and myself, walked back towards the main hall. "Now how long will you be staying and how is Thomas coping without his beloved Sarah?"

Once I started talking I found I couldn't shut up as I filled them both in on the mundane events of Maiden Bower. It was only then that I realised how much my manor meant to me. It was the only home I called a home since I shared a bedroom with my grandmother. I found myself missing it and the loyal workers who lived there. That night, as I lay in bed with my wife for the first time in months, it felt uncomfortable. Gytha turned her back to me, after saying goodnight. I had not expected to make love but I had assumed that Gytha would. I was confused and, what made it worse, was the knowledge that there was a woman just down the passage who was desperate for me in her bed. All my thoughts of home became amplified; their life was simple and there I was in command. Here I was a victim of other's desires and my own lusts.

The next morning, I left a sleeping Gytha to go to the hall for some food. I had talked more than I had eaten the previous evening and was unnaturally ravenous. As I walked to the hall, I put my head around Harold's door. Sarah was dressing him and I went in. He hid behind Sarah and that, for some reason, really upset me. Sarah gave me a half-smile, "Never mind, my lord, it will take some time for him to get used to you."

I nodded unable to speak. Had the few months I had been away made me so strange to my own son? I had a sudden flash of inspiration; I would take them back to Maiden Bower. There I would not have the distraction of the Queen and my son and Gytha could become used to me again. Sarah half opened her mouth to speak but, looking at Harold she closed it and carried on dressing him. I had finished eating the porridge and bread when Gytha came in with Harold.

"Good morning my husband."

"Good morning my wife. I have been thinking. Things are not as dangerous at Topcliffe now. Why don't the three of you return with me? You would be in your own home then and far more comfortable."

Outlaw

A look of panic passed over her face and Sarah threw a strange look at her. Gytha quickly recovered. "I would my lord but the Queen relies on me so much and, in truth, it is a comfortable here. Perhaps next year when things are more settled?"

With that, I was dismissed and she began to feed Harold. Next year might be a dangerous time if Edwin and Morcar went to war with the King. I resolved to leave as soon as I could for I was far from comfortable. "I will go to make sure Branton left for home."

As I walked towards the stables I heard footsteps behind me and saw Sarah hobbling after me. "My lord, a word."

"Yes, Sarah?"

She looked ill at ease. "My lord I er..."

I smiled, "Come now Sarah; you know you can speak openly with me."

She nodded. "My lord, could I return with you to maiden Bower?"

I was surprised, "But I thought you had wanted to be with the bairn and my wife?"

"Well he does not need me now, you see how my lady was feeding him and I, well, I miss my husband." Her eyes began to well with tears, "I do not like it here sir. Please!"

I enfolded her with my arms. "Of course you may return with me. We shall leave tomorrow. That will give you the opportunity to say goodbye and pack your things."

"Thank you, my lord, I am grateful."

Branton had left before dawn and I relaxed a little. I had fulfilled my part of the task and I returned to the main hall. The Queen and Calum were at the table. The Queen was nibbling on a small piece of bread.

"Good morning my lord, your majesty."

Calum nodded, his mouth full of cold meat. "You slept well, my lord."

"I did your majesty. And you?"

"No, I was a little restless, it was a warm night and I was hot."

She flashed me a flirtatious look unseen by the others and I felt myself redden. To cover my embarrassment I launched into an explanation of my decision to leave. "Sarah has asked to accompany me to Maiden Bower, she misses Thomas so I will be leaving in the morning for the journey will be slower and…"

The Queen looked at me, an angry look in her eyes, "Tomorrow? So soon?"

Calum and Gytha looked at each other with a confused look and Gytha said, "But you have only just arrived."

"Have we upset you Aelfraed?" Calum looked quite worried.

"No, no it is just that there is much to do at home and, well Harold seems to be uncomfortable with my presence and, perhaps in a few more months he will be old enough to, well, old enough to be able to talk to me and…"

Gytha looked relieved. "Perhaps you are right my lord and perhaps in a few months we might be able to return home."

"Perhaps."

The sound of chewing and spoons on metal platters filled the air. I hated the atmosphere. I was used to men where they spoke their minds. This must be like the court where everyone wore a mask to hide what they really meant. "My lord Aelfraed, I will have a letter for you to take to Edwin. Come to my chamber after noon and I can explain to you what I wish Morcar to be told and my instructions for Lord Aethelward."

"I obey you in all things majesty."

It was well after noon when we lay, spent, on the bed. I had learned that the Queen was a slave to her passion and, as soon as I had entered the room she had begun to devour me; I was the sheep to her wolf. Now, as we lay together, she admonished me. "Why are you leaving so soon? Am I so unattractive to you?" She looked down at me. "Your body says that you do."

"Of course, I do but think about it. If I stay here then people, Gytha and Calum will become suspicious and talk."

"I am the Queen, I care not."

"That is the point Ealdgyth, you should care for you are the mother of the future King of England and lewd behaviour, especially with the warrior who is to lead the fight against William, would jeopardise your chances of achieving your aim."

She rolled on top of me and straddled me. "I have spent my whole life in politics. I thought that, with Harold, I had a lover and a husband but he was with me for too short a time and then you came along, even better than his father and I became happy. Let us run away Aelfraed. I have money and we will find somewhere away from England where we can live together and be happy."

I sat up. "I swore an oath to Harold and to my men. I am a Housecarl and I must do my duty."

She hurled a pillow at me. "Damn men and their duty! If the world were ruled by women then it would be a better place with more peace and a lot more loving."

I kissed her and began to dress. "But the problem is, my love, that it is ruled by men and if we fled abroad we would be followed by those who wish you harm." I kissed her again. "I will return with more messages, I promise."

"Then make it quick. I need you."

Sarah was silent for most of the journey. She kept looking over her shoulder, back towards Fife and then at me and then she would burst into tears. My guilt surged through me as I desperately tried to remember if she could have been seen and the Queen but I could not; the journey was miserable. I spent the time thinking about military matters to take my mind off the women in my life. I reflected on the armour we had and that of the Normans. Once we reached Maiden Bower Thomas made such a fuss of his wife that all thoughts of the journey evaporated. Branton was a little surprised to see me as he and Osbert filled me in on the events of the past two days.

"Lord Aethelward left with four new men at arms as was suggested. He told us to watch the woods for spies and to continue to make weapons."

He said it as a question rather than a statement. "Yes, Osbert that is excellent. Come with me while I speak with Ralph. I have an idea for our armour." Intrigued he followed me. Ralph stopped working when we entered and walked away from the noisy fire. "I have been thinking. Osbert, do you recall Earl Edwin's men at Fulford?"

"Aye, they ran."

I laughed, "Yes Osbert, but they only wore a mail byrnie such as we wear."

"Yes my lord." I could see him becoming interested.

"The Normans protect their legs with metal greaves." Ralph looked puzzled and I demonstrated. "Metal plates attached to the front of the legs." Enlightenment filled his face. "Could you make them?"

In answer, he went to the back of his workshop and brought out four dagger blanks. He put them across his massive palm. "Sort of like this."

"Like that but attached to each other."

"We would need to use wire to secure them and they would need to be checked and repaired every couple of days." It was my turn for the puzzled look. "The movement on the wire will weaken them and they will break."

"You could cover the wire in leather or cord. It would extend their life a little."

Ralph slapped Osbert on the back. "Good answer. You shall have to smith with me." He nodded approvingly. "It will be much easier than making a mail byrnie."

"Could you do them for the upper arms? They would be a little shorter." Osbert looked at me. "It would give more protection for the upper body. I noticed after Stamford that the most serious wounds apart from the ones which killed were to the shins and the upper arms."

"Aye, I could do that."

"Good. Then make a set for Osbert and me. We will try them out and if they work then they can be made for the rest of the men."

"The only thing my lord is the expense. Iron is not cheap."

"No, but it is cheaper than my men's lives. Buy the iron, no matter what it costs." In my mind, I was envisaging another visit to Reuben.

The next month passed very quickly for I threw myself into being the lord of the manor. The harvest was a good one and I took my men at arms to help the farmers and villains to gather it in. The men at arms did not moan over much and Osbert had them making it a competitive game to see who could gather the most. The people loved it mainly because they had never seen it happen. We had a much better work rate when the fyrd was training and we had the best yield that Thomas could remember. We would have a healthy surplus and Reuben could remain unvisited.

Outlaw

It was early December when events began to move quickly and was the start of the momentous events which would irrevocably change our lives. The first arrival was Aethelward and, thankfully, he was unharmed as were the men at arms. As he dismounted he turned to Osbert first. "They are good men, dependable. Thank you, Osbert, it made my task safer."

Osbert beamed with pride. The men at arms were his life and I saw him striding off, a good head taller. He turned to me. "Well, the Queen was right." We went inside for there was a chill wind blowing from the sea and it chilled to the bone. He went to the fire and turned his back on it to warm himself through. "I am getting too old to ride these roads in winter. But I fear I will need to ride tomorrow to Jorvik to see the Earl." There was little point in hurrying him for he would get to the meat when he was ready. "William comes north next year and he is marrying his sister to some lord from Burgundy. And there is more, Edwin is to be replaced by Copsi." Copsi had been a supporter of Tostig and had fled to Orkney. I had thought he was dead.

"So the Queen was correct."

"Aye, and she had better watch out for I saw Edith Swanneck with that Robert of Jumièges together and they had the look of plotters."

I remembered that the Norman lord had been involved in an attempt to kill King Edward and Edith had already tried to kill Ealdgyth. It did not take a genius to work out what they were plotting. "I am pleased that she is in Fife."

"I am not so sure Aelfraed. There were Scottish lords at William's court. You did right in building up your forces. William is building a huge castle on the river in London. He is here to stay."

The next day Aethelward and I rode with Osbert and ten men at arms to Jorvik. Aethelward suggested we ride armoured when I asked him why he was a little vague, "Let us just say that the Queen is not the only one that was talked about in London. There are many Norman knights who would like to claim you as one of their victims. Guy of Evreux has, apparently many friends." He sniffed. "I cannot see why. I have shit tougher turds than him."

Outlaw

Osbert almost fell off his horse laughing. Uncle was a witty man but he chose his moments. It certainly lightened the news that I was the target of so much Norman animosity. When we reached Edwin's palace I spoke with Osbert, "Stable the horses and have the men secure places in the warrior hall. Make sure they understand there is to be no trouble. I do not want another man murdered because he wanders off alone. There will be time enough for ale at Yule."

"I am here with them, my lord, there will be no trouble."

I smiled and tapped my nose, "However, Osbert, anything you can discover whilst you are here would be useful."

I think that the guards on the walls had spread the word of our arrival. We seemed to be the cause of interest and incident each time we visited. One of Edwin's lieutenants found us and took us to the Earl's private chamber. As the door opened, I saw, to my complete surprise, Ealdgyth. I was stunned. She took my breath away. She had dressed as a Queen with sumptuous furs and jewels on her fingers. She was making a statement. Her whole body was wrapped in layers and she had applied colour to her lips and eyes. For once I was tongue-tied. I only had eyes for her and she stared at me but no one seemed to notice. Edwin and Morcar stepped forward to clasp our arms. Edwin, in particular, seemed excited.

"Well, Aethelward? What did you discover?"

We sat around a table and Aethelward went through the information he had, including the invasion plans of William. "Well sister, I was wrong to doubt your news and it is now clear that we have no option but to fight."

"There is more my lord. He has replaced Earl Morcar with the traitor Copsi. Even now he is with William planning his rule of Northumbria."

I thought Edwin would have an actual fit he became so red. "That black-hearted traitor. That decides it. We fight."

Aethelward held up a hand. "Yes we fight but first we plan. How many trained men have you?"

"Enough."

"Let us be blunt. You did not have enough at Fulford did you." Both brothers coloured at this while Ealdgyth just smiled. "I am not criticising but there is no time to mince words. Have you men who can stand in a shield wall and face the Norman horse? Have you archers to thin their ranks? Have you improved Jorvik's defences?"

Their faces told the truth. They had done nothing but talk. Ealdgyth spoke. "We do not need to be ready yet Lord Aethelward for William will not travel in winter. We have until the spring."

"We have two months, at the most."

Morcar nodded. "You are right. What should we do?"

"Do as Aelfraed has done. Buy arms and armours for your men. Enlarge your armies."

"That costs money."

Ealdgyth said sarcastically, "Which you will not have if William takes your lands from you."

"Very well it will be done." Edwin looked at Morcar. "Will you command strategos?"

I knew that he did not wish to do so but I also knew that he would if only for the Queen and me. "I will but you will do exactly as I say."

Morcar answered for them both, "Of course. And now, a toast, to the restoration of the line of Harold."

We all touched glasses and drank. "Your majesty, I did not expect to see you here. When did you arrive?"

"I came by sea. King Malcolm had a ship already sailing for Jorvik and I came." She looked directly at me, "Your wife is caring for the twins."

Aethelward leaned forwards. "Your life is in danger, your majesty. I believe that Robert of Jumièges and Edith Swanneck are plotting your death."

"Do not worry sister. You will be safe here."

"As she was when Edith tried to poison her last year."

"Security is tighter now. That will not happen." I somehow did not believe that. I had come to learn that the brothers were talkers, not doers.

Ealdgyth held up her hand, "Please, do not trouble yourself over me. If you are so concerned Lord Aelfraed then take the room adjacent to mine. As I recall that was how you saved King Edward's life, by being on hand."

"Whatever I can do to serve your majesty."

Outlaw

"Good, it is settled. I will dress for the feast." She swept out of the room and when she had gone, it felt emptier.

"I still like it not. She was safer in Scotland."

"I know Lord Aethelward but she is the Queen and does as she wishes, even when we do not agree with her."

As we went to our rooms Aethelward took me in hand. "I will be no use tonight to guard the Queen. Should we use Osbert?"

"No uncle. I can do without sleep for one night at least. First I will find Osbert and see if he has discovered aught."

I knew that he had when he was nervously awaiting me at the Mickelgate. "My lord, I was in The Saddle talking with the landlord and he told me that those knights who killed Branton's archers are back in the city."

"But Morcar banished them."

"I know but they are not in the halls, they are staying elsewhere."

"You have done well. Keep your eyes open and have some of the men patrol the walls tonight. I will be in the chamber next to the Queen for Aethelward feels that she may be the target."

"I will divide us into two groups. One can sleep early and the other late. We will be there if you call us."

"Thank you, Osbert. I rely on you much as I did Lord Ridley." That was one of the greatest compliments I could pay my sergeant.

I told Morcar, Edwin and Aethelward of my news and they were shocked, especially Morcar. "But I forbade them to return!"

Aethelward smiled wryly. "You are to be replaced by Copsi so I do not think he will worry overmuch about obeying your law."

"I will warn the guards."

I was not confident. I had seen killers at work and watched guards on sentry duty. They only saw what they expected to see and many drifted off to sleep in the wee small hours. I would need to be alert. The Queen, of course, had other plans for me. After the meal, the Queen was escorted to her room by her brothers. I strapped on my sword and dagger and stood outside the room Morcar looked at me curiously. "Surely waiting outside a room is not a task for a lord?"

I smiled. "When I last did this I was a Housecarl. The King certainly thought it was a worthy task but I will not remain outside

Outlaw

all night, I will retire but I am a light sleeper. If I hear anything I will be able to reach the Queen in minutes."

The Queen must have been listening inside the door for when she heard the silence she opened the door and dragged me inside where she showered me with kisses again. "Come to me. I grew tired of waiting for you and I have followed you here."

I barely had time to remove my sword and dagger before she wrapped her naked body next to mine and we made our usual, passionate, frenetic love. "It is not safe here."

"I am safe in your arms my love, is that not safe enough. Besides I had news."

I sat up. "You did not mention it earlier."

"No, my love, news for you. You are to be a father."

I looked at her and I know that I must have looked like the village idiot for I was slack-jawed and wide-eyed. "Gytha!"

She laughed her dancing laugh, "No you goose, me! I am with child. You and your father are certainly potent."

I did not know what to make of it. How could I be a father and what would the world think. They would ask who the father was and what would her reply be? She saw the look on my face. "Do not worry, people will not notice for a while at least. You saw how I dressed before; I cover up my shape with fine furs. By spring they will all have more to worry about than who has been making love to the queen."

"What happens when the child is born?"

"By then we will either have won or lost and the baby will be forgotten."

"And Gytha."

"I would not worry about your wife Aelfraed." She was running her nails up my chest and stroking me when she said that and, at the time, I ignored it. Soon we were coupling again and this time we both fell asleep.

I was suddenly awake and alert. I had heard something. I slowly opened my eyes. The door did not look to be closed any longer. I slid my left hand to the side of the bed. I sought my sword but all I found was my dagger. It would have to do. I slowly slid from the bed. I hoped that whoever was in the room would take the movement to be the Queen sleeping. I crawled to the end of the bed and saw a shape. It was a leg, looking up I saw two men with daggers drawn stalking the Queen. I had no time to think; I had to act. I lunged upwards stabbing towards the place I thought the neck would be. When my hand was suddenly engulfed in warm blood I knew that I had struck well. There was no light in the room but I caught a lighter shadow and jerked my head back as the blade came towards my neck. With my left hand, I reached out and grabbed the killer's dagger arm. His momentum took us both forwards. He had not been expecting a warrior in the room and as he fell forward with his hand he encountered my naked groin. He involuntarily recoiled in horror and I took my chance. I was holding his dagger and I stabbed upwards with mine. The blade entered his body just below his ribs and it slid upwards into his heart. I jumped to my feet and quickly put on my tunic. It would not do to have a naked Aelfraed in the Queen's chamber. "Guards! Guards!"

Amazingly Ealdgyth had slept through our silent dance of death and when she saw me standing with a bloody dagger in my hand she screamed. Aethelward and the guards were the first in with burning torches. I saw my uncle relax when he saw the bodies on the floor. Both of them still leaking blood. He took the scene in quickly and when he saw the dagger in my hand he nodded and smiled. Then he glanced at my clean tunic and looked puzzled. I quickly shook my head as Edwin and Morcar arrived.

"Are you safe sister?"

Ealdgyth was quick. "Yes Edwin, thanks to the bravery of Lord Aelfraed."

They saw the bodies and the bloody dagger. "What happened?"

"I thought I heard a noise and seeing the Queen's door open I entered and managed to dispose of both of them."

Aethelward turned them over. "From their hair they are Norman, but I do not recognise them. Do you nephew?"

I peered down. "No uncle. It seems Guy and Robert of Jumièges like to get others to do their dirty work."

"Get these bodies out and get this cleaned up."

Aethelward said, "When the bodies are gone, majesty if you would like to use my room. I will stand guard until dawn. I have managed some sleep and Aelfraed has done enough for one night."

Outlaw

Edwin and Morcar patted me on the back as I left the room. I was a hero once more and I had given the Normans even more reasons to hate me and to seek my death.

Chapter 7

The whole city was talking about the attempt on the Queen's life. I sought out Osbert and asked him to do something for me. He disappeared. Aethelward kept giving me strange looks but he said nothing. How I would explain myself to him I did not know. We had put the bodies in the stables; Morcar and Edwin were keen to know who the men were. No one recognised them. A guard approached Morcar, "My lord, Lord Aelfraed's sergeant requests entry."

They looked at me and I nodded. "Send him in."

Osbert came in bowing, along with the landlord of The Saddle. I had sent Osbert on the errand for I had an idea who they were. "Landlord, look at these bodies. Have you ever seen them before?"

He had been a warrior himself and did not blanch at the sight of the whitened bodies. "Aye, my lord. These are two of the Normans who caused trouble last year. The ones who killed your lad. I saw them yesterday with some others."

Edwin and Morcar became even more interested. "Where?"

"Down by the river."

Osbert, go with him and take my men to find them and bring them here." I suddenly realised that this was not my manor, "With your permission my lord."

"Of course."

When Osbert returned it was with the news that the Normans had fled from the city and were, probably, heading south to tell the Norman and his ally that their plot had failed. "Gather the men. We leave for Topcliffe later."

Aethelward joined me at the stables. "I have asked Osbert to gather the men."

"You would leave now nephew?"

"I would return home to prepare for war; warn Ridley and the other Thegns…"

"And the Queen?"

"Now that her brothers are alert to the danger they can protect her." I did not look him in the eye. The real reason was the Queen, I could not stay so close to her, she had entranced me and I could not focus on protecting her because of who she was. I had been lucky on the previous night. I could have been lying in a pool of my own blood, all because of my lust and my desires.

He put his arm around me. "Do not take what I am about to say as a criticism of you. Last night you performed a brave and heroic deed but do not try to tell me that you were outside the room when the murderers entered. You were inside and you were naked. You were in bed with the Queen." I turned to him. "Do not try to deny it. The others believed your story but I saw the tunic without blood. We are warriors Aelfraed and know that the blood goes everywhere."

I dropped my head in resignation. "And that is why I must leave uncle. If I stay then people will know and they will talk. Our situation is parlous enough without impugning the Queen's honour."

"I am not condemning you but your actions have made the Queen's position even worse. Her brothers cannot protect her. They think they can but they have not the ability. We must persuade her to return to Fife."

"We can try but I do not think we will succeed. She needs to be close to the action and, I am sorry to say, close to me. There is something else," I paused, "she is with child, and it is mine."

He shook his head, "One thing about you Aelfraed, you do not do things by halves!"

We returned to the hall where everyone had one topic of conversation, the attempt on the Queen's life. When I entered I was greeted with cheers, pats on the back and applause. I felt like a cheat. I had been lying in a woman's bed but they thought I was the hero stalking the corridors. The Queen rose to greet me, "My Lord Aelfraed, you have saved my life. This is the second time you have done so." She reached up to chastely kiss me on the cheek. "You are the Queen's champion!"

Morcar and Edwin were equally effusive in their praise. "With warriors like you Aelfraed they can outnumber us two to one and we will still win."

Aethelward took the Queen's arm. "Your majesty, a word with you and my nephew in private if you please." He forcefully led us both to a small antechamber normally used by the night guards. "You will have to be more careful, more discreet your majesty."

Outlaw

She turned to stare at me. I shrugged, "He knows."

Aethelward smiled, "Your majesty, your brothers might have believed that story last night for they are not warriors but I know that Aelfraed was naked when he killed those killers."

She managed a wan smile. "My naked hero!"

"The point is if Aelfraed is to protect you he cannot bed you, at least not here."

She pouted and, suddenly became a young girl once more. "But I am Queen."

"And if you wish to remain Queen and if you wish your warriors to fight for you then you must behave as the widow of King Harold and not the lover of his son." Aethelward's blunt words brought home the truth to her and, her shoulders sagging, she nodded. "We will remain here until the New Year. After that time we will need to return to Topcliffe to prepare our forces. Should you wish to visit Topcliffe…"

She leaned up to kiss Aethelward. "What a clever general you are!"

We remained in Jorvik until the middle of January. The Queen and I kept our promises and nothing happened, neither between the sheets nor an attempt on her life. We did hear that Copsi had been confirmed as Earl of Northumbria which meant that Morcar was no longer in command of Jorvik. We had, to all intents and purposes become a rebel city, much like Exeter. Just before we left we declared our support for Harold and Ulf as heirs of King Harold and asked all loyal Thegns for their support. To us it was inevitable but, as we later heard, the court of King William was surprised by our action. They had expected that Copsi would just arrive and take over as William's vassal. The north had spoken and there would be war.

We left Jorvik with my men at arms and ten warriors given by Morcar and Edwin to be the Queen's guards. I suspected that at least one of them was Edwin's spy but it mattered not. At Topcliffe I was master. We travelled back via Coxold so that I could inform Ridley of the events and actions which had taken place. He grinned. "We fight alongside each other again eh, Aelfraed? Good. I have increased my forces and they are almost as well armed as yours. The Normans will get a surprise when they come." Ridley had become a much more confident man since he had ruled Coxold. Thegnship was good for him.

As we rode the last few miles to Maiden Bower, I hoped that this was true. A visitor in Jorvik had told us of other Normans who had travelled to Italy and Sicily and were carving out their own kingdoms as big as King William's; they were not a people to attack lightly.

I had sent a message telling Sarah to prepare rooms for the Queen and to provide her with servants for she had left hers in Scotland with the twins. It was a frosty afternoon when we rode into my citadel, my refuge from the world. The sentries on the towers had seen our arrival and Thomas and Sarah had Branton organise the men into two lines so that we rode down a liveried line. I was impressed with my men. We looked like warriors and not the usual rabble.

Sarah took the Queen to meet her new servants. Once again, she looked a little tearfully at me as she bowed to me and I determined to find out what was on her mind. I was master of Topcliffe and I did not like this strained atmosphere which had existed ever since we had returned from Fife.

Branton sought out Aethelward and myself. "My lord, we have seen tracks in the forests. There are armed men scouting and watching the castle."

"Have you done aught?"

"No my lord, we waited until your return."

"Hunt them and, if you can, bring them to me, if not then kill them."

"Are you sure nephew?"

"Uncle, we are at war. If they are friends they will not be skulking around the forests and if they are enemies then…"

He nodded and Branton left. I think he was pleased to be able to do something. He hated being idle and, like his brother Osbert, was a man of action. I knew that Sarah would take some time to show the Queen around and I went, with Aethelward, to visit Ralph. "How are the improvements coming along Ralph?"

He grinned, "Excellent, my lord. We have adapted them since you and Osbert had yours. I have now made the ones at the shoulder narrower at the top and wider at the bottom. It makes it more comfortable and yet gives more protection. Here is the one I am making for Garth."

He showed me the shoulder protectors made of iron and I could see that they were better than the prototype he had made for us. "Very good. Have some made for us."

"If you will just stand still my lord I will measure you." He took a stick and held it to my arm. Using a lump of old charcoal, he made a mark. He then took a piece of cord and looped it around my arm. He tied a knot and slid it off. He smiled at my puzzled look. "We found that not all warriors are the same and it is just as easy to make a specific piece rather one that fits all."

As we walked back Aethelward spoke warmly of the idea. "That is an excellent idea Aelfraed. Your men will all be much better armoured against the Normans. You at least have prepared for this coming war. Well done."

I saw Sarah walk towards her hut and determined to follow her. I wanted to get to the bottom of her attitude since Fife. With Ealdgyth in my home, things would only become worse. I tapped lightly on the door as I walked in. I knew that it was right to go where I pleased in my land but I respected the privacy of my people. "Thomas, Sarah."

They both bobbed and said, almost as one, "My lord."

"Sarah I am here to speak plainly with you. What have I done to offend you? Since Fife, you have all but shunned me."

In answer, she burst into tears and would have fled the room had not Thomas restrained her. When he spoke he was quite stern. "Sarah, tell the master. This has gone on long enough and he does not deserve this. Either you tell him or I shall."

I was even more confused than I had been. If Thomas knew then what had this to do with Fife?

Sarah spoke, but it was between sobs. She dabbed her eyes with a cloth as she poured out her story. "My lord, you have done nothing wrong. It was the wrong done to you which caused my upset. It is the Lady Gytha." my heart leapt up into my mouth. Was my wife ill? "She has taken the Thegn of Fife to her bed. They live as a couple when you are not there."

I sank into the seat which was behind me. I had not seen that coming but as I watched the fire flicker and flame things suddenly made sense. Harold had been running to Calum and not me; no wonder he was upset. The flustered looks on their faces and the sudden tidying of the bedchamber; they were getting rid of the evidence. The turning of the back in the bed; it all became clear as though someone had removed a veil from my eyes. Then suddenly another thought hit me; if Sarah knew then so did the Queen! I felt doubly used and deceived. All her protestations of love were empty. "Sarah. Thank you for telling me." I stood and enfolded her in my arms. "Let us go back to how it was, where you and Thomas are my friends." She thanked me through a flood of tears.

"Thank you, my lord."

"In future Thomas, I would prefer to know things sooner rather than later."

He nodded, "Yes my lord but you know what wives are like." He heard the words he had said, as though spoken by another and he reddened.

I smiled. "Yes, Thomas I think that I can say now that I do know what wives are like."

When I left the hut I headed directly for the Queen's chamber. I opened the door and pointed to the two servant girls. "Out!"

They fled fearing my wrath. The Queen lay coquettishly on the bed. "My lord, is this to be the future? You come here demanding me at all hours of the day and night?"

I was so angry that I ignored her flirting. "Just when were you going to tell me about Gytha and Calum."

If I had poured a bucket of cold water on her I could not have had a bigger effect. She sat up and covered herself with an animal skin. I have no idea why. Perhaps she thought I was going to attack her and it would, in some way, defend her. "Who told you?"

"Well, obviously not you. Not the woman in whose arms I have been for so many nights. Not the one person I thought would tell me. Why did you not tell me?" I could not understand it. She would have had more chance of my attention if I had known my wife had another.

"I wanted them to be together for I wanted you. I knew that Gytha would not question your presence with me for she and Calum were lovers and then, when I came to England," she tailed

Outlaw

off weakly, "I knew you would be angry and I did not have the courage to tell you."

"Well, I am angry now my Queen. No man likes to be made a fool of, especially not by a woman or in my case two women!"

"It doesn't change things between us."

"Doesn't it? I don't know!"

With that, I stormed out. I was so angry that if I had stayed I would have hit her. Walking across the yard I shouted, "Osbert! Training swords. I am out of practice."

By the time I reached the barn, which we used to practise in during the winter, Osbert and Branton were there. I picked up the small shield we used for training and the wooden sword. Branton placed my training helmet on my head and I faced Osbert. I had not had the opportunity to fight since I had blinded Duff in the summer. I had been too busy organising and plotting. I needed this!

I swung my sword hard at Osbert's head and he just managed to get the shield there in time to protect his head. The blow was so hard that he took a step back and I heard the sharp intake from Branton who had rarely seen his brother forced backwards. Before he could recover I punched forwards with my shield before he could swing and then swung the sword at his knee. I felt it connect and he sank to one knee. I swung the sword up and hacked at his neck. When I saw that he could not counter with his shield I stopped the blade as it touched his neck. He put down his sword. "Well my lord. I do not think that the Normans will stand up to that onslaught."

Branton came over and looked askance at his brother. "Were you letting Lord Aelfraed win?"

In answer, Osbert stood and hit his brother in the stomach with his wooden sword. "Fool!" Then he looked at me with concern in his eyes. "Are you alright my lord? I have never seen such fire in your eyes and I feared for my limbs. I have never felt such blows before."

"I am sorry Osbert. Let us just say that I was taking my anger out on you. I am sorry."

"No, my lord. When I follow you in battle from now on I shall have an inkling of what the poor sod on the other end of your blows is feeling. My job will become a lot easier. God help the Normans when they come!"

I put my arms around the brothers. "Come let us broach one of Goody Sarah's casks. I have a thirst on me." That is the way it is with men. None of this putting on a face and a show; none of this deceit but just simple honesty. I began to yearn for the chance to fight the Normans. The sooner they came the better.

In the event, it was late spring before we heard of the arrival of large numbers of Normans in the north. It was a rumour at first. Refugees fled to Earl Morcar's city telling of being displaced from their lands by new Norman landowners. In some cases, the owners had died at Senlac and Stamford but others were forcibly ejected from their homes. The warning was sufficient for us to rally the lords in the north and prepare for war in earnest. Aethelward held off calling the fyrd up until they had their crops in the ground. We organised, instead, scouts led by Sergeant Branton and incorporating men from all the other lords. They roamed the land for thirty miles south of Jorvik and we knew that we would have enough time to call the fyrd and meet them. Strangely Edwin returned to Mercia, ostensibly to raise his troops but he chose the moment that the Normans began to filter north. Perhaps I was judging hin on his past performance, who knows? The advantage was that Morcar did everything which Aethelward asked of him.

We held a conference at Jorvik. "We need to meet them on a ground of our choosing, one which does not suit their horses." He looked at us all. That means north of Jorvik!"

Morcar paled. "You would abandon Jorvik?"

"No, my lord. We place in Jorvik men to defend the walls and evacuate those others who would just eat the garrison's food during a siege. If their leader is foolish enough to besiege you then that suits us for we can attack his lines and have the advantage we desire. We will withdraw north to the hills close to Helmsley and Osmotherly. The ground favours our shield wall and there are many streams there where we can anchor our flanks,"

Had Edwin been there he would have argued, I knew that but Morcar saw the wisdom in the plan. "I will send away those who are not fighting and begin to bring in the stores."

Outlaw

"Your men at arms we will need. Keep archers and spearmen. We have a sufficient number from Lord Ridley and Lord Aelfraed."

We then returned to our homes. The Queen was now noticeably pregnant and it had reduced her demands for my body to a mere once a day rather than all night as it had been. I tried to persuade her to go to Jorvik or even Fife but she was calm as she explained her reasoning. "I do not wish to be in a place from which I cannot run because it is under siege and I do not want to move. It is uncomfortable. Sarah and the girls are excellent servants and they will deliver our child. I am safer here than I am in Jorvik."

Neither of us could fault her logic but we left a garrison of twenty warriors to protect her. We had begun to move east when Branton's riders rode in. "My Lord, the sergeant sent us. There are Normans close to Wetherby and they are heading for Jorvik."

I turned to Aethelward. "Continue organising our men. I will ride to Branton and organise the archers. We will meet you by the white horse." The white horse was an ancient carving in the hills and seemed appropriate bearing in mind it had been Harold's sign.

Aethelward agreed. "No heroics boy. I need you as the rock in the shield wall. Remember you are still a Housecarl. You and Ridley are the last of the Housecarls now."

I wore my mail armour and took Sweyn, my biggest horse. He was not fast but he could carry me long distances. I also had Boar Splitter, my spear and Death Bringer, my axe. I was going to war and I knew not when I would return to Maiden Bower. The Queen and I always parted each morning as though we would not see each other for a while. She enjoyed the passion of our goodbyes and I was happy to play along.

Branton had gathered all of his scouts together and I could see that they were a healthy number, sixty of them. Each man with a bow and a quiver. "Well done Branton. Where are they?"

"They are heading for Jorvik down the Selby road. There are two thousand of them. About a hundred knights, another thousand light horse, a hundred crossbowmen and eight hundred foot. We still have six scouts out but they are well to the west and have not reported in yet."

Outlaw

"Send a rider to bring them to the white horse." He shouted an order to one of his men who galloped off. "Any siege weapons?"

"No, my lord."

I was relieved. Siege weapons would have caused a problem for us. "Who is their leader?"

"William of Perci."

"Is our Norman friend with them?"

He knew I meant Guy of Evreux and he grinned. "No my lord, I saw many little pricks today, but he was not one of them."

"Good. Now we are going to meet them north of here. When they reach Jorvik they will find it barred. Do you have any of Earl Morcar's men with you?"

"Aye, sir, about nine or ten."

"Right then, send them to Jorvik with a message for the Earl that the Normans are coming."

While Branton went to issue the orders I looked at the fifty men who remained. We could ride and be with Aethelward within a few hours. We had time, before they camped, to cause a little mayhem.

"Branton we are going to annoy the Normans. I want your men to use the old arrows, not the ones we intend to use against the knights. Is that clear?"

Branton looked disappointed but he nodded. I then explained to him my plan and he grinned. "That should upset them. And I have the perfect place. There is a valley which runs parallel to the road. If we take that we and appear like wraiths above them."

We could hear the rattle of armour from the other side of the low hills and I placed myself at the head of ten mounted archers. The archers were all from my demesne and I made sure that their shields were on their saddles and mine was on my arm. I wanted them to try to capture the hero of Fulford. I was counting on my notoriety and their impetuosity. The other forty men waited below the crest of the hill.

I turned to address them. "Men of Topcliffe, today we begin to regain our land and we are the first to do so. Remember we are here to hurt them and I do not want any of you to get yourselves killed. If you do then you will be in serious trouble!" They laughed and that gave me confidence. "Topcliffe!"

Outlaw

We burst over the skyline and we could see them less than a hundred paces away. There was a thin line of mounted scouts who had not seen us. We halted and Branton ordered the men to fire. The scouts fell to a man as horses and men were struck with arrows. They then changed their aim to the foot soldiers behind them and two flights struck them before the horsemen at the rear and the front reacted. "Withdraw!"

The men were awaiting the order and we galloped off in good order. Their crossbowmen were busy trying to load their cumbersome weapons and the light horse only had spears. We were safe. They were, however, good horsemen and they began to catch us. As we crested the rise the other archers waited with drawn bows. Branton led his men through gaps in their ranks to wheel around and fill in the gaps. I wheeled to the left of the line and readied Boar Splitter. A hundred men thundered over the top of the hill to be met by a withering rain of arrows. I saw many men plucked from their saddles and fall to their death. Branton's men kept up the rate. One knight had accompanied them and he galloped directly at me, his spear held in front of him. I kicked Sweyn hard and he lunged forwards. I knew that I had to avoid hitting the shield for it was designed to deflect blows, my uncle had told me that. I chose instead the less honourable but more effective target, his horse. I held the weapon overhand and stabbed down just as his spear struck my shield. The wicked point flicked up but the metal rim turned it from me. As I withdrew my spear I saw it was covered in blood. I had hit his horse. He turned amazingly quickly, far quicker than I, and I saw him draw out his sword. I had no time to do so and I kept my hold on Boar Splitter. He hacked down at me and his sword struck my new shoulder armour. The blow hurt but it did not penetrate as the blade slid down. His horse caused the brave knight's death for it dropped its head and I could see his young face. I thrust Boar Splitter straight at the man's eye and as it went in I turned and twisted. He gave a high pitched scream and fell to the floor, dead.

I heard Branton's voice, "My lord!"

I looked up to see the knights now attacking. "Retreat!"

Had there been no dead they would have caught us but, as it was, they had to negotiate the dead and dying as well as riderless mounts. Within a hundred paces they had given up to reclaim their dead. I reined in as soon as I could, "Any casualties?"

"A few scratches that is all."

"How many of theirs?"

"I think there would be at least twenty dead and perhaps half of that wounded."

"A victory then."

"Aye sir, but your combat against the knight, I thought he had you with the sword."

"Thank Ralph and his new armour. It saved my life."

Aethelward and Ridley had already set up the camp below a small wooded knoll. I could see that it had been chosen with defence in mind and I envisaged the shield wall atop the knoll. The fires were already burning and I could see the ditch which had been dug in front of the camp. A warrior directed us to the safe piece of land which crossed it. As we looked down I could see the wooden stakes sticking viciously up. It would hurt both horse and rider.

Aethelward was pleased when I told him the enemy numbers but less happy that I had risked death. "I said no heroics."

"There were none. I was never in danger."

Aethelward raised his eyes to the skies, "They will not be here before the day after tomorrow which means we have time to prepare our defences."

Ridley was always deep and thoughtful and he looked awkwardly at Aethelward, "My lord, how do you know they will come here? They could just besiege Jorvik, or go elsewhere."

"They could; which is why Branton is going to draw them on by harrying them tomorrow. They cannot besiege for they have no weapons and thanks to my nephew they know that he is north of them. When they see the shields of Branton and his men, they will come."

We had just over a thousand warriors that day. Two hundred were armoured men at arms and a hundred were archers. The rest were an unknown quantity, the fyrd. Aethelward had been told what caused the disaster at Senlac Hill, the fyrd pursuing the Normans, and he sought to obviate that by placing the fyrd behind the thin line of men at arms and archers. If we were successful then

Outlaw

they could pursue the enemy. "Your men," he said to Ridley and me, "will be the key to success or failure. You will have to endure their horsemen. This is why I have placed us, as Harold did, on an upslope. Their horses will have to slow down but they will be looking for a weakness."

I looked at our men at arms; they were sharpening weapons and talking easily to each other. They were confident for they had never suffered a defeat. Those who had been at Fulford and Stamford, the few who remained, had left the battlefield with their weapons and the dead enemy remained. They would not worry about the Normans.

Branton and his archers arrived shortly before dusk. He was grinning from ear to ear, "They are coming, my lord and they are angrier than a wrecked wasp's nest." He pointed to the south, "They are about a mile away."

"Did you lose any men?"

"Just one archer, his horse fell and he was surrounded."

Aethelward looked at me, "They will know our numbers then."

"Rafe will not talk."

Aethelward shook his head. "He will for the Normans are a cruel people and they will torture him. It matters not Branton, in fact, it may aid us for they will know that they outnumber us. Place your men on the flanks and put your horses at the rear with the boys. They are the horse guards today."

I turned to Osbert, "Now Osbert."

"Stand to arms!"

Every man took his place, eager to face the enemy. I nodded to him, "Unfurl the banners, and let them know who we are."

Sarah and the women had busily sown the red horse on a white background and the huge banner looked magnificent as it fluttered overhead. Ridley signalled to his sergeant and his banner, slightly smaller but no less magnificent, was unfurled. He had two smaller red horses on a green background. The Normans would have an incentive to close with us and that is what we wanted.

One of the sentries on the hill shouted, "Riders coming in."

Every weapon was readied and then we saw that it was the last of our scouts coming from the west. The other archers recognised them and began hurling ribald insults at them.

"Where the fuck have you been? Shagging sheep?"

"Overslept?"

"You'll be late for your own funeral."

The leader rode up to me; he was one of Branton's men. "Sorry we are late sir, we found a column of men. They were heading up the Roman road towards Ripon."

Aethelward frowned. "How many and who was their leader?"

"There were about fifty knights, a few hundred horsemen, thirty crossbowmen and two hundred foot. They had no banners but were led by an older man dressed like you my lord and that Norman tosser from Jorvik; the one who doesn't like you."

"Guy of Evreux!"

"And I would guess that the man dressed like you is Copsi."

"Uncle if they join with these then we are in trouble."

"No, but I worry about Topcliffe for Guy of Evreux knows where you live."

That thought had not crossed my mind and now it infected it. The few men we had left to guard it could not withstand an assault by almost a thousand men. I prayed that they were heading for Ripon. My thoughts were interrupted by a shout from the sentry again, "Enemy in sight."

Chapter 8

The thundering hooves of the approaching horsemen confirmed the sentry's warning. The line of light horse reined in when they were five hundred paces away. They had expected to fall upon a few archers and suddenly they saw a wall of iron facing them. The numbers grew and we saw the Norman knights with the Perci banner come to the fore. They surveyed the scene and we waited for their attack.

Aethelward said, confidently, "They will not attack tonight."

"How do you know? "

"Look at their horses. They have ridden hard carrying armoured men. I can see that they are lathered. If they do attack I will be surprised for they will lose."

He was right for we saw them withdraw to a low hill about a mile away in the lee of the white horse. They set up camp. I turned to Osbert, "Stand the men down but I want a screen of sentries to warn us of their approach. Light the cooking fires on the other side of the hill." He looked at me strangely, "We need our sentries to have no distractions."

Ridley nodded, "I remember in Wales, Aelfraed. Those sentries did not see us for they had fires burning."

"I will do so my lord."

The three of us watched the Normans for a while until night fell completely and all we could see were their fires. "Do you think they will come tonight?"

"I would, nephew if I were Perci. If only to see what the terrain is like. If he does not then he is a poor general and tomorrow will be easy. If he does then we will have our work cut out on the morrow. But as a precaution have the men take water from the stream and soak the ground behind the ditches on the flanks. It will not hurt us but it will slow down any advance."

I ate as I walked around our lines. I wanted my men to see me and gain confidence from that but I also wanted to be close to the front line in case they did come. Ridley copied me and followed me around but Aethelward was tired, and if I am honest, not well. He retired early leaving the watch to us. We saw the fires dim and then the night was black. "Ridley, you get some sleep now and I will wake you at moonset. You can have the early watch."

Reluctantly my friend went to bed. "Osbert. You sleep now and I will wake you in an hour or so. I may need some company then."

I could not sleep anyway. My mind was filled with the worry of Maiden Bower. Should I have left more men to defend it? Could I have sent the Queen and my people to Medelai? None of this was any use for it was in the past but it tormented me that I had been so keen to bring the Normans to battle that I had forgotten my weakness, Maiden Bower. I wandered amongst the sentries, ensuring that they were alert. Their teeth showed white in the night and they nodded their respect. Suddenly we heard a cry and we drew our weapons. There was another noise and a second cry. I turned to the sentries next to me and held my finger to my lips. I then signalled for them to go forward with me. When we reached the ditch we saw the scurrying shapes of the enemy scouts who had fallen foul of the ditch and the stakes. It was dark and I could not see but when morning came I expected I would see some blood on the sharpened spikes. Our defences had been effective.

When Osbert relieved me I fell into a sound sleep. The fact that they had come meant that it would be a hard day and I knew that we had to defeat them quickly to enable me to find out where Guy and Copsi had gone. If the Normans did not attack the next day then we would have to.

We were up and fed before dawn, anticipating an early attack. They had seen how few we were and they would have identified the fyrd, distinctive by nature of their lack of uniformity. Of course, they did not know that our fyrd were better trained and prepared than those who had died with Harold. Branton and my archers each had two quivers; one held the mail breakers and the other the normal missiles. Aethelward sat astride his horse just behind the men at arms, the better to survey the enemy ranks. It was he who saw them advance.

"Here they come."

William of Perci had brought bundles of faggots which they intended to lay in the spike-filled ditch. "Archers, take out those men."

The range was just over a hundred paces and the archers sent over flights of fifty arrows at a time. Even though each faggot bearer had a warrior protecting him with a shield, they took heavy casualties. They were brave men for they succeeded in covering the stakes, some of them with their dead bodies. William's herald lowered a pennant and the light horse, armed with a spear and shield and covered in leather armour, galloped forwards. Osbert began to bang his shield with his spear and it was taken up along the line. I knew how unnerving that sound was. It was a message to the horsemen that we were not moving. As soon as they crossed the ditch the land began to rise and that allowed Branton's archers to aim at the horses on a flatter trajectory. It also visibly slowed up the charging horses. The front rank was decimated and the few who threw their spears and javelins did little damage to our shield wall. When they retreated there were dead and dying horses scattered along our front and the dead horsemen amongst them.

"He is sending the crossbowmen against the archers."

Branton nodded his acknowledgement. I saw that the foot soldiers began to advance steadily towards us. William of Perci was no fool. My archers were not numerous and could only fire at one target. He was sacrificing his crossbows to enable his infantry to weaken us. I turned to Ridley and Osbert who were standing just behind me, "As soon as the first men are across the ditch we will charge them. They will not be expecting that."

They both grinned and Osbert shouted, "Shield wall!" I stepped back between Ridley and Osbert. If we went into wedge formation then we would be the tip. The line which approached us was ragged and not continuous. The men in it had not trained as we had. They might outnumber us but we were organised.

The first fifty had crossed the ditch and Osbert yelled, "Forwards!"

We moved quickly, but without running towards the line of foot soldiers. I held Boar Splitter above my shield and identified the warrior I would be hitting. He too had a mail shirt and the Norman helmet with the nasal. His shield was a shorter version of the kite shield used by the knights and in his hand, he held a spear. We were a solid line and the brave man advanced towards it. I could see that I was taller and I mentally adjusted my aim so that I would

Outlaw

strike downwards. The advantage of a round shield was that any blow which struck the top would slide around the side. The man before me had no such aid and when I stabbed down he reacted by pushing his shield up. He was too slow and all he succeeded in doing was driving the spearhead into his skull. I twisted the blade out and looked for another enemy. I saw, from the corner of my eye that Osbert and Ridley were slightly behind me. We had ended in a wedge formation. Around me, I could hear the sounds of battle, cries of joy and death screams. When I saw the ditch a little way ahead I shouted, "Charge! Push them in the ditch!"

Even though they had filled in the ditch it was uneven and, as we hit them, they fell to be stabbed as they lay on the ground, pinning their writing bodies to their own faggots. "Withdraw!"

We pulled back steadily to our original position. I turned to look for Aethelward but I could not see him. I checked down the flanks and saw that the crossbowmen had retreated and most of Branton's men remained. Branton himself came running over, "Lord Aethelward has been struck by a bolt. He lives but he cannot direct the battle." He saw the shocked look on my face, "He will live my lord."

There was a lull as the Normans regrouped. We had taken few casualties but they had been badly hit and their confidence dented. They still outnumbered us. I watched as they divided their horse. The knights took their right flank while the lighter horse took the left. The mauled foot and crossbowmen began to advance up the middle.

"Branton use your mail breakers against the knights and send the other archers to the right."

There were only a hundred knights and they thought they would ride through my archers and attack our flanks. They would have a shock coming. "Ridley, go to the left side of our line, Osbert, take the right." I needed two experienced heads if the archers did break. I glanced behind me. There was now no one to command the fyrd now that Aethelward had fallen.

I was gratified to see that the foot moved cautiously towards us. Their resolved weakened the closer they came to us they clambered over their dead comrades. I was able to watch the knights as they rode up the hill towards Branton. I say rode rather

Outlaw

than charged for it was, perforce slower than they would have liked, for the ground was wet and the horses carried a heavy load. I wondered if Branton had delayed his men too long for the horsemen were but sixty paces away and he had not given the order. The men before me were a hundred paces away and trudging rather than marching towards us. I heard, "Loose!" from Branton and turned to see the twenty arrows fly towards the Normans. Ten knights were plucked from their saddles and two horses veered away from the deadly missiles hurtling towards them. The rest of the knights halted and covered themselves with their shields. Whoever was in command decided that discretion was the better part of valour and retreated down the hill. It did not save them for Branton and his men continued to pour arrow after arrow at them. Only half of their force reached their own lines unscathed.

The archers on the right had not fared as well and I saw fewer flights flying from their arrows. Luckily Branton saw their plight and I saw the resourceful sergeant send ten of his archers to reinforce them. Then I was too busy to notice as we became engaged. Crossbow bolts flew over our heads and began to strike the fyrd. I turned and roared, "Fyrd! Up shields"

My men already had their shields up but some of the less well trained paid for it with their lives. We strode forward to engage the men at arms. Boar Splitter stabbed and jabbed at all before him and I could see the fear in men's eyes. No one wished to confront the Red Horse and the deadly spear. I was in that happy state warriors sometimes achieve; I was in a rhythm stabbing and punching. One of my victims fell sideways clutching the shaft, my weapon was torn from my grip. In one fluid motion, I slid my shield around and took up Death Bringer. Our line was looser but my men, who surrounded me, knew my action and they moved out of the circle of death as the axe began to weave a path before me. The warriors before me had terror in their eyes. They stabbed their spears at me but my new armour deflected most of the blows and those that did strike me did not penetrate Ralph's excellent work. One warrior, braver than the rest, attempted to step inside my swing; with a slight correction, the axe head sliced through his helmet and into his skull. The soldier behind tried to take advantage as I withdrew

Outlaw

my blade but the warrior next to me thrust his spear into his mouth, already shouting his triumph.

That was enough for most of them and they began to retreat. "After them! Do not let them regroup. Branton! Keep your eye on the knights."

I knew that Ridley and Osbert would warn me of danger to our flanks and my only fear was a charge by the knights. I never, for one moment, thought that Osbert and Ridley were harmed. The men we fought were not the Welsh Housecarls, they were not good enough. We passed beyond the ditch and still, they retreated, the ones at the back running away. Our archers began to shoot arrow after arrow into their unprotected back. I wondered if we would be able to reach their leader, still sitting impassively on his mount behind the rest of his men. I heard, "Ware right!" Looking over I saw the light horse preparing to charge.

"Fall back. Keep in good order."

We managed to reach the security of the fyrd and we gathered our breath. The field was covered by their dead. There appeared to be mercifully few of our men lying in the mud and I saw Ridley and Osbert safe on the flanks. This was where I missed my uncle and his advice. I had no idea how many we had killed but assumed we were almost even. "Branton!"

"Yes my lord?"

"Mount up all of your archers. We are going to attack them. You keep the horse away from us. Ride at them and shoot your arrows." I grinned, "They have learned to fear you. Osbert, Lord Ridley." When they reached me I was pleased to see them whole and without wounds. "Have we lost many?" I was aware that I only had two hundred men at arms. We could not afford high losses.

"A handful."

"We are going to attack them. Ridley, take half of the men at arms on the left, Osbert the rest of them on the right. I will lead the fyrd."

Osbert cocked his head, "Are you sure, my lord? They are unpredictable."

"I will have my fyrd behind me and Branton will keep watch on the horses. I will give the command when I have spoken to the fyrd. Let me know if Perci makes a move."

Outlaw

I moved up the hill towards the fyrd. The wounded had been taken behind the men and I wondered how my uncle was. I was desperate to speak with him but time was of the essence. The men of the fyrd looked eager and, as I approached, they began to roar my name. I held up my hands for silence and they all stopped. "Today we get revenge for King Harold. Today I will lead you to attack and defeat these Normans. Some of you know me, others do not." I glared at them, "No one goes ahead of me. Is that clear?" Some said 'yes my lord' and others nodded. "Keep together and make sure your shoulders touch your neighbours. The men of Topcliffe will be behind me, watch them." I saw my own people visibly grow a head taller. "Form your lines and follow me."

I walked down the slope and saw that the Normans had still to move. That, in itself, gave me confidence. We had them worried. I carried Death Bringer for I wanted to inspire fear in these foot soldiers. "Let them know we are coming!"

Ridley and Osbert began banging their shields and those in the fyrd who had them, mainly my men did the same and then a single voice started a chant which they all took up, "Aelfraed! Aelfraed!" I moved forwards and the whole ungainly line headed down the slope. The chant and the banging help to keep the rhythm and when I glanced down I saw that they were all marching in step. The bodies were a minor inconvenience as we stepped over them. I saw the pennant dip and the remnants of the light horse charged. It was a weak charge for the horses were blown and Branton's archers kept up such a withering rate that they soon withdrew. Crossbow bolts began to strike the men and Branton changed his target. I actually saw one heading for my face, I slightly inclined my head and felt it fly along my cheek.

Perci had recognised the fyrd and me. He obviously saw his chance and he and fifty knights rode in a wedge towards me. I roared, "Shield wall!" noticing, as I did so that William of Perci was in the third rank. He was a careful warrior. Branton's men were using their mail breakers but I knew they would have few left. The whole battle would be determined by the men of the fyrd and Death Bringer. Fortunately, he was aiming his wedge at me and my men had spears- I, of course, didn't. I would be facing the most powerful weapon of the age with just an axe and a mail shirt.

Outlaw

I began swinging, watching, as I did so, the spear held out by the lead warrior. He had a golden star on his shield. I was aware of other knights being struck by arrows but the one at the front bore a charmed life. Suddenly the spear struck my shoulder just as my axe bit, savagely, into the horse's neck. My blow was so hard that it almost severed the head. The spearhead caught in the metal plates and was torn from the rider's grip. As he tumbled to the ground I raised the axe and in one blow decapitated the surprised knight. I quickly swung again and this time connected with a knight's leg. He screamed in agony and wheeled his horse around. I was suddenly facing William of Perci. His horse had stopped and he held his spear in his hand, without warning he threw the spear overhand at me. I reacted without thinking and Death Bringer pinged off the head of the spear making it spiral away and behind me. He actually smiled at me and nodded acknowledgement. Shouting something in Norman the knights rode away as quickly as they had charged. My fyrd cheered and we continued our descent towards the cowering foot soldiers. I knew that the time was right and I shouted, "Charge!"

The moment that we broke into a run the enemy just broke and fled, following the departing horsemen. "Branton! After their horsemen. Harry them."

Soon the only Normans left were those who were dead or about to be dead. The fyrd crossed the field, slitting throats as they went and picking up pieces of armour and weapons. Ridley made his way towards me, "I think your grandmother was watching you this day Aelfraed."

"I think someone was. Find out the butcher's bill. I must find Aethelward."

Aethelward was awake, lying amongst the wounded. His shoulder was bandaged and there was blood seeping from it. The farmer who had repaired him was more used to animals. "Well?"

"We won and they fled."

He closed his eyes, sighed and lay back. For a moment I thought he had expired but, after what seemed an age, he opened them and said, "Thank god for that. I was worried when you attacked their line. That was not our plan."

"No Uncle, but as there is another column near Ripon I knew we had no time to sit and wait for them to attack. We had to strike quickly. The arrows worked and that took the heart from their knights. They are used to taking arrows and still winning. Branton's arrows kill!"

When we tallied up our losses, they were lighter than we could have hoped; sixteen archers, thirty men at arms and forty of the fyrd. There were many wounds but all but three of them would survive. The Normans had lost heavily. We found eighteen dead knights, almost a hundred and fifty of their horsemen and two hundred foot soldiers and crossbowmen. Perci would have to head south and lick his wounds,

I held a war council, "Osbert, take the fyrd back to Topcliffe and half of our men at arms and archers. Lord Ridley and I will follow them south and then take Aethelward to Jorvik for I do not like the look of his wound. Although Osbert did not like splitting our forces he knew that I was worried about Maiden Bower. We lashed a sling together made from cloaks and spears and put Aethelward between two horses. Our progress was slow but I still felt every bump as my uncle winced. I was grateful when we reached Easingwold and he passed out. I suppose I could have taken him to the priory just ten miles north but I did not trust Morcar anymore. He needed to know that we had won. We had our first victory against the Normans.

It was dusk when we reached the northern gate of the city. The sentries wondered at our state for men were covered in Norman blood. We were quickly admitted and I sought the nuns at the house of healing. The looks on their faces when they beheld my uncle's wounds were not hopeful. He woke and murmured, "Go find Morcar. I am in good hands now."

Morcar was beaming from ear to ear. "I have heard that you have trounced the enemy."

"They fled the field if that is what you mean but they are still around and there is another column heading for Ripon." I paused, "William has sent Copsi north."

Had I slapped him I could not have effected a bigger change. He paled. "It is not over then?"

Outlaw

I laughed. "No, it has not started. But at least you will be safe now and we have the chance to build up the army. You can allow the people back into the city now."

He looked shamefaced. "They never left. They would not go."

I was about to become angry but there would have been little point. It was in the past but it just proved that Morcar was not a leader. "I will remain here tonight and then take the army to Ripon to find this Copsi."

When I returned to the house of healing Aethelward was looking a little better. He grabbed my hand. "Find Reuben and fetch him here." I was about to argue but he just said, "Do it, please."

I owed my uncle all and I did as I was bid. Reuben looked a little nervous as he entered the house of healing. The nuns had little love of Jews but my presence and Reuben's kind and ancient face made it easier.

As we entered his chamber one of the nuns who was leaving touched my arm and gently shook her head. I hoped that I had misunderstood the gesture. Perhaps she meant that Reuben should not be there but in my heart, I knew what it meant.

"Reuben, Aelfraed, I am dying." He held up his hand to silence my arguments. "I am a warrior and I know these things but I have had a good life and I have seen my sister son become the greatest Saxon warrior of his age." He turned to Reuben, "Old friend, for that is what you are, you have my monies. I hereby bequeath them to my nephew."

"It will be done my lord and it has been an honour to serve you." He then did something surprising, he leaned forward and kissed Aethelward on his forehead. "I will leave you with your nephew now for it is time for those things we leave unsaid, to be said." He turned to me, "Before you return to your home my lord if you come to my home, I will apprise you of your assets." He stood in the doorway looking at Aethelward and then he left.

"Come, closer Aelfraed, we have little time." I sat on the bed and leaned my ear so that it was close to his mouth. "You will no longer have me for advice but I saw today that you do not need it. You are a strategos. I know not how things will turn out. That is *wyrd*, but I hope that we will prevail and return England to its rightful rulers. If events turn out ill then use your money to buy safety in another land. I was happy in Constantinople and they would make you welcome."

He sighed and lay back. "Uncle!" He opened his eyes and gave me a wan smile. "I want to thank you for coming back for me all those years ago and making me the man I am. I love you as the father I never knew and I promise that I will not rest until I have ended the rule of the tyrant."

"Do not waste your life. Unless you can raise the country behind you then you will lose. At the end of my life, I realise now that life is precious and not to be thrown away. But I shall now be with Sweyn and Ulf, Osgar, Wolf and Harold and we will watch your deeds....."

And he was gone. Lord Aethelward, the Varangian Guard, the Thingman, the strategos and my best friend, died in the house of healing in Jorvik.

The next day we laid him to rest in the churchyard of the cathedral. Reuben, Ridley, Branton and Morcar were the only mourners present at the interment. I wanted it to be quiet with those who had known the great man. As we stood in silence, each saying goodbye in his own way, I suddenly felt very lonely. There had always been someone for me, Nanna and then Aethelward and now I was alone; I still had Ealdgyth but she was not someone who could replace Aethelward but it made me desperate to see her again for with her I could cry, with her, I could seek comfort.

The men at arms had all respected Aethelward and we marched in sombre silence across the Ouse, and north-west to Topcliffe. Yesterday's victory now seemed hollow. We had paid a bigger price than I had wanted and I was even more determined to rid my land of these invaders. Reuben had given to me a list of my assets and I was a rich man. He had given me a small box of coins. When I had asked him why he had inclined his head and said he had a feeling that I would need it sooner rather than later. It was only a tiny part of my money but money was not important to me; people were.

We were still ten miles from Maiden Bower when we saw the thin tendril of smoke spiralling into the sky. Branton had his scouts out but we were all on edge. One of his scouts suddenly appeared,

Outlaw

waving his arms. We halted and readied our weapons. "Riders approaching!"

We relaxed when Branton recognised them as two of his archers. Their faces were ashen as they reined in their mounts. "My lord, Sergeant Osbert sent us, Maiden Bower has been attacked and destroyed."

I turned to Branton, "Take charge and bring the men along. I will ride ahead."

"I will come with you Aelfraed."

Ridley and I rode as though the devil was chasing us. I cared not if Sweyn suffered, this was far more important. The smoke grew as we drew closer. I could see that the wooden walls had gone long before we reached it and, of the settlement, neither a stick nor stone remained unburned. We could see the fyrd, under Osbert's direction, moving the bodies into neat lines. When he heard our approach he turned to come towards me and dropped to his knees. I dismounted and lifted his face. Tears were coursing down his cheeks. "Rise Osbert and tell me all. But first, were there any survivors?"

"No my lord, all are dead." He stood, "All." The emphasis on the last word told me all that I needed to know. I nodded to him to begin.

"It was late when we reached here last night for the men were weary. The fires were still burning. We ran the last mile but we could not save any of the buildings. We found one survivor, Ralph's boy, Ralph. He was hiding in the river, hidden by the stream. He sleeps now but he told us the story. Norman knights arrived the day before yesterday with a proclamation which took Topcliffe from you and gave it to a Guy of Evreux. Thomas argued that you were the rightful ruler and he was slain when Sarah tried to intervene she too was slain. The men on the walls had opened the gates to see what was happening and the Normans rode in unopposed. They slaughtered all who were within. Ralph told his son to hide and then he fought the Normans with his hammer. We found his body surrounded by much blood. He died well."

"And the Queen?" He took a breath. "Come on man. She is dead. Tell me how?"

"She and her servants were raped and then they had their throats slit. I have placed her body with that of Ralph, Thomas and Sarah." He looked at me tearfully, "I knew that they were special to you."

I waved a hand around the dead. "They were all special to me." I took him and embraced him. "Thank you old friend, I know that was not easy. Take me to the Queen."

As I gazed down on the wife of my father I suddenly realised that I was the only one who knew she was with child. That secret died with Aethelward and Ealdgyth. "We will bury them all in the morning in the ruins of Thomas' home." This was a new way to wage war. This was the Norman way. All had been killed, men, women and children. It gave us a foretaste of what was to come when William himself came north.

As we went out into the setting sun I asked Osbert. "Who was with the Norman knight and where did they go?"

"Ralph son heard one say he was Copsi, Earl of Northumbria. He said they headed north-west. "

"Which means Ripon or Medelai. Tomorrow, send a rider to Medelai to see if they are there and then you and I will visit Ripon."

He and Ridley looked shocked. "You cannot take the army to Ripon…"

"Never fear Ridley. I will take just Osbert for the army is in no condition to take a city and I would not risk innocent Northumbrians dying. If we waited for them to come to us then we would be trapped between them and William of Perci's force. No, I have to strike quickly. We will go in disguise to Ripon if the curs are not at Medelai. And then Ridley, old friend, I would like you to care for my people as this land has been given to another."

"Of course. What will you do?"

"Do? Why when I have finished with these murderers I will continue to fight this Norman tyranny. When I have disposed of these two murderers then we will raise the north. This is not the end of the war. It is the beginning. Morcar had better decide if he is part of it or not for I have finished playing at war. Now it is to the death!"

Chapter 9

Branton was as angry and distraught as any when he arrived later in the evening. All of us just wanted to hurt someone. All the elation of our victory had been sucked from us by the deaths we had suffered. It was aggravated by the fact that our losses on the battlefield had been so light but the ones we had suffered were grievous.

The dead were laid to rest in separate graves. I put silver coins from my box on their eyes. It was the second funeral in as many days and I had had enough. We placed stones at the head of each grave and we had ensured that the graves all faced east. When we had time we would place proper headstones but we had more pressing matters on our mind. As events turned out we never did put the headstones there and the four graves still have a rough stone to mark them as far as I know. Ridley took Ralphson with him to Coxold for the boy had no-one. He had been his father's apprentice and when Ridley offered him a post as a blacksmith he was delighted. Ridley was the kindest man I knew. The rider from Medelai arrived soon after the funeral. "The Normans are not at Medelai, my lord."

"Then they have gone to Ripon. Branton, take the men to Medelai and await your brother and me there."

He didn't move. "My lord, with respect I would rather go with you," I opened my mouth to speak, but he put his hand up. I saw Osbert reach for his blade but I shook my head. Branton was loyal and he must have had a good reason to be so insolent. "You wish to sneak around Ripon, my lord. Good. That is what I do best. If you were to stand in a shield wall then my knuckleheaded brother is a far better man than me." He said it with a smile to take out the insult and I saw his brother give a half smile. "With me, we would blend in but with my brother, you would both stand out like sore thumbs because, with respect, my lord, you are big. And finally, I know Ripon better than my brother, for I served there for a short time."

There was silence and then Ridley said, "He makes sense; Aelfraed and I know that Osbert would go with you but if you want to succeed then you need Branton who is stealthier but I want to ask what you hope to achieve?"

"I will kill Guy of Evreux and I will kill Copsi."

"You know what it is you do?" I nodded. "It will not be in battle, this will be murder. Are you ready for the consequences?"

"I am for I know that you will look after my men should aught happen to me."

"What about Gytha and your son?"

I looked at the three men; I was now as close to these as any since I fought with Ridley, Wolf and Osgar in the shield wall. I took a breath. "Lady Gytha now makes beast with two backs with the Thegn of Fife." The shocked look on their faces was mixed with sympathy and revulsion. "So you see, this is now my world. And I have to do something about it. It is *wyrd*." That they understood and they nodded. "Branton I will take you. Osbert, take my men to Medelai but tell them that if they no longer wish to serve me then I will understand." I handed him a heavy purse. "In that is enough coin to give each archer and man at arms ten silver pieces. They can serve Lord Ridley if they choose."

Osbert was appalled. "My lord they would serve you."

"Give them the choice, Osbert, for I am stepping over the line and where I am going I cannot guarantee that they will have a lord."

"I will do as you ask my lord but to us, you will always be a lord and you will always be our leader."

"Thank you for that. Take my armour and weapons with you to Medelai and we will meet you there when this is finished. Now, Branton, tell me, how do I become anonymous?"

By the time we left Maiden Bower, I had been transformed. He took a tunic from one of his archers and tied it with an old belt. There was a hood on it and it would help to disguise my face. Its colour was a nondescript browny green which would blend in well with a range of backgrounds. More importantly, it was a common colour and a common design. I would look like many other men. We found a sword which had been used by one of the defenders who had died and I took my own dagger. Around my shoulders he placed one of the wolf skins we used to keep us warm and on my head, he put a leather helmet, much as I had worn when I first left

Outlaw

Medelai. He changed Sweyn for one of his nags and we both looked like itinerant warriors seeking employment. It was not far from Topcliffe to Ripon and we took it slowly. "We need to get there just before dark before they close the gates, my lord."

"If you spend the whole time my lording me then we will soon give the game away. I will take your brother's name eh?"

He smiled, "Right, Osbert. We will see if there are rooms at The Swan and keep a low profile. I always find that if you sit and drink you will normally hear more than if you ask questions." I nodded. That was how he and his brother had first come into my employment when Ridley and I had stayed at The Angel for a meal all those years ago.

Ripon is a fine city and an old one but it is much smaller than Jorvik. The warrior hall stood next to the river and it was where, I assumed, the Normans would stay as it was the best accommodation in the city. Branton was worried about our venture, I could see that. He nervously scanned the road ahead and behind. When he caught me looking at him he gave me a false smile; it was not like Branton.

"What is on your mind, Branton?"

"I understand why you want to rid the world of these Normans but why not bring our men at arms and we could ambush them and kill them in battle."

"Because, Branton, I feel responsible for all those who died at Maiden Bower. I gave the Queen my protection. If we came to Ripon with our men at arms they could wait us out and besides we do not have enough men, at the moment, to fight them." I looked at his quiver. "How many knight killers do you have left for your bow? "

"A few."

"And with Ralph dead where will we get them? No this must be done in dark of night to tell these Normans that they cannot do as they have done without punishment. I want them to fear us and to fear me in particular."

"It is a huge risk my... Osbert. They will all hunt you."

I laughed. "And that is what I want for then they will have to fight us. As long as I am with the army then we know where the battle will be. I want no more innocents to die for us."

Outlaw

"I think I understand."

"Good, and Branton, you just have to watch my back. I will not soil your hands with my crime."

There were two guards at the gate; one was fat and sat on a small stool. His companion had a narrow cruel face and when he looked at us I could see that he was dismissing us as vagrants. "What do you want? We want no tinkers here."

I bit back the retort and played the role. "We are not poor men." I jingled the small purse. "We have money to pay for a bed and food."

The fat one belched, "Well you'll be lucky. The city is filled with Normans." The thin one stood aside and we rode in. The streets were busier than I had seen in many a year. The alehouses were filled with noisy and boisterous voices. The Norman soldiery were celebrating their victory at Maiden Bower and that gave us a chance for they were relaxed and that made them vulnerable. We struggled to find a stable and had to settle for a smithy where the blacksmith knew Branton and allowed us to stable the horses, for a few coins, of course.

Once we left the smith we wandered the streets to see if we could see where the Norman knights were housed. It was, as I had expected, the warrior hall. We stood in an alley forty paces from the door while we sought a way in. There was none for there were guards on the doors and they challenged all who approached. "If we can't get them in then we must get them out."

We found an alehouse which had the sign of barley outside. It was crowded and, thankfully, dimly lit by a fire and a few tallow candles which emitted a smoky, thin light. There were no seats and we stood against a wall watching all those who were drinking. We were looking for a Norman, any Norman, so long as he was alone. Most of the ones we saw were in groups but then Branton noticed a solitary figure who was seated by the door. We approached him.

"What do you two want?"

"We see that you serve the Normans we would like to know if they are recruiting."

He laughed as he looked at the two of us; we made a sorry scruffy pair. "Why are you warriors?"

Outlaw

I shrugged, "We were. We served with Aelfraed of Topcliffe until he was beaten."

The man's interest was piqued. "Beaten? I did not know he had fought."

"Aye we ran into William of Perci and his knights and we were whipped. Aelfraed fled and we came here for we heard that there were opportunities here."

"Oh, there are opportunities. All sorts." I could see his greedy mind working out how to profit from our information. He beckoned us closer. "Listen, I like you. I am from London myself and these Normans pay well for the right men. Do you know where this Aelfraed is?"

Branton nodded, "We know precisely where he is hiding."

"And you could take us there?"

"Well, we could but he still has men with him and we wouldn't want it known that we betrayed him."

He leered at us, "Afraid of him, are you? Well, I can see that. He is supposed to be a big bugger. How about this then I will see one of the knights and then meet you, say by the river?"

"When?"

He shrugged, "That depends on the knights. You might have to wait a while but then again there might be a reward for you."

"We will be there."

"Good. See you, lads, later."

The warrior hall backed onto the river and there were some elder trees and blackberry bushes there. We secreted ourselves in them. Our tunics and hoods hid us. I wanted to see them before they saw us. Copsi would not know me but Guy and the other Normans would. I had no idea who would come. If it were not Guy then we would have to think of something else to winkle him out. I was beginning to think that no one would come as cramp and hunger pangs began biting into me. Branton hissed, "Someone coming!" and I shrank back into the tree.

"Where are you?"

"We are here."

A heavily accented Norman voice said, "You may go. We will reward you in the morning if this proves to be valuable and reliable information."

I still could not see how many men there were but I slipped my dagger out just in case. An English voice then spoke. "Come from the trees so that we can see you."

It was now so late that there were few people around. The warrior hall was a hundred paces from us and the river gurgled and hissed behind us. Branton went first and I kept my head down and followed him. From under my hood, I saw that there were two men. Neither wore armour but they both had swords at their sides and one of them was Guy!

The older man spoke. "We hear that you know where Aelfraed is to be found."

"We do my lord. We served him until recently."

"And you say William of Perci defeated him. I had not heard."

"We fought close to Osmotherly a few days ago. I believe that they went to Jorvik."

The man spoke to Guy in French then he turned to Branton. "And where is this Aelfraed?"

"He is in the hills beyond Medelai at a secret camp."

"How many men does he have?"

"Twenty, thirty? Others may have left him."

Guy said something in French. The man smiled. "This is Guy of Evreux and he is keen to find Aelfraed. There is bad blood between them. If you take us to him you will be rewarded."

Branton boldly asked, "How my lord…?"

"Copsi, Earl of Northumbria. Money? A place serving with us. There are many opportunities for bright men who are willing to be flexible." He came closer to Branton as though to lead him away.

Now that I knew who he was I could wait no longer. I lunged forward with the dagger and plunged it into his neck. He was dead even as I withdrew it. I changed hands with my dagger and drew my sword. Tossing my head back my hood fell back revealing my face. Guy took it in a moment and drew his sword. He was a brave man for he could have shouted for his guards but his face filled with fury and he hacked at me, spitting out words in French. Branton slipped to the edge of the wood and nocked his bow. I deflected the clumsy hack with my dagger and sliced down towards his leg. Even as he took out his dagger, I felt the sharpened sword connect with his leg and, in the moonlight, I saw blood on it. He was wounded.

"Make it quick my lord, the guards will investigate this noise soon enough."

I stabbed forwards with my dagger and my sword at the same time. Our blades clashed and our faces were close. "You are a murdering bastard and you are going to die." As I spat out the words I head-butted him. He was slightly shorter than me and I heard his nose crack. When you are headbutted your eyes close, automatically, and I took advantage of this by stabbing down with my dagger into his upper arm. He was a brave man but he was used to fighting from a horse and this close combat was new to him. There are no rules and I brought my knee up between his legs. He doubled up, the wind was taken from him and I chopped down with the blade. It was not a good sword but it was a sharp one and his head rolled to the ground, resting next to Copsi.

"My lord, guards!"

"To the river."

We slipped into the river and waded in the shallows downstream, next to the warrior hall. The guards were coming the other way but any noise we made was masked by the sound of the river. The water was only up to our knees but we were not swift and when we emerged close to the smith's we could hear the uproar from the warrior hall. Time was now of the essence and we quickly retrieved our horses. We had left them saddled for just such an emergency. The problem would be getting out of the gates which would be guarded. We lead the nags through the narrow, empty streets. There were two guards at the gate. Branton held his hand up to me to halt me and gave me his reins. He quickly ran around the corner shouting as he went, "Quick! Lord Copsi has sent for you. He wishes to ask you about the people who came in tonight. There has been a murder. I am to guard the gates until you return."

"Thank you, brother." The two men were so worried about what they might have done wrong that they did not question Branton's authority. By the time I reached them Branton had opened them. We mounted and kicked our mounts on. Unfortunately, there were two guards outside and when they heard the gates open they came to investigate. We rode our horses at them and they scattered but then they raised the alarm. There would be pursuit and we were not mounted on the best of horses. We headed down the road towards Medelai. It was not as good as the road we called the Roman road, but it would take us closer to safety. The ground rose once we left the city and I risked a glance back. I saw eight riders emerge from the gates. Four of them headed south towards Topcliffe whilst the others took our road. There would be others following but it was those four who would be the main problem.

"There are four of them Branton. Let us try to keep a lead until we reach the forest." The forest began three miles along the road and, once in there, we could lose them. It was a mile further along the road when we knew we were in trouble. My horse began to favour his left fore and Branton began to pull away. He saw my dilemma and returned to me. "We'll never outrun them, my lord. You take my horse."

"And leave you to be captured? That will not happen." I stared around, desperate to find something to help us. I saw that a little way ahead the road turned right and was hidden from view for a few paces by a large rock. "Up there, we can ambush them."

As we rode up Branton questioned my tactics. "Ambush? Two against four?"

"They will not be expecting it. You can easily take one with your bow. I will stand before you. If you fire swiftly then we may get a second and then the numbers would be even."

I knew that he was not convinced but as long as there was a chance we would survive I would try to the end. We tied the horses to a small bush and prepared to meet them. We had another advantage, we would hear them before they reached us. Branton had only four arrows left in his quiver; we would have to rely on his accuracy. I wished that I had Boar Splitter rather than the functional sword I held but it would have to do. I held my dagger in my left. I did not know if they had shields but I might well be fighting two of them. Suddenly we heard their voices as they thundered along the road. When they emerged they were in single file. Branton's arrow was loosed from no more than twenty paces and the surprised rider flew backwards from his horse, I actually felt the arrow whiz next to my ear. I swung my sword at the second rider's horse and felt my arm jar as I connected with the side of his head. Its rider launched himself at me as his horse tumbled over. I put my dagger out, more in hope than expectation and, as the warrior fell on top of me, the dagger slid into his ribs. I struggled to push him off as Branton fought with the fourth warrior. I rolled the warrior from me and stabbed him in the throat. We had no time for niceties or honour and I ran my sword into his back.

"Quickly, let us take their horses before others join them." I suddenly saw that Branton had been wounded and had a gash in his leg. I quickly tore a piece of tunic from one of the bodies and tied it tightly around the leg. He winced as I pulled on it but I knew that it would hold until we reached Medelai. We led the horses for, if we were pursued, we could change to fresher mounts.

The nights are short in late summer and soon the first rays of sun peeped over the hills to our left. I recognised where we were for I had played in these woods as a child. "Almost there, Branton. Hang on."

He was pale but still smiling. "Don't worry my lord. I am tougher than I look."

The manor at Medelai was busier than it had been since my family had lived there. I retained a reliable steward to manage it for me but I rarely visited. Now, with my men at arms and archers in residence, it was almost bursting at the seams.

"Can't let you alone for a moment without you getting into trouble." The humour in his voice could not disguise the concern Osbert had for his little brother.

"Just a cut from a sword."

"Come we will see to it while Lord Aelfraed tells us all."

"Copsi and Guy of Evreux are dead."

"Then Edward the archer is avenged."

"We were pursued. We will need to ride to Coxold. With Ridley's men, we could evade capture."

"They have many men?"

"Aye, the place was crawling with them. If they join with William we will be hard pushed to defeat them. We need Earl Morcar to raise more troops." I took Osbert to one side. "Did you give the men the choice I asked of you?"

Outlaw

"I did my lord and they laughed at me saying they would serve you as a penniless lord." He shook his head. "Then they said that with you as the leader they would not need pay for there would always be plunder!"

"I hope they are right."

With the extra horses we had found and by taking all those from the estate we were able to ride to Coxold before dark. I felt much better inside Ridley's solid walls and we now had a sizeable force that could see off any but a full army.

As we sat before the fire, Ridley and I talked of Aethelward and our travels through Wales. "It seems such a long time ago Aelfraed."

"It does and we have changed so much."

There was a comfortable silence and then Ridley asked, "How easy was it to slide your blade into an unsuspecting man?"

He meant no insult although many men would have taken it as such. "No different to combat. We have both killed warriors who were not watching us and so it was with Copsi. I fought the Norman blade to blade. He was tough but he had little skill. If the Normans are unhorsed, they become weaker. It is worth remembering Ridley."

"What are we to do now that Aethelward is dead? It seems bleak at the moment."

"It does but I am heartened by my uncle's words on his deathbed; he said he had been preparing me to take his place. If Morcar can raise an army then we stand a chance."

"Why does not William come north?"

"I think he is too busy controlling what he has and he is trying to raise money through taxes. We now know how expensive it is to keep warriors."

He smiled wryly. "It is that. My steward is always complaining."

"Which is why we employ stewards so that they can worry." I suddenly remembered my steward. "Thomas, he never complained. I shall miss him and dear Sarah."

"And the Queen?"

I nodded, unable to speak for my heart was filled with sorrow for my dead child and that I found sad, that I missed someone I had never seen more than the women whose bed I had shared.

Outlaw

"We will need to visit Jorvik if only to keep prodding at Morcar, or he will sit on his arse doing nothing."

"Succinctly put Ridley. I think he enjoys the title but not the responsibility."

"And what of Edwin?"

"I think he is trying to hold on to Mercia without actually fighting."

"Will William of Perci come again?"

"I think he will have to and if he comes soon then there will be no fyrd, they will be gathering in the harvest."

"We did not need them at Osmotherly."

"We needed their numbers. If we just had our men and arms and archers then he would have surrounded us and attacked on all sides. We would not have lasted long." The logs flamed and flickered throwing sparks across the floor. "How many men can we muster?"

"I spoke with Osbert, to get an accurate tally. Sixty men at arms and thirty archers."

"Not a huge force then?"

"No. I just hope that Morcar has recruited."

We spent a week at Coxold repairing armour and making arrows for the archers. Ralph Ralphson took over the making of his father's knight killing arrows and Branton was happy again. When we finally reached Jorvik we were disappointed. Morcar had done little but celebrate that the new Earl had died! He thanked me but kept giving me strange looks. I disliked the politics and the verbal dancing he engaged in and I bluntly asked him. "Earl Morcar speak plainly with me. You know something. If you do then spit it out."

He sighed, "It is hard to tell you, especially with the news of the Queen and, Gytha. "

So the news of my wife and Calum had leaked out. It was inevitable. "They are minor issues compared with the rule of the tyrant."

"Well, here it is then. You are and Lord Ridley have been declared outlaws for the murder of Copsi and Guy of Evreux."

"But Lord Ridley was not there! That was Branton."

"You were identified by someone who saw you in Ripon and the description of the man with you fitted Lord Ridley." He shrugged,

"Your lands are forfeit. They have been given to Lord William of Perci."

"I can swear that it was not Ridley."

"But I am no longer Earl. I sit in this city under false pretences."

"While you sit here then you make the law. Make a proclamation telling all that Ridley is innocent."

"I will do so but it is meaningless."

"It is only meaningless if you make it so. We have nothing to lose now Morcar let us rise against William. Send a message to your brother and ask him to rise. You owe it to your sister!"

I think that what decided Morcar was my statement that he had nothing to lose. That day saw a change in him as he began to behave as an Earl and for the next few months, we had a chance.

By early winter Edwin had risen and we had raised an army. It was not huge but it was big enough to frighten William of Perci. He had based his army at Doncaster and we marched down to meet him. Earl Morcar had mounted men and we left the fyrd at home. I meant that we had fifteen hundred warriors, all of whom were armoured. Even with his reinforcements from Ripon he still only had two thousand men. We knew that we had the advantage of our earlier victory and when we arrayed our forces before the new motte and bailey at Doncaster, we were in high spirits. The cold morning and the harsh wind blowing from the east did not hurt us. This was our land. I unfurled my banner in the centre of the line and made sure that my men art arms showed their shields with my motif. I wanted William to know that I was coming for him.

He had just over a hundred knights; they were lined to the right of their line. In the middle were their foot soldiers and I could see that he had given them all spears so that they looked like an armoured hedgehog. He had fewer light horse and they were to the left. Thinly spread out, in a long line, before the whole army were sixty crossbowmen. That was his biggest mistake for he could not concentrate their fire on any one part of our line and I knew that he would fight a defensive battle.

"Branton, take your archers to get rid of the crossbowmen in the middle. Osbert, give your brother ten men at arms. They can protect them with their shields. Earl Morcar, send your horse to face the enemy light horse. If they attack, then charge them."

Outlaw

This was my chess game now and I would use my pawns in the middle while threatening his left. I was inviting him to charge us with his knights. "Ridley, form a shield wall, William of Perci will be along shortly."

Ridley never questioned, he just carried out orders calmly and efficiently. I hoped that Morcar would do the same. Branton's fifty archers poured arrow after arrow into the sky. There were so many that it looked as though a rain cloud had appeared overhead. The bolts were ineffective because of my men at arms and soon there were only a handful of crossbowmen left on each side.

The light horse made a perfunctory effort to charge the retreating archers but a quick charge from Morcar's horse made them run for the safety of their foot. "The line will advance."

Banging their shields, we headed towards the Normans. Just as I had expected William of Perci saw his chance and his pennant dipped three times. The light horse charged towards our cavalry and his knights, riding knee to knee charged our left flank.

"Branton! Knight killers."

Branton and his men did not have many arrows left and they chose their targets well. The knights seemed better prepared this time, no doubt remembering the effect of the weapons at Osmotherly. They held their shields tightly and protected their bodies well. It did, however, unsight them a little and that gave my men an edge. The men on the left braced themselves as the knights struck them. Their wall of spears found a few horses and the line halted. Soon I could hear the melee from my left as both sets of armoured men tried to find a weakness.

In the centre, I prepared to meet the foot. We were heavier and I counted on our two lines to punch a hole in their defence. We struck with a clash of iron on wood. My well-trained men were soon stabbing and jabbing at the less well protected Normans. Suddenly I heard a shout from Osbert, "My lord, the cavalry!"

I looked to my right and saw, to my horror, Earl Morcar and his horsemen riding north. They had broken. "Osbert, back right."

Osbert's part of the line began to edge around to form another side to our line. I roared, "Halt!" We were winning in the middle but if we advanced we would be surrounded. I turned to look for a way out of this trap for Morcar's desertion had given Perci the advantage of numbers. Our only chance was to defeat the knights and hope that William retreated. I turned to Edwin of Malton next to me, he would be the next sergeant, if we survived this disaster. "Edwin, hold the line whilst I aid Lord Ridley. Listen for my command and do not advance!"

He grinned as he hacked a foot soldier with his short axe, "Aye my lord."

I extracted myself from the line and trotted to the left where the knights were still heavily engaged. I saw Branton. "Make me a hole in the middle of their line on my command and then be prepared to cover our retreat!" He nodded and I stood in the second line, men made a gap for me and I found myself just behind Ridley. It was a stalemate. "Branton! Now!"

Suddenly eight arrows flew dangerously close to our heads, striking the four knights at the front of their line. There was a gap and I pushed myself to Ridley's left. "Wedge!" Stabbing forwards with Boar Splitter I felt the blade slide into the horse's throat and through to embed itself in the knight's gut. Horse and rider fell to one side and there was an even bigger gap. I slid my shield around and held Death Bringer. As I began to sing, I felt Ridley to my right do the same and soon the singing blades were carving a path through horses and knights who had no answer to the scything blades of death. Their lances lay shattered and they could not reach us with their swords. It was with some relief that I heard the Norman voices shout and the remaining knights fell back. I quickly looked to the right. The attack there was being held.

"Topcliffe! Fall back! Branton, harry them."

We had lost many men and as we closed our lines to retreat, I saw that we would do well to survive the retreat. I took Boar Splitter from the dead horse and held my shield before me for the danger now would be the crossbowmen and the light horse. I heard a horse behind me and Branton's voice, "My lord, there is a small wood half a mile north."

Without turning I shouted, "Good! Keep the crossbows and horse away from us, we can deal with their foot easily enough."

Even though we were retreating we killed more of them as we slowly trudged backwards. When we could we rotated our men so that fresher men were in the front and it was heart-breaking to

Outlaw

leave our dead littering the field but we had no option. Branton's archers did a magnificent job, riding to any who threatened our flanks and their horse became wary of them. By the time the sun was setting we had reached the safety of the woods and it was with some relief that I saw Perci's pennant dip and his men retreated. The last fifty men at arms sank to their knees in exhaustion. We had tasted defeat and retreat and, I for one did not like the taste.

Chapter 10

When Branton returned he had many empty saddles. "You have done well Branton and saved us this day. I will not forget it." He nodded. "See how many horses you can find and, if you are able, bring any of our wounded from the field."

We knew there were wounded for we could hear their pitiful cries as they lay amongst the carnage. I did not know if the Normans would bother with their own dead but we had so few men left now that every man, even the wounded, was worth double. Osbert spat on the ground as he bound a wound on Edwin's arm, "With respect my lord, Earl Morcar is a prick and if I see him again..."

"Do not worry, Osbert, we have fought alongside that coward for the last time."

"With whom will we fight then, Aelfraed, for we have few men left?" Ridley's voice of reason chilled me to the bone.

"I do not know. What is the alternative? Submit?" I looked at Ridley and suddenly realised that he had a future. "You could take your men back to Coxold and continue as Thegn."

He smiled sadly. "Aelfraed, it has always been the same, my world and yours are tied together with a bond which has been determined by *wyrd*. Where you go, there go I."

"But Ridley, I am an outlaw. You know what that means?"

"Aye my lord, it means that every man's hand is turned against you. You have no home and you will be shunned by all."

"And you choose that?"

"I choose that."

I turned to the circle of warriors who watched us and listened to the conversation. "And all of you, do you choose that. I will give coin to any who wish to go home. It is only Aelfraed of Topcliffe who is an outlaw."

In answer, they all banged their shields and roared, "Aelfraed." None left me and we were all outlaws from that moment on. The sign of the Red Horse became the symbol for rebellion and resistance to all invaders.

When Branton returned he had managed to acquire thirty mounts, some of them Norman. He also found eight warriors who

Outlaw

were wounded. Two of them would not see out the night but, at least they would die amongst comrades. "My lord, we cannot stay here. We must move."

"I know, Osbert, place the wounded on the horses, Branton, lead us out and have four men as scouts to watch our rear. We trudged north all night, eventually collapsing at Knottingley where we begged some shelter and food from those in the small village. I felt honour bound to tell them who we were and that we were outlaws. Cnut, the headman, nodded. "That is as maybe my lord but I stood with you at Stamford and to us, you will never be an outlaw. You are welcome to stay as long as you wish."

"Thank you, Cnut but we will leave on the morrow for I would not wish harm to come to you and your people."

When we finally reached Jorvik three men had died of their wounds and we had buried them with weapons and honour. Ridley took the majority of our men to Coxold where Ralph Ralphson could repair the damaged armour. We knew that every day was precious. Soon William would come north for all resistance lay with my depleted band of warriors and we needed to find somewhere to winter. Our lives would change irrevocably. I went with Osbert, Branton and six men to Jorvik. I needed money from Reuben but, more importantly, I needed to speak with Morcar, if only to tell him how I felt.

The sentries on the gates looked shamefaced as we approached the Mickelgate. They looked at each other and then crossed their spears, barring us from entry.

"I am sorry, my lord but you have been declared outlaw and cannot enter."

I felt my men reach for their weapons and I held up my hand. I did not want to spill Northumbrian blood. "You know who I am?"

"Yes my lord, Lord Aelfraed of Topcliffe."

"No, I am Aelfraed Godwinson, son of the last legitimate King of England, Harold Godwinson. I do not recognise a Norman declaration." They looked at each other, confused. "Who commands here?"

"Earl Morcar!"

"Then we will see him." I looked at them both sadly, "I do not wish to end your lives for you are merely doing your duty but at

Outlaw

my command, these warriors behind me will slay you in the blink of an eye. Do you want that?"

I could not see the expressions on Osbert and the others behind me but it must have terrified the two sentries who stood aside, "Very well, my lord."

"Branton, take two men and find Reuben, explain that I need a letter to obtain money in Eidyn Din and Constantinople. A thousand gold pieces from each. He will understand and tell him we may not be able to meet again." I would have preferred to say goodbye to the old Jew personally but I did not know what reception I would receive at court. "Then meet us on the Coxold road."

When we reached the court I saw Norman mounts and at least one Norman warrior. We were still armed as at the field of battle. "Osbert, leave the men guarding the horses. You come with me. I fear there may be bloodshed ere long."

Osbert spoke with the men and I heard them draw their swords. I doubted that any of the garrison in Jorvik would cause them any trouble but the ones inside were a more serious threat. Even as I went into the hall I wondered why I was risking our lives. I could have just taken my money and ridden away but I needed to look Morcar in the eye if only for the dead who lay at Doncaster and Fulford for this was the second time he had let me down.

The guards at the door looked at our swords. "My lord your weapons…"

Osbert walked up to the man. "Aidan of Easingwold. You and I have stood behind this lord and defended him with our lives. You have a choice, let us enter or die where you stand." Osbert was known as the toughest of my Housecarls and many said that he could have stood with honour at Senlac. Aidan nodded to his companion and stood aside.

When the door opened, I saw four Normans speaking with Morcar. There was an audible gasp from them all. Morcar went white. He stood with a weak smile on his face. "Aelfraed, good to see you. I thought that you were…"

"Dead? I would have been had we not fought our way out after you deserted us and now I see that you are consorting with these Normans."

"The day was lost."

"The day was not lost until you ran again. Know this Morcar that you live only because of your sister whom I loved but the next time I see you. You will die."

"You do not understand, Aelfraed. King William has built a castle at Warwick and Edwin has submitted. Harold's mother has surrendered as has Hereford. There is only you and Hereward in East Anglia who fight. It is over. We have lost."

I was not surprised by the news but I was disappointed. "It matters not to me. This will be over when Death Bringer is prised from my cold dead hand."

Over in the corner, the four Normans were speaking with, what looked like a servant. Osbert spotted their agitation. He said, quietly, "I don't want to alarm you my lord but those four look like they have just worked out who you are."

"Earl Morcar unless you wish to see bloodshed in your hall, tell your new friends to sheath their swords."

The four mailed men had drawn their swords. Morcar spoke to them in French but they still advanced. Osbert and I drew our swords and daggers out and faced them. "No! Please, Aelfraed. Put up your sword."

I glared at him. "What and submit? I know not what runs in your veins Morcar but it is English blood which flows in mine."

Even as we were speaking the four knights launched themselves at us. They had deigned to use daggers. I parried a sword away with my dagger and blocked a sword with mine. Instead of retreating, I advanced for I was bigger and heavier than they were. I punched with my sword and the surprised Norman tumbled to the ground in a heap. I swung the blade at the second man who ducked. I stabbed forwards, instinctively with my dagger, and felt it slice along his cheekbone. He put his hands to face his face to halt the bleeding and I kicked him in the groin to add to his misery. My first opponent had risen to his feet and, angrily, advanced on me. His eyes filled with fury and humiliation. Aethelward had always taught me not to fight angry and I never had. The Norman raised the sword to crash it down on my unprotected head; unfortunately for him, there was a wooden wheel hung with candles suspended from the ceiling and his sword stuck. This was

Outlaw

no time to be generous and I ran him through with my sword. Osbert had disposed of one of his men and the other stood there facing two bigger men armed with double his weapons. I stepped forwards and, roaring, "Fuck off!" hit him in the middle of his face with the hilt of my sword. I heard the nose break as he crashed to the ground. "Morcar, choose your friends more carefully in future." Although no one else had a belligerent look about them, we backed out of the room with drawn blades. Once out of the chamber we strode quickly out of the hall to the gate. Branton was already there with our horses.

Osbert turned to me and grinned, "I do not think we will be invited back there in a hurry."

"Let us ride!"

As we kicked our horses a crossbow bolt flew from the door of the hall and struck me on my shoulder. The armour saved me but it felt like being punched by Ridley. Branton smiled, "Have you been upsetting people again, my lord?"

"It would appear so. Perhaps Earl Morcar does not know how to get the bloodstains from his floor."

We rode hard until we reached Coxold. Ridley had organised a magnificent feast. I had forgotten how hungry I was. I had barely slept for two days and I could not remember the last food I had taken. We all ate in one of Ridley's barns. It was rustic and it was rough but it felt like a feast of kings. We were depleted in numbers but not in spirit. We spent the whole night talking of those who had fallen and remembering them. Stories were told of their deeds and it was good to know that, when we fell, others would talk of us and keep our memory alive.

The next morning we rose late and we rose stiff. My shoulder ached and, as we dressed Ridley laughed, "It looks as though someone has painted your shoulder green and blue."

"Those bolts are more than a nuisance. If I had not had the armour I fear I would be dead by now."

"I will see if Ralph can make some for the other men."

The four of us, Ridley, Osbert, Branton and myself held a council of war in Ridley's hall whilst the men had their armour and weapons improved. "The question is now what do we do?" I had included Osbert and Branton for they felt like family and I respected Osbert's views. Ridley would listen and soak all the information up like gravy and a piece of bread. Branton had the ability to see things from a different angle. They remained silent and I think they expected me to give them some choices. "We could do nothing, and hope that William ignores us. We could journey to Ely and help Hereward fight them. We could try to raise an army against William and… well, that is my range of strategies exhausted."

"I do not think, my lord, after our experience in Jorvik, that William will forget us. We have damaged him too many times."

"I know Osbert and we no longer have the security of Jorvik for the Normans control Morcar."

Branton played with the feathers of one of his knight killers, "We could go abroad, my lord. I assume that the message to Reuben was to provide you with funds in Scotland and Constantinople. I assume that they are in your mind?"

He was clever; was he questioning my motives? "They are the last resort Branton and I would not travel alone, I would take as many with me as wanted to. Aethelward suggested the East and I know that our skills are held in great regard there but I do not wish to desert our people. Thomas, Sarah and the others still burn in my memory and my nights are haunted by the spectre of their deaths."

"We could just stay here Aelfraed. We could defend Coxold against the Normans. We have enough time to build up the defences."

"Aye my lord. It would be a hard nut to crack."

"You are right. We could defend this manor and your people; they would aid us?"

Ridley almost bristled with indignation. "Of course, they would, they are loyal."

I lowered my voice, "And if we lost Ridley and they ended up like my people at Maiden Bower, you would be happy about that and you could live with the deed?"

He visibly paled. "But if we did not lose…"

"Lord Aelfraed is right, my lord, if the King does come, he will have more men that William of Perci and even William of Perci now has enough men to defeat us. We could hold out for a while, possibly even weeks but then we would run out of arrows, and food and the will of the fyrd would weaken. We would be left with fifty of us to fight against a much larger army. We would lose. Many Normans would die but we would lose and then what would happen to the people of Coxold?"

Ridley's silence was eloquent. "I suppose we could go to Ely and join Hereward."

No one seemed excited by that idea. Branton continued to look at his arrow. "There is one other alternative." We all looked at him. I could see that Ridley was desperate for any solution which would mean his people would survive. "We do not think that William will come before next spring. We spend the winter building up our weapons and making places in the woods where we can live."

Osbert snorted, "Live in the woods?"

"Think about it brother. We know the woods to the east and the west of the road. The main road north is here. We could make the Norman's life impossible if we harried them along the road and when they travel around the north. We nearly have enough horses now and we have time to mount all of the men. We could strike in one place and, when they come to look for us, find another sanctuary. Move and strike. They would need a bigger army that they have to control the land."

Osbert nodded, "Aye, my lord, and remember, the people at Knottingley are not different from any others and they welcomed us and helped us."

"I would not wish to put anyone in harm's way."

"Nor would we, my lord."

Ridley smiled for the first time, "They have named us outlaws. Well, let us live as outlaws. Strike, where they do not expect us. Make them fear to go to bed at night."

"And, my lord, if they do come into the woods after us then we can make them dance a merry dance. Their knights will not have the advantage then."

"Nor would my men at arms."

"No my lord, we would need to change. I think we can change but can the Normans?"

I thought about it. This was not the glory of a shield wall but that glory had perished with my friends and my father, far to the south. The day of the Housecarl was over if only because the remaining

Housecarls were Ridley and I. Was it even worth staying to fight? Would we not have more riches and fame if we travelled to fight as mercenaries? Aethelward felt it was important to fight and I owed it to the dead. We would have one last attempt at wresting the land back from William's greedy fingers.

"If you are all foolish enough to follow me then we shall do as Branton suggests." Their smiles were as though we had already won a victory. I shook my head in disbelief. "Branton you had better scout out two camps quickly before winter falls. Osbert and Ridley we will need to prepare ourselves for living in the wild. Weapons are vital but we need to think about armour which is less heavy and yet still affords protection."

"When I served my other lord, he was not a rich man and we had leather armour with metal pieces. If we used a mixture of leather, disks, such as we have on our shields and the shoulder protectors of iron then we might move easier through woods."

Ridley nodded, eagerly, "And the Normans, they use a mail hood beneath their helmets to protect their necks and backs. They would not be too heavy."

"Both good ideas see to it and I will take some of Branton's men and look for good places to ambush the enemy."

So we spent the late autumn into early winter busily making our preparations and hoping that the King would not come north. It seems he was a cautious man for he spent a long time building a solid castle at Warwick. Uncle had told me of his White Tower in London and it seemed that this King would control the land through stone and iron; the stone of his keeps and the iron of his men. That suited us for it meant he would have few men to hold on to this land and that gave us the land between castles. Branton found two good camps, one was close to Helmsley and the old village of Griff. It was in a valley that was hidden from view but which had good access north and south along the valley. The other was east of Medelai where the river tumbled over rocks and there was a high cliff. The forests stretched to the hills many miles to the west and we could roam at will. Both had water and wood; both were well known to us. As the first frosts of winter gripped the ground we planned the spring and the camps we would build.

Outlaw

Six of the fifty men we had brought from the field of battle were too badly wounded to serve as men at arms. Despite my offer of money they implored me to still be able to serve me. Branton came up with the idea of stationing three men in each camp as caretakers and hunters for we would be too busy to gather game for ourselves and it seemed to suit everyone. Osbert organised stores of salt and the pans we would need to cook. Ridley had his steward buy in materials to help us repair our clothes and make new ones. We had plenty of time to plan and think of unexpected events for the Normans spent the winter in Jorvik and far to the south.

On my forays, I saw that they had defended Jorvik with many crossbowmen and the city had become Norman. I saw, before the snows came, that they had started to build a huge motte close to the river a mile or so from the old warrior hall. Already it would be too big for us to assault. The road to the north was quiet and all that we discovered were traders. Once they found that we were not bandits they became quite friendly towards us and they were the source of much of our intelligence as they travelled south to Lincoln and beyond. We knew that Hereward still held out and that Edwin had submitted, living at Warwick, probably as a prisoner. We discovered that the Scots had strengthened their border fortresses ready to repel any invasion from the Normans but of Edgar and Sweyn we heard nothing; it was as though they had disappeared from the land. I still visited Medelai and my steward still supplied me with my dues for no-one had done, as they had with Thomas, and told him that he had a new lord. He was a loyal man whose son had fallen with us at Osmotherly. These tributes I retained for a future time when things became desperate.

When we travelled close to Maiden Bower it saddened me as I saw the desolation that had been my home. Each time we came down the road to travel to Coxold I found myself drawn to view the graves of those that I loved. We always ensured that the ground above the graves, which still bore just a rough stone, was undisturbed and that the carrion feeders were chased away. It is strange to think of it now but none of us ever spoke as we went about the manor that had been Maiden Bower. It was as though it was a holy place but when we left, I for one, felt an inner peace. Perhaps it was the spirits of those that I had loved watching me from beyond the grave. We learned that others shunned the place as they felt that it was haunted. We did not fear it and it may have been haunted but those ghosts would not harm us.

It was close to All Saints when we had our first action since we had fled Doncaster. We had been to the east of Jorvik and were approaching the road to the south when one of my scouts drew my attention to the small column heading north for the safety of Jorvik. It was coming on to dusk as the days are short at that time of the year and they were hurrying. The light from the thin, setting sun, silhouetted them and hid us in the darkened east. We could see that they were Normans by their mail and their helms. There was a knight, six men at arms and a small wagon. There were but eight of us and none of us wore mail but it was too good an opportunity to miss and a chance for me to see how ambushes would work. Four of my men were archers and the other three armed, as I was with shields and spears.

"Edward, you take the archers and ride ahead to that oak tree. When they come in sight aim for the knights. We will attack from the rear." I was pleased to see the grins appear in the dark; they were not afraid and looked forward to the break from dull patrols. We trotted down the left of the road to come behind them. "You two take out the two men behind the wagon. You take out the driver and I will attack the others. Come to my aid when you have disposed of your men."

We still had the round shields we had always had. I know that the kite shield was better for a horseman but the shield was familiar and we had retained them. The advantage we had was that you could use it offensively and that was how I would try to overcome the two or three men I might be facing depending upon how lucky my archers were. As soon as the wagon passed our place of concealment we charged down, silently, in a single line. I did not see but I heard the cries as my men did their job. I was busy concentrating on the three riders who turned to come to the aid of their comrades. They too had spears which they held overhand as though to throw. That suited me. It would take a very lucky hit to hurt me. I ignored the one to my left, my shield would take care of him and I held Board Splitter ahead of me. The warrior grinned in anticipation as he raised his spear to strike me but Boar Splitter thrust up under his arm to mortally wound him. I felt the spear strike my shield as I withdrew Boar splitter. The next warrior thought he had an easy victory until the two arrows plucked him from the saddle and he fell dead. And then it was over. The man who had struck my shield was killed by the two men at arms behind me.

"Gather the weapons and armour, put them in the wagon. Edward, collect the horses. We will head to the woods to the west." I wanted the contents of the wagon but I did not want to leave the wagon tracks for them to follow. We could pack the horses with the contents and ride back to Coxold during the night. I realised that it would be closer to the putative camp at Helmsley but that was in the future.

While my men packed the horses I examined the wagon. It contained boxes of crossbow bolts. They were useless to us. There was a small box with papers in and a smaller box with money. "Edward, throw these bolts into the river. They are no good to us but they will be missed by the garrison." When we left the wagon it was as though the foxes and crows had picked it clean; there was nothing left to aid the Normans.

Ridley was worried when we arrived back so late. "You are becoming an old woman like Sarah, my friend."

He did not smile at my attempt at humour, "Aelfraed, you do not know how important you are. If you fell then there is no one left to fight William. You are the symbol which holds us together."

I could see that he was genuinely upset. "I am sorry Ridley and I will try to avoid getting killed."

Osbert had been checking the goods we had acquired. "You had a good haul. How did you do it? Edward says they outnumbered you?"

"Aye they did but we attacked from the dark into the sunset and we attacked at the front and the rear. It worked this time."

"They are all dead my lord, it will work again. The money is useful but I cannot read these documents, they are in French."

I cursed. That was our weakness. Anything in French was as good as code. "How about Oswald?"

Oswald was the priest from Topcliffe. He had robbed the estate before I arrived and I had had to be stern with him but once the manor became successful he became a loyal and faithful priest. His church had benefited from the manor's success and now, without a lord at Maiden Bower, he was the focus for the people and acted as an agent. More importantly, he could read the documents. "We will visit him on Christmas Eve for it will seem normal to attend church then." I did not want people to know that Oswald still aided us and we would go as hooded men, anonymously.

I had not been in a church since my own wedding in Jorvik; I was not a religious man and too many good people had died badly for me to believe too strongly in a kindly, caring God. If we had had such a God then I would not have had to kill Guy and Copsi and my child would live still. I stationed men at arms around the outside of the church and I went in with Ridley and Osbert. We kept the cowls over our heads; as much to protect our people as ourselves for, this way, they could deny all knowledge of us. I recognised some of the fyrd who came in with their families. We sat in the shadows at the back. The church was dimly lit in any case. Oswald chanted the Latin litany and the congregation responded. We rose, knelt and sat as the others did. Eventually, after what seemed an eternity, it finished and we sat as everyone left. There were some curious looks and I suspect that some of the fyrd recognised me but, thankfully, no one spoke.

Oswald returned and we threw back our hoods. "My lord! I wondered who the hooded men were at the back and, to be honest, I feared that you were Norman killers."

I looked at him curiously, "Norman killers?"

"There have been rumours of Normans seeking out those who fought with you, men at arms and archers. You have a price on your head as do your men." That was news to me but then we avoided towns and congregated places.

"We need you to translate some French for us. Could you do that?"

"Of course, my lord. Come to my home, there is a fire there and I am too old for this cold."

He was right, his hearth was cosy. He lit a candle and took out the first document. His eyes opened and then he shook his head. "Aye, well I know who the new lord is, William of Perci. He is coming in January to take over the manor."

Outlaw

I shrugged. We knew that it would be someone, at least this way we knew who it was. "Does it mention Coxold?"

"Yes, he is to have that one and Medelai." He looked sadly at us, "It seems, my lord, that you are dispossessed." Again that was no surprise and we had, in effect, prepared for it. "There are other manors close by. It seems that he rules all but Jorvik."

He put the letter to one side. "If there is nought else in that letter then I would burn it. Then there is no trace."

He nodded, smiled and threw the document into the fire. "As a man of God, I would not have thought of that, my lord." He took out the second document which appeared to run to several pages. "Ah, now this is interesting. It informs a certain, Odo of Bayeux, that Earl Morcar is to be arrested and held in anticipation of King William coming north in March to begin the building of his castle and to rid the land of the last remnants of Saxon rebellion." He put the paper down. "It seems, my lord, that he is coming for you."

We decided to have the best Christmas that we could. Ridley and his steward slaughtered all the animals which we had kept for the winter. There would be little need now. We left only the food for the steward and the household. We had deprived ourselves of rations for some time to eke out the reserves. If Coxold was going the way of Topcliffe then we would dine on geese and duck, mutton and chicken. Only the breeding pairs were left and every village and tenant of Ridley was invited. It was a truly jolly occasion. We did not know it then but this would be one of the last times that we would enjoy the pleasant company of women. The women and girls loved the fact that they had so many men to dance with and their husbands and fathers were proud that the last of the Saxon warriors were in their company.

When the nights lengthened, even though it was frosty and the ground was hard, we bade farewell to Coxold. Ridley was tearful for he had become fond of the place and its people. Had the Normans not come then he would have made a good lord and his benevolent rule would have benefited the people. As it turned out, no one in Northumbria enjoyed that but then few in Northumbria would survive the onslaught of the next few years. We loaded the horses with everything that we would possibly need and said goodbye.

Outlaw

Ralph Ralphson had grown considerably and bore a huge grudge against the Normans. He was desperate to join us and fight but we persuaded him to stay if only to continue to manufacture those weapons and armour we would need. In the end, he agreed only if he was allowed to bring the weapons and armour himself. I reluctantly agreed for I needed the goods he would bring but I was not happy about letting someone from outside our tightly knit band of brothers have access to our hideaways. I trusted the boy but he was a weakness and I prayed that it would not come to haunt us.

We rode east, mainly because the other refuge we had was a little close to Medelai. We knew that there would be a hue and cry to find us; we could use the western camp when they had searched the area. Sixty men left Coxold, men at arms, archers and six camp guards. It was not a huge army but it was one of only two who were fighting the Normans.

Chapter 11

By the time the nights had lengthened and our waists grown thinner, we had two well-made and well-hidden camps. It had been hard building them in the winter but, as Osbert had pointed out, it meant that when the plants began to grow our shelters blended in and looked natural. We tried, whenever possible, to build our shelters out of living trees and bushes; bending and shaping branches and weaving in other materials. In the depths of winter, we had to augment these with cloaks and clothes to keep us dry. The forest, however, contained much game and we used this whenever our supply of salted meat grew short. We still visited Coxold and Medelai until they were occupied and the two stewards kept us supplied but in early March, Branton, who had been sent to Medelai, galloped in with bad news, "Perci is at Medelai and he has begun to build a castle at Topcliffe. He has put every man woman and child to work."

"But it is Spring! What about the crops? The lambs?" Ridley was incensed; they were not his people but he knew what would come next.

"They do not care Ridley. This is what happens when you lose a war. But at least it means we can move to our western camp and see if we can annoy the Normans a little." There were just our three crippled warriors at the camp and they were pretending to be itinerant charcoal burners. It was an acceptable enough story and their injuries should provide an excuse for them not to build the castle walls. "We will move out tonight. Branton, you take the archers and make sure our way is clear."

The ride was not short but we were lucky and had a fine moon to guide us. The night was frosty but not icy and the horses made good progress. The hardest part was the slope leading down to the Vale of Jorvik. We had not seen any Norman occupation of Thirsk, which was a small place anyway but we avoided it as we did Masham. We rode through the night like ghosts for everyone was inside their homes, including the Normans. As the coldest part of the time came and went, I wondered how we could use that to our advantage. We could move freely along roads during the night and be ready to strike as dawn broke and tired sentries saw what they expected to see.

We found Branton waiting for us close to the old Roman town of Catherick. He spoke quietly, "There is a Norman conroi ahead. They are in Catherick itself."

"We will go around but tomorrow you and I will find out who this conroi belongs to."

Edward, Branton and I rode to Catherick the next day. It was but a handful of miles from our camp and there was plenty of cover for our horses. We spied the Normans at work on the motte and bailey they were building. I say Normans, but they were on their horses supervising the thralls and villeins who toiled away. There would be much hunger this summer if the lambs were not cared for and the crops not sown. We counted five knights or, at least, horsemen who were dressed as knights and fifteen men at arms. We could see no crossbowmen. This looked like our first opportunity to strike at the invader who was spreading across the land like a disease.

The men rested all day and we rose in the middle of the night at moonset. We took all the men we had for we wanted no surprises. We left the horses in the stand of trees with two men and then we split up. Ridley and Osbert took half the men to wait close to the construction site in case we failed in our mission whilst Branton and me took the others to hide close to the river and the village. The Normans had obviously occupied the old warrior hall for there were armed sentries outside. The huts of the villagers were further from the river. We spread out in a thin line. The two sentries at the main door appeared to be the only guards which meant that there should have been eighteen men inside. Branton had six archers and they each aimed at one of the sentries. As I nodded, six arrows found their targets and the two men fell silently into oblivion. One of the horses neighed but there was no other sound. Branton and the archers went to the horses while I took the fifteen men at arms with me. I was counting on surprise. Once we entered the hall then we knew that all inside were Normans and therefore enemies. Branton waved at me to show that he had secured the horses. With his archers mounted they could catch any who escaped our trap. The door opened with a slight creak; I hoped that the sentries coming and going during the night had made the noise before and it was familiar enough to ignore. All of us wore our shields at our backs and carried swords, axes and maces.

I stepped into a world lit at one end by a glowing fire that had slowly died down during the night. The Normans were spread along the sides but I assumed that the knights would have taken the prime positions by the hearth. I made my way through the sleeping bodies. If they woke it would be unfortunate but the closer I got to the leaders the better it would be. One of the men three back from me slipped slightly and stepped on a man. He woke with a roar and took in the armed spirits who had appeared, he began to roar a warning before he was despatched by a warrior but they were all awake. There was no time for honour and I slashed at the warrior next to me who had crouched, prior to rising. The next man was splashed by his blood and struck by his head as I decapitated him. We now outnumbered them by two. I ran towards the Norman knight I could see drawing his sword. He still had his tunic on but that was all. He advanced towards me with the sword held level with his shoulder. I slipped my dagger in my left hand and hacked at his sword; there was a clash of sparks and I stabbed up at him with my dagger. It sliced through his tunic and into his side but the knight just gritted his teeth and swung his sword at me again. It was a two-handed sword and longer than mine. It meant that he could keep me at bay. I feinted with my dagger and he reacted by turning with his blade. I took the opportunity to stab forwards with my sword and struck his thigh. I knew it was a deep wound as I struck a bone and deep red blood gushed from it. It had hurt him and he staggered back. I smashed down with the sword and again he staggered, this time into the fire. Without meaning to he rolled away from the fire into the point of my dagger which entered his throat and ended his life. I turned quickly to see one of my men fall to a knight's sword. Unfortunately for the knight, his side was facing me and my blade entered one side of his body and exited the other. The remaining warriors were quickly slaughtered for each faced three or four of my men.
It was like a charnel house. "Take our dead and wounded and then gather any weapons, armour or documents. We need to be away before dawn."

Outlaw

There were not enough horses for us all and so I had the wounded and dead placed on the horses along with the arms and the weapons and the ten warriors with me backed out of the village. "Put your hoods up, disguise your faces." As we left I saw the tiny glow from doorways as the villagers fearfully peeped out. I hoped they did not recognise us. I wanted our identity to be a mystery. We made our horses and met up with Osbert and Ridley. We quickly and silently headed east towards Topcliffe. The ground was hard now but the hoof prints would be clearly visible when the Normans came to look for their lost patrol. We rode to the road and then headed south for a while. When we came to the small river over which the road passed, we headed west, into the river and thence home.

"Too many men died there, my lord."

"I know." We had lost three dead in the attack and then another had succumbed to his wounds. "It was a major blow to the Normans but, you are right Osbert, they have more men to lose. The knights are fine warriors, even without armour. We will limit ourselves to ambushes along the road for a while. You never know, we may get more men who wish to join us."

Osbert was not convinced. "Anyone who joins us would be a potential spy. We have to be careful."

I could see what he meant for, with a price on my head there would be many men willing to risk all to make their fortune. As it transpired, there were no volunteers and we spent the next month watching for travellers. We devised a method by which two archers would wait as close to the Jorvik road south of Topcliffe as they could manage. If they saw a likely convoy then one rode up to the place we waited to fetch us whilst the other trailed them. I was there with Osbert and twenty men, a mixture of archers and men at arms when Edward galloped in. "My lord, a column of men at arms and knight. "

"How many? "

"Twenty men at arms and four crossbowmen but only the knight is mounted."

I turned to Osbert. "They can't be making for Catherick, they wouldn't make it. They must be going either to Topcliffe or Medelai."

"Then we have to take them." We rode along the road for four miles and then turned off into the scrubland adjacent.

Edward held his hand up. "I think that they should be just down the road around the stand of trees."

"You and the archers secrete yourselves next to the road. We will attract their attention. Take out the knight if you can or his horse and your next target will be the crossbows."

We had discovered they were the Normans best weapons and although we did not fear them, we respected them. "Right Osbert, I will ride down the road with four men and see if he will attack us or at least draw close to us. You and the others hide in the bushes and close with them."

"With respect my lord, you cannot carry on like this."

I saw the others smile, "Like what?"

"Always putting yourself at the fore as you did in Catherick. Always the first one in. I know you are our leader but we can't afford to lose you. Let me have a go this time." He grinned to take any insolence out of his words. "See if I can manage it, eh sir."

He was right. He was as good a warrior as I was and perhaps I was hunting glory too much. "Very well, but don't get yourself killed, I don't want Branton pissed at me as well!"

We found some bushes and hid the horses. My horse, Sweyn, neighed; he always did that when he heard strange horses. They were approaching. Osbert and his men were in the distance riding down the road and I spied the Norman column. The knight had spotted Osbert and he showed his caution by forming his men into a defensive circle with him in the middle. Osbert halted and we had a stalemate. Edward and his archers had no target yet, at least not a target they could hit effectively. Osbert must have read my mind for he spread his men out into a line and began to trot down the road. I heard an order in French and then four crossbowmen stepped forwards to aim their weapons at Osbert. Although Edward's men could not see the knight well enough to hit, the lightly protected crossbowmen were an easy target and they fell to the ground dead.

The men at arms turned to their left to protect against the new enemy and I shouted, "Now!" We sprang from concealment and struck the rear of their line with our spears. "Withdraw!"

Outlaw

The knight was a brave man and he charged at the archers. They knew better than to stay and they quickly mounted and sped away. Osbert galloped up and his men at arms exchanged spears with the men at arms, leaving another couple dead. When the knight reorganised his lines it was stalemate again and we withdrew. I felt disappointed but it had been a good ambush. We had killed or wounded at least eight and not lost a man. Osbert was cheerfulness personified as we rode back to camp. "Now that is how we should do it. Annoy them. Slow them down. Make them look behind every bush for us."

By the end of the month, the convoys had increased in size to protect them against our incursions. Each one had mounted men and crossbowmen to escort it. But we did notice that they cracked their whips even harder and the castles rose inexorably to dominate the skyline. I could see a pattern. They were controlling the roads. It was the chess game again; the castles controlled the board to enable their knights to attack. Luckily we received some intelligence from an unexpected source when Ralph arrived with more arrowheads.

He appeared to have grown by at least four fingers! "They have almost finished the castle at Maiden Bower and Aux Gemons…"

"Who is Aux Gemons when he is at home.?"

"That is William of Perci or as he is now called Baron Topcliffe. His nickname is Aux Gemons because of his moustaches. He is now at York building that castle and William has raised the taxes. They have been doubled. He has tax collectors all over the land."

"You have done well Ralph. Have they been to Coxold yet?"

"Aye, they came there first."

"You be careful when you return to Coxold and we will call in to the manor to speak with the steward."

When he left I drew Osbert, his brother and Ridley to one side, "We will move camp."

"What was that about visiting Coxold?"

"We will Ridley but it will be from our other camp." He looked at me with a puzzled look although I could see that Osbert had worked out my meaning. "If Ralph is captured he will send any Norman west."

"Ralph will not talk."

Outlaw

"We cannot take that chance, besides, they are alert to us here. It is time to collect some taxes of our own."

To the east, there were many more small villages and settlements nestled in and around the foothills. There were few forts and castles although I suspected that William would change all that soon. The road to Scarborough wound through a fertile gap in the hills and, with my military eye, I could see that a castle built at Helmsley would prevent any progress that way. It was one reason why I had selected the camp as our hideaway for it enabled to strike quickly and yet still remain hidden.

The nights were becoming shorter when we began our forays and this emboldened the Normans. It suited us too for the new growth on bushes and trees afforded us more shelter. Branton and his scouts spent the first three days watching for the tax men. He found them on the second day. They were to the south-east of us around the small village of Malton and Norton. I suppose they felt secure for there was a good Roman road to York but they had reckoned without my men. We left ten in the camp to improve its disguise and we led the others to ambush the small column. There were thirty men in the column and Branton had reported neither crossbows nor knights. He did tell me that the men at arms had more armour than hitherto.

"It seems we are annoying them then Ridley! We will split the force and await them either side of the road in and out of Malton." We knew that they were in Malton and had been to Norton but we had no idea if they would return to Jorvik or continue to bleed the villages dry.

It is gently sloping land around these villages and the trees were sparse; the dips and hollows, however, suited us as there was no clear line of sight over long distances. I waited with Branton and half of the men on the road back to Jorvik whole Ridley took the iothers north. I had a scout on the outskirts of the village ready to warn us of their approach. When he did come, however, it was to tell us that the men had headed north towards Ridley. We mounted and trotted through the village; we saw some distressed villagers to whom we waved but we had no opportunity to speak with them. Ridley and Osbert would be outnumbered by the Normans we knew they would need us.

Outlaw

"Branton, send two men ahead to find the end of the column."

The two men were still in sight when we heard the clash of weapons. I kicked hard and Sweyn surged forwards. My men needed no command, the sound told them their comrades were in battle. We crested a rise in the road and saw that there was a furious battle going on. The tax collector was cowering behind the line of men battling with mine. "Branton!"

My sergeant nodded and, calling to his archers wheeled left. I grinned as I turned to my men, "Charge!"

The increase in speed coincided with the first flights falling on the backs of the Normans. They were armoured but it is highly disconcerting to have arrows falling behind you. I saw the tax collector yell something and the line began to turn. The line of men who faced us was not continuous and certainly not prepared. I stabbed down with Boar Splitter as I tugged back on Sweyn's reins. It was a trick I had taught him; it helped me to remove my spear and his hooves normally terrified the men on the ground. As I withdrew it I saw that two men lay dead and I stabbed again at the back of the man before me. He fell to the side taking my blade with him. I unsheathed my sword and looked for an enemy. A rider aimed his horse at me, his spear levelled. I waited patiently and as the head came close, swept it aside with my sword and then swung the blade back to sever the man's arm at the elbow. He screamed as he rode past me. I looked around for another enemy but they had surrendered for we had surrounded them.

I could see some empty saddles but the ground was covered in dead Normans. The tax collector was still cowering beneath his tiny vehicle and I dismounted to confront him. "Who is your lord?" I spoke in English for I knew that the Normans would need someone who could speak with the villagers.

"Baron William of Perci, my lord."

He was English and I was tempted to kill him outright for being a traitor but something told me to hold my temper. "Then when you return to your master tell him that William collects no more taxes from these people." The surprise in his eyes told me that he thought I would kill him. "Tell him and tell your comrades here that any Norman I find in this land will die. Tell him also that no castle and no town are safe. We can strike anywhere as your men

Outlaw

at Catherick discovered." I turned to Osbert. "Disarm them, take their armour and helmets, take their shoes and release them." I raised my voice and pointed. "Jorvik is that way."

The twelve men who accompanied the tax collector looked unhappy as they trudge down the road. I wondered how they would fare in the village they had just robbed. Osbert and Ridley rode up to me, "I am surprised you let them live Aelfraed."

"Ridley, we need them to fear us and I want them to know that we struck at Catherick. They will be looking for somewhere between the two. I am also gambling that they will think that the east is safe for them and this is the extent of our control." I looked at Osbert, "Did we lose many?"

"Aedgar died and we have a couple of wounds." He nodded at the weapons and the cart, "Good haul though."

The Normans had disappeared down the road. "Right, back to the camp. Branton, send a couple of men to see where they go."

The coins the tax collectors had gathered were substantial in number but in such small coins that it reflected the poverty of the people. Ridley and looked at it and then each other, "We cannot keep it Aelfraed."

"I know but apart from Malton and Norton we know not who paid them."

Osbert came over and ran his hands through the coins. "We could always just return it to the people as payment, overpayment."

"What do you mean?"

"We need goods that they have in the villages, food, clothing and the like. If we go in to buy them we can pay much more than they are worth. We may not be repaying the exact villagers whose money was taken but at least we would put money back into the villages."

I patted him on the shoulder. "That is a good idea. Edward!"

"Yes my lord. Disguise yourself and find out which villages have been taxed. It may take you a couple of days."

As they were heading north I would work south from Norton but avoid the road and the Normans."

Edward sniffed, "You'll be teaching my grandmother to suck eggs next! My lord."

Outlaw

I laughed, my men needed no instructions about avoiding detection, we were like spirits of the night. "Osbert find someone who did not fight at Malton and send them with a horse to buy things from the two villages. Take a third of the money. Ask the camp guards what we need."

When Branton returned at dusk he was grinning. "They were not happy bunnies by the time they reached Hutton. Luckily for them, they found some other Normans there building a small fort."

"Is it worth us visiting?"

He shook his head, "I think it is just a place to tax those who use the road. Stupid really, for there are ways to avoid it."

For the next month, we continued to seek out William's collectors and we robbed them. They increased the guards they used but, as they rarely used knights and crossbowmen, we always came out on top. Word came to us, in early summer, that the castles William had been building were nearing completion and that William had his knights with him, searching the land around Medelai and Topcliffe. "He is looking for us, my lord."

"Yes, Osbert, which means it is time to move back there."

I think I saw Ridley's jaw actually drop. "Back there but didn't you hear? William is looking for us there."

"But we aren't there, we are here and by approaching from the east we will see him before he sees us. Once he has searched and found three charcoal burners only he will head here, to the area around Malton where we first struck."

Osbert nodded. "Makes sense and we move at night. "

We had noticed that the Normans feared not the night but those who prowled at night, the human wolves, us! I also wondered about some mischief on the way over to Medelai. The castle at Topcliffe was not yet finished and I had an idea how to slow it down; it was probably a petty gesture but the Normans had taken everything from us and I wanted to repay them.

We travelled light and left just before sunset. We skirted Thirsk for there were signs of construction there too. We headed south towards Topcliffe. We were approaching from the side away from the rivers and we knew the land well. We dismounted in a wood, a mile to the north of the castle and, leaving five men to guard the horses, travelled across the fields to the construction site. We had bows and swords for the work would be close in. Our dull clothes and lack of helmets meant that we were almost invisible as we scurried towards the mound rising in the distance. I sent Branton and Edward forward and when we reached them they pointed to the ramparts and held up three fingers. They only had three guards there! We approached slowly. There was a ditch and the spoil had been used for the mound. They had yet to complete the outer wall and the keep was a wooden affair with a small inner wall. Two of the guards were talking above the small gatehouse. I pointed at Edward and signalled for him to take an archer and deal with the other guard. I pointed to the two guards and then at Branton. He and four men aimed at the two men. They allowed enough time for Edward to get around the other side and then they loosed. Branton's men were good and the two men were hit in the throat and fell to a silent death punctuated only by the thump as they hit the ground. We ran to the walls and, using two of the shields we had brought, two men were hoisted above our heads to climb over the walls. A few heartbeats later the gate was opened. Once inside we would see that there was a stair leading to a door halfway up and the ground floor had the horses. Branton led the horses to safety while Osbert quietly climbed the steps and jammed four spears against the stairs and the entrance. Ridley and I went into the stables where there was a ripe smell of horses and hay. The Normans had fodder in there for their steed and it was dry. My men brought in some of the wood we found outside, obviously ready to build the ramparts, and they stacked it in piles. Using a flint we sparked a few flickering flames which we fanned until the hay and the wood caught. We quickly left the stable as an inferno erupted. Once outside we watched the tower burn. As soon as the smoke rose we heard coughing and then the men inside tried to get out of the door. The spears held them for quite a while and, when the flames began to consume the ladder, we knew that they were doomed. Two men managed to break open the door but Branton's archers' arrows, mercifully, ended their suffering. When no one else emerged we mounted Norman's horses and rode northeast to where ours had been left.

When we rode we went in a northeastern direction, as though heading for the Tees. When we found the stream I was seeking we turned and continued west. All the while we could see the red glow in the south that marked the end of the tower at Topcliffe. Ridley still thought that I had been reckless.

"No Ridley, just the opposite. When the fire is seen, perhaps even now, then William, either Perci or the Bastard, will send men south and east to find out what is amiss. They will find the burning tower. If they have good trackers then they might follow us northeast and then they will lose us. Or they may not have good trackers and search around Topcliffe. Either way, the one place they will not search is where they were for they would have travelled over that ground and not seen us."

Ridley nodded. Osbert said casually, but showing that he had been paying attention, "What if he only sends some of his men and the rest still search the forests?"

"Then we skirt further north and approach from the west." He nodded. "I know it is a risk but this way we have damaged William of Perci and his castle and we keep William the Bastard guessing."

I had Branton and Edward further south from our line of march to watch for any Normans and, as dawn broke and we found ourselves crossing the Roman road close to the Swale, the two of them rode towards us.

"You were lucky my lord. A column of knights and men at arms, all mounted, travelled down the road just an hour ago."

"How many?"

"It was still a little dark but it looked to be over two hundred."

"And it would be too dark for banners. Good then ride to the camp and see if the road is clear. If one of you does not return then I will assume that it is."

The ride over the last fifteen miles was the most nerve-wracking of all for it was daylight and the open vale meant that we could be seen from a long way away. If I were William, I would have a castle along the road but so far it was devoid of castles and men. We received no word from my scouts and as we rode into the hidden camp, we all breathed a collective sigh of relief.

We remained hidden in the camp for a few days and then I sent scouts out to the villages to see what they could discover. As usual, they took some of the Norman tax money to buy things we needed and they were more than happy to give us information. I suspect

Outlaw

they knew who we were but none knew where we hid and, for the moment we were safe but I knew that, before winter set in, we would need to build two new camps away from these two sites. William the Bastard had returned south, apparently less than pleased with my work. We heard that there was a healthy reward for information about Aelfraed the Outlaw and his rebels! At least he knew who we were. William of Perci, Aux Gemons, had begun work on his castle and the downside of our raid was that the people of the manor, my people, were put to work rebuilding. For my part, I concentrated on the north of the land around our camp, up towards the Tees and the old Roman fort. William had sent his tax collectors there, for it was rich farmland but it was a long way from Jorvik and we were safer from reprisals. By the autumn the collectors had stopped travelling north of Topcliffe but the land to the east and west was heavily patrolled by mounted men. It was as though they were saying that north of that line was mine but the rest was Norman. Although we had not had any more deaths we were all getting older and our numbers were not increasing. It was again, a stalemate, and then Edgar the Aetheling finally invaded and brought with him Sweyn, King of the Danes. We had two enemies in the land.

Chapter 12

They landed close to Riccall just as Harald Hadrada had. They were not as numerous as Tostig and the Norwegian King's horde but then there were no Saxons to oppose them. As the Normans decided not to use the fyrd there were just the Norman troops in the region left to fight. Baron William retreated to the partly built castle at Jorvik. It freed us to move around at will for the Normans were too busy with a real army to worry about my ragtag band. I had a dilemma. Should I throw in with Edgar? Fight alongside the Danes and overthrow the Normans, or, join the Normans?

The night before we left the camp we sat around the fire debating the issue, "We cannot fight for the Normans, my lord?"

"Yet if we help the Danes might they not be tyrants like the Normans?"

I just listened and the memory of Aethelward came to me. I wondered what he would have done. At least he would be proud of my silence but I was still unsure of how he would view my actions. I closed my eyes and remembered my mentor and listened to the words of my friends.

"But they are both our enemies!"

I opened my eyes and sat up, "I remember Aethelward telling me of when he fought in Byzantium. There was an Arab wise man who said to Aethelward, *'the enemy of my enemy is my friend'*."

Ridley looked confused which made Branton and Osbert smile. "Huh?"

"Who do we fight?"

"The Normans."

"Who are the Normans enemy?"

"Now? The Danes."

"Then they are our friend. It may well be that they prove to be as bad as William the Bastard but we will deal with that later."

"We join their army?"

"No, but we make hay while the sun shines. We attack and harry the Normans. We burn their castles and we rob them of supplies. The advantage we have now is that we do not need to hide. We can ride in mail and unfurl our banners."

Outlaw

And so, as the year petered to a wintry end, my small army went to war. We headed to Coxold, mainly because Ridley had not seen his people since the previous Christmas and Ralph's reports were not as detailed as he wished them to be. We rode close to Topcliffe and, seeing the new ramparts on top of the blackened mound we detoured to see what mischief we could cause. The four men left to guard it ran off when they saw the column of men with the red horse shields. "Fetch a couple of them back, Branton."

They had only had time to put new wooden stakes in ready to attach the ramparts. They pulled out easily. When we went to the new hall built close by the river we saw that they had built this of stone and wood- it burned well. Branton returned with one of the men. I lifted one eyebrow and he shrugged, "They wouldn't stop."

"Do you speak English?"

"Yes my lord."

"You know me?"

"Yes my lord, I was one of Thegn Skipton's men. I fought at Fulford."

"And yet you fight now for the Normans?"

"The Thegn is dead and his land belongs to William of Perci. I needed to eat."

I looked at the man who was shivering, not with the cold but the fear of imminent death. "What is your name?"

"Tadgh my lord."

"Tell me, Tadgh of Skipton, how many men does the Baron have?"

He shrugged, "I was never a counter my lord, more of a fighter but he has many horsemen. He came here with, oh must have been fifty armed horsemen and five hundred foot soldiers, I was one of them and thirty or so crossbowmen."

"Why were you left here? To make sure the castle wasn't wrecked again?" He gave a half smiled, "That really pissed him off."

My men laughed. "He expects much of his men. Four of you to defend against my men?"

"That's why we run sir. The lads and me, well we can't fight the men of the hood, no-one can."

Osbert asked, "Men of the hood?"

Outlaw

"Yes sir, that's what they call you. Well, they say, *'Hommes de la Capuche'* or something but one of the lads said it means men with hoods or of the hood he wasn't certain. They think you are the ghosts of the men who fought at Hastings."

I was curious. "Why do they call us that?"

"Well first off there's never any bodies after you fight and then you appear in places where you shouldn't and disappear as you did at Catherick."

I looked over to Osbert who was as interested as I was in the man's story. "So, he went to Jorvik."

"Yes, my lord, he was collecting his men from the other castles on the way. The Vikings are back they say."

"That they are. Now then Tadgh you present me with a dilemma. We should kill you. Indeed, there are men behind me already whetting their knives in anticipation. On the other hand, you are an old comrade. I will give you a choice, death, and I will make it quick and as painless as possible or become an outlaw and join us." I heard Osbert snort behind me. I turned, "Remember Aedgart? He fought against us and proved to be a valuable comrade did he not?" Osbert nodded, Aedgart had been one of his truest friends.

"Well sir, you give me a choice of life or death, no contest. I am your man."

I smiled cynically, "Just as an hour ago you were Baron William's man. You may join us but you will be watched so do not think of running. Branton here can hit the eye of a hawk at four hundred paces." That was an exaggeration but Branton enjoyed the compliment.

"Yes my lord."

"Find yourself a horse; there are some spares at the back. Edward, keep an eye on him."

Leaving the burning building behind, we headed for Coxold. Ridley rode knee to knee with me, "Men of the hood eh? I wonder how we can use that."

"What do you mean. use it?"

"They think that we are supernatural creatures; let us use that idea. Strike more at night and make them fear their own rooms and chambers."

Outlaw

"I prefer a stand up fight. I miss the shield wall and fighting alongside you, Osgar and Wolf."

"As do I old friend but those days are gone. There will be no shield wall again; William the Bastard has seen to that."

The pall of smoke rising in the distance told us that Aux Gemons had struck again and I saw the anger rip across Ridley's face for he knew the land and the only manor nearby was his. We found the first corpses on the outskirts of the village. They had been running away and all bore wounds in their back. Here the buildings were Ridley's buildings. The Normans had not claimed it yet but they were all burnt. There was a smell of human roast which made some of the younger men gag as we approached the village of the dead. The smithy was ashes and the warrior hall had four timbers left and the rest was blackened debris. The only building which still stood was the church. We could not see any bodies but we searched anyway. Tadgh nervously edged closer to me as the men began to stare with open hostility at this man who had been with them until a short time ago.

"Tadgh," I said loudly, "were you here?"

"No, my lord."

"Do you so swear?"

He put his hands between his legs and said, "I so swear."

The open hostility stopped but the men still did not take to the stranger. The men searching the church came back shaking their heads. There were no bodies in there. Suddenly we heard a noise and every man's hand went to his weapons. I held my hand up for calm when I saw that it was fifteen or so women and girls. They rushed, crying, up to Ridley, "Oh my lord! I curse the day that you left."

He dismounted and took the woman in his arms. It was the most gentle I had ever seen Ridley. "Tell me, Edith, what happened."

"One of the boys, young Alan, came and said that the Normans were coming, lots of them. Ralph heard and told the steward to get everyone to run away or be prepared to fight. He said that the Normans were the new rulers and we would have to get used to it. Ralph just told us to run and he looked so fearful we did. We ran to the trees overlooking the village and Ralph got his hammer. They just started killing everybody. There was only Ralph with a

Outlaw

weapon and he hit a few of them, then he went into his smithy and he never came out," she began to cry once more.

"You are doing well my pet, now what happened next?" Ridley's voice reminded me of Nanna's, soothing and gentle, encouraging confidences.

"Well they set fire to the smithy and then some of them found some of the girls who hadn't run and," she looked up at Ridley and blushed, "and did things to them. Oh, sir, some of them were only nine or ten and they screamed." She shook her head. "I can still hear them and then when everyone was dead they threw the bodies in the buildings and set fire to them."

I felt so sorry then for Ridley for this had happened to me and I knew the dark pain which now ripped and gripped him. His eyes were filled with tears. I turned to Branton, "Branton, bring the box with the coin." He went to the pack horse at the rear. "Osbert, detail eight men to escort these women to…" my mind went blank. Where was safe? Perhaps the lucky ones were the dead, the dead who had died quickly.

"How about Medelai sir, that should still be standing and the Steward, well he will know what to do."

"Good idea, well done Osbert. Here ladies. There is coin here so that you will not be poor. Go with these men to Medelai. They will watch over you and the Steward there is a kind man, rough but kind." I shrugged, "Neither Lord Ridley nor myself can offer you any comfort save that we will be revenged on these killers of children." She kissed my hand and then Ridley's and led the women off. Each one bowed to Ridley as they passed and each one kissed his hand.

There was an eerie silence after the crying women had gone. Ridley had a determined look upon his face as he stared at the burnt manor, "I let these people down Aelfraed. We all let them down."

"What could we have done old friend. We had no defences; we would have died with your people."

He turned on me, suddenly angry, "Well perhaps that would be better because we would have killed some of those bastards. There was a time when I felt sad for Wolf and Osgar now I know that they are the lucky ones for they do not have to look on this

Norman world. They died defending an England that was worth defending. What do we do? Sneak around in the night. Burn a few bits of wood and feel like heroes. Well, I for one do not feel like a fucking hero!"

Something changed that day in my relationship with Ridley. He was still loyal and fought as hard as any warrior but he was never as close to me again. His people had suffered and he blamed me. The sad thing is this was just the beginning. The scene would be repeated but on a far larger scale. The world we had known had ended and we were about to enter a world that was more like a nightmare than a reality.

We had planned on staying the night in the comfort of the warrior hall but that was out of the question. Instead, we made a camp in the hills some five miles south of Coxold. The hunters shot some game but we did not enjoy the meal and ate only out of habit. There were none of the ribald stories or songs for almost a year ago we had shared our food with these people. The women who had been raped had danced with these men and we had been happy; they had been happy. We would never dance or eat again without thinking of Lord Ridley's people. Branton began keening a lame, quietly at first and then as others joined in it became louder but still a gentle hymn to the fallen. When it finished the last notes seemed to echo around the hills and then there was silence as each man remembered in his own way.

As we prepared to ride I sought out Osbert and Branton; Ridley had barely said a word since the previous night, "We will need to watch Ridley today, especially if we run into Normans."

"I think that we have more chance of running into the Danes, my lord."

"That is my intention, not to fight with them but to let them know we too fight the Normans. Branton, have Edward and two men ride to the south of Jorvik towards Riccall. When they find the Danes return to me and then I will go and have a talk with them."

"Is that wise, my lord?"

I laughed, such an unnatural sound that every man looked at me as though I was mad. "Not wise? Tell me one sane thing that we have done since Fulford." I put my hand on his arm, "I no longer know what is wise and I just do what feels right."

Outlaw

The trail of William was clear to see as we neared Jorvik, dead bodies and burning buildings. We camped close to the western end of the city and I waited for my scouts to return. We approached the city walls and saw, immediately, the improvements they had made. The towers and gates had been strengthened; the ditches were deeper and there were sentries patrolling the length of its walls. It was obvious that Morcar was no longer in charge. We were seen when we approached for I wanted them to know who we were. Ridley was with me and I could feel his seething anger as he stared intently at the walls as though he could see through them into the black heart of William of Perci. One of their crossbowmen tried a shot but it fell short. I turned to Branton, the range was four hundred paces but I thought he could attempt the shot, "Branton see if you can hit the walls, a man would be a bonus but the wall would be good."

He spent some time selecting an arrow and only then did he string his bow. He pulled it back to his ear and I felt sure that the bow would snap and then he released it. We watched it arc high into the air and, amazingly, the Normans watched it too. They were so intent that the crossbowmen who followed his flight had a real shock when it plunged into his upper arm and they all dropped from sight. All of us, apart from Ridley, laughed with the relief of the tension. Although the other archers were not as good as Branton, we outranged the crossbows which they used.

The scouts returned the next day. Edgar and the Danes were moving towards Jorvik, taking the same route the other Norsemen had years earlier. I took Osbert to one side. "I would take you with me but I worry that Lord Ridley will do something foolish if left alone. You know how to handle him. I will take your brother and Edward. They both keep their wits about them."

"I will watch him, my lord." He hesitated, "If you don't mind me saying so my lord, Lord Ridley worried about you when the Queen died. You came through it and I am sure he will too."

Osbert could be surprisingly gentle for such a bear of a man and he understood people. I suppose that was what made him such a good leader of men. The three of us left the next day; we were lightly armed for if the Danes chose they could take us easily. Branton had been with me before and for some reason appeared

Outlaw

confident when with me. Edward was a little more nervous, glancing at every bush and looking for enemies who were not there. I did not think that the Danes would bother with ambushes; their aim was to take Jorvik. We headed for the road south of Jorvik for that would be the route they would have to take. I had my helmet back from my face so that I could be recognised but the prominent shield told the world that I was Aelfraed Godwinson, Housecarl.

There were scouts who were out and they raced up to us with weapons readied. "Steady lads, just hold your arms away from your bodies."

When they saw that we were not aggressive they took our reins and led us down the road. Edgar and Sweyn led the army. Edgar had filled out in the last two years but he was still young to be leading such a force. Sweyn looked like a more rotund version of Hadrada and I knew the two had been great rivals. Sweyn's warriors closed around their King and then Edgar smiled, "Fear not King Sweyn. This is my half brother Aelfraed. He fought at Fulford and Stamford."

Sweyn's face opened into a grin. His English was good, far better than Hadrada's, "Ah this is the famous Housecarl whose men killed my great enemy Hadrada."

I nodded, "And it is good to meet the man who has come to rid us of the hated Normans." I was careful in my choice of words for I was still a warrior and would not lie. "This, mighty King, is Branton, the archer who slew Hadrada."

Sweyn dismounted and turned to speak with his men. I signalled to the other two to dismount. Suddenly they all cheered and Sweyn strode up to Branton and grabbed him in a bear hug. "We owe you much Branton for Hadrada would have taken our land had you not killed him." He disengaged himself and took a golden bracelet from his arm. I could see it was intricately carved. "Take this as a token from the Danish people. You will always be honoured in my land." Branton looked at me as he held the object and I nodded. Sweyn then took my arm, "Come Aelfraed Godwinson, walk with me and we will talk."

Edgar turned to me eagerly, "We heard that you had not submitted and you continued to fight."

"Who told you that?"

"The warriors of Earl Morcar who joined us."

I spat, "Then I would watch those carefully my lord for I have fought with them twice and both times they ran." I shrugged, "That may have been their leader I know not but they could have joined me ere now."

Sweyn and Edgar exchanged glances. Sweyn nodded, "I have heard Aelfraed that you were well trained by Aethelward and I see it now. You are known as a fearless warrior and a leader of men. How many men do you have?"

It was a blunt and honest question and I gave it a blunt and honest answer, "Not as many as the days following Stamford for we have fought, alone, against greater numbers. We number less than fifty but," I added proudly," I would back those fifty against any hundred others."

Sweyn said something to the men behind and they laughed and answered their king. "My men say they would like to try such valiant warriors."

I grinned, "Let us beat the Normans first."

"Tell me Housecarl, how do you defeat the Norman knights? Are they not impregnable? Did they not defeat Harold?"

I shook my head, "No, they did not defeat my father. He had too many untrained men with him, the fyrd, and when they became out of control, he was surrounded and my brothers died. And we defeat them by only using trained warriors. And we have a secret weapon. Show him, Branton." Branton took a knight killer from his quiver and handed it over. "This is Branton's invention. It penetrates the mail. Of course, you have to be a good shot for they use their shields for protection. And when you face them in a shield wall then use your weapons against the horses. Once they are on foot they are easy to defeat."

Sweyn passed the arrow back to his men and translated. Edgar took the opportunity to speak with me, "My sister Margaret is now Queen of Scotland." I had not heard that but it made sense and also gave Edgar a refuge. "I was sorry to hear about the Queen." I looked at him sharply. He held his hands up, "I swear to you Aelfraed I had no part in the plot of my mother's. The old bitch is deranged. I am sorry, genuinely."

Outlaw

I relaxed a little, his words sounded like the truth. "In the end, it was that bastard William who was responsible for their deaths but the men who killed her now lie dead."

"I heard that they were killed. I would not like to be your enemy Aelfraed."

"Then rid the land of the Normans and you will not be." I think I saw him actually shiver then.

Sweyn was still talking and we walked north. He bit his lip and then looked at me, "I visited Fife and met your... I met Lady Gytha."

I gave a wry smile. "I am a warrior Edgar, you can speak openly with me. My wife Gytha now plays the Dane with Calum, Thegn of Fife."

"Men speak truly of you Aelfraed."

"Why what do they say? That I am someone without the gift of gilded speech?"

"No, they say that you do speak the truth and men trust your words." He smiled, "In my world that is a rare thing for all men flatter me and promise me everything."

"You have to be true to yourself and true to your men. We are on this earth for a short time but our deeds live on after us. Our father Harold was a great warrior, betrayed by a brother but at the end, his men were still loyal to him and died in brotherhood. I lost many friends that day."

Sweyn's voice next to me almost made me jump as it boomed out, "And it is good for England that you did not die that day for you have kept the spark of rebellion alive. I have heard that William has a higher price on your head than either Hereward or Edgar here. He fears you Aelfraed for you are undefeated and you have never submitted."

We had reached Fulford and I recognised the hill from which Hadrada had launched his attacks. "If you would take some advice I would camp here. It is the field of Fulford and many brave Housecarls died here on that day but it is a good place to defend. You are close enough to Jorvik to smell the shit in the drains."

Sweyn laughed and slapped me on the back, "I will take your advice and then we will eat and we can get to the bone of your visit and decide how to take this city."

Outlaw

Branton was feted like a hero by the men of Sweyn's bodyguard. An intelligent man he quickly learned some of their words and, with the aid of sign language, they began to communicate. I sat with the two leaders; Edgar wisely said little and listened much; Aethelward would have liked him. "They have begun a new castle and they have deepened their ditches. Their horsemen are within the walls but they cannot sally forth if you are closer to the gates. They have, however, deepened their ditches and an assault would be costly. Their crossbows are deadly and can be sent at you so that you do not see the man."

Sweyn nodded and chewed on the mutton bone he held in his huge fist. "Well strategos, what do you suggest?" I looked up sharply. "Yes Aelfraed, I had heard of your uncle and knew his skill. You have such skill and you are, I can see, an honest man. Advise us."

"If you have archers then use them to clear the walls. Have your men make shields that are oblong, like the ones the Romans used and man-sized. They can shoot from there. Attack at night. They are vulnerable to those kinds of attack."

He laughed, "We have heard that you and your men are called ghosts, what is it, men of the hood?"

I shrugged, "When you only have a handful of men you do whatever you have to. Jorvik has fine Roman walls but they stretch a long way and they cannot defend all of them equally. If you attack a gate on one side then men could climb over the walls."

Edgar looked puzzled. "How? They are higher than a man."

"We have done it. You have two men hold a shield above their head and a third man climbs on to that. He can reach the battlements and pull himself up. Once you have a few on the walls it becomes easier."

Sweyn shrewdly watched me, "You are a thinker Aelfraed. And how would you attack the gates, without losing too many men?"

"Cut down one of the oaks hereabouts. "I grinned, you have axes I assume."

"Aye, and when we have a moment I would like to view Death Bringer."

"You shall. Cut down a tree and sharpen the end. Fashion four wheels and then have your men pull it towards the gates. I would

Outlaw

suggest the Mickelgate, to the south of the city. The road slopes down to it a little and should make it easier to pull. Have the men pulling protected by men in mail with shields. You will suffer casualties but if it is night time there will not be as many. Remember you only need to draw men to the gate. You do not need to force the gate. Then when your men have captured another gate you attack there."

"So I split my forces?"

"I would have my better, more experienced warriors at the northern gate. You will need fearless men with the ram but…"

"It is an acceptable risk. And you Aelfraed where will you be?"

I smiled, "I will attack the western wall with my men."

Edgar almost coughed up his food, "But you only have fifty men."

"Aye Edgar, but they are my men! Besides, it increases the odds of success. With two attempts at a breach, we may succeed."

Sweyn laughed. "I like that plan. I am glad we met, Aelfraed."

"One more thing; the people of this land have suffered greatly at the hands of the Normans. They suffer them in their city they do not welcome them. Kill only Normans or," I added darkly, "you will have to answer to me and my men."

Edgar coloured and Sweyn went silent. "In other men, I would find that boastful but in you, Aelfraed Godwinson, I heed the warning and you have my word, the people will be safe."

We spent the next few hours discussing how we would coordinate the attacks. It would take the huge army some time to reach the northern and gate and for the southern attack to manufacture its ram. While Sweyn was asking Branton about his arrows I took the Aetheling to one side. "I understand why you have brought the Danish king to help you regain the thrown," I did not mention that I had as much right to the throne as he, perhaps more, "but when you are king, what assurances do you have that Sweyn will honour them?" He looked shocked but I continued, "I do not doubt that Sweyn is an honourable man, I like him but I also know that when men gain power they can change. Our father did."

"I envy you Aelfraed for I did not know my father. You fought with him. What was he like?"

"He was fearless. The Housecarls loved him. Why else would they have given their lives for him? Did you know that at Stamford Bridge he rode alone to the Viking lines to speak with them? And he was funny too. He made men laugh for he could talk with them as one of them." I shrugged, "When he became king he became a little more distant. Power, you see."

Edgar looked at me with suddenly wise old eyes, "It is strange Aelfraed but that is the description men give of you and when I saw you I shivered, for it was as though our father walked the earth again." He stared directly at me. "Perhaps you should be king."

I laughed and put my arm around him. "No Edgar, you say I am like my father and I am honoured that you think so for he and my uncle Aethelward are my models. But as much as I would like to be my father I would not wish to be king. No you can be king and I will support you but first, we have to defeat these Normans and that will take iron from you. Can you do it?"

"Aye brother, with your help we can do anything."

Chapter 13

Edward made sure that he told all of our company of the esteem in which Branton was held. The men at arms and the archers had a healthy competitive streak and loved to mock each other. Branton's rank amongst the Danes put a sour look on his brother's face. I took the two brothers and Ridley to one side as Edward regaled the others with tales of the Danes. Branton even allowed him to show the golden bracelet which impressed all. Branton himself cared not for such rich trinkets but he loved the sentiment which came with it.

"We are to attack the eastern gate in two nights' time."

Osbert wrinkled his nose, "With fifty men?"

Branton smiled, "Lord Aelfraed told the Danish king that his men were worth two of any other warriors."

"Huh, even with a hundred we would struggle."

"I will happily charge!"

"Yes Lord Ridley, but the bolts would bounce off that thick hide of yours!" I could see that Osbert was trying humour to enliven Ridley to his old self; it was not working for Ridley just ignored the attempt at banter.

"Perhaps if you listened to my plan?" They nodded as they saw that they had dismissed out of hand what they had not heard. "The Danes will assault the Mickelgate while others scale the walls. The Danes will use a ram; we will not. Nor will we strike at the gate but at the walls to the side." Even Ridley looked interested and intrigued. "Mickelgate is situated at a bridge over the river which concentrates the enemy's men we, on the other hand, will go to Petergate to the west. This is but newly built and is not yet stone finished. The upper parts are made of wood. Branton and his archers can shoot fire arrows at the wooden parts. They will catch fire."

"But, my lord, they will douse them with water and put them out."

"True Branton, but if they are dousing them out, in firelight, they become targets for ordinary arrows and this will be night time. We will be shooting from the shadows, over the ditch. At the same

Outlaw

time, the rest of us will close with the walls and, using our shields we will send up the lightest warriors to scale the walls."

"How high are the walls?"

"Good question Osbert. If memory serves they are almost the height of two men. We may need to use three shields supporting two men and two shields held aloft."

Osbert looked dubious. "Which means that we could only gain the battlements with eight or nine men. They would have to be good warriors."

"Well as at least three of them will be us, I should hope so." He looked a little more pleased with that. Ridley just nodded. "The key to this is that they will send many men to the main gate. The Danes attack will be obvious. Branton's attack on the gate will be annoying for them rather than dangerous but it will draw many guards to the gate where they think we will be attacking and, even if we fail, it should ensure that the attack on the Monkgate will have a greater chance of success." I looked at each in turn. "Can anyone see a problem which I may have missed?" I allowed them time to think. I remember when I was a Housecarl and had been asked my views, the questioner never gave me time to think. Eventually, they all shook their heads. "The target for the men at arms will be the gatehouse. Branton and the archers can keep them busy so that we can slip down the stairs and open the gates."

"What if we are seen from the walls whilst we climb?"

"Then we will have failed so pray that it is a cloudless night."

We spent the next two days preparing. We would all need to be fully armed and armoured. The odds, at the Petergate, were stacked against us. The other problem I had foreseen was that William would be on his way north. Harold had made it in a few days; the disaster would be if he arrived whilst we were assaulting but we could do little about that and I realised, somewhat dispassionately, that it would be the Danes who would be the first to know and to suffer.

Edgar had obviously acquired some horses for one of his English warriors rode to us with a message. "My lord asks is all prepared for tonight?"

"I am, what is the signal to be?" I could see, from the blank look that he did not have a clue. Edgar and Sweyn had not thought of

Outlaw

that. "Ask him to do two things, one to send you when he is about to begin his attack and secondly to shoot a fire arrow high into the sky when the ram rolls."

Relieved he grinned, "Yes my lord."

I hoped that, as the gates were less than a mile apart, we would have a chance of seeing the arrow but the human signal would be just as effective. I was now relying on a Viking to make the correct decision about the time of the attack. I hoped that Sweyn was a good enough general to choose the best moment.

We watched the sun set to the west of us and when it was dark before the moon rose, we slipped forwards keeping to the sides of the old road leaving two men to whistle when Edgar's man arrived. Branton and his archers went to the right and we went to the left. Edward carried a covered pot containing coals; its lid hid the fire. We walked through the sparse bushes, constantly watching the walls for signs of movement. Osbert held up his hand and we froze. We could see a sentry walking from the Petergate to the small turret fifty paces from the tower. We watched as he completed a full circuit and saw that he was the only guard. We ran forwards in spurts when his back was to us and then became stationary. Lying flat on the ground, our cloaks hid us from view. I kept one eye on Branton for they needed to be in position before us.

When we were twenty paces from the ditch Harald of Thirsk crawled along the ground like a serpent and peered into the ditch. As soon as it was safe he returned to me. "A few wood spikes on the bottom but you can put your feet between them," he whispered, "They haven't cleared the grass and weeds from the sides so we can pull ourselves up if we need to." I nodded and he slid into his allotted position. As soon as the guard moved I signalled and we moved forward quickly to the ditch. Harald and I went down first and safely negotiated the obstacles. I waved the others down and they joined us on the other side of the ditch. I hoped that the shadows in the ditch would disguise our presence but we had to wait until the guard moved. We could now no longer see him without presenting a white face and we had to wait for Branton's signal. He waved his arm and we pulled ourselves up next to the wall. The only way we could be seen now was if he looked directly over and I hoped that soon he would be too busy for that. We took off our cloaks, which had served their purpose and we split ourselves into the groups of six. I hoped that two men would be able to thrust one over the top but I had planned six so that we could ascend higher. Then we waited. It seemed an age and I wondered if Sweyn had missed his opportunity; we need to strike in the middle of the night when the garrison was deep asleep and they were not expecting it. Suddenly there was a whistle. I peered back into the darkness and saw a movement. Branton could still see the key and I relied on him now. He had been given discretion when to loose. It was with some relief that I saw the glow as they took the lid off the pot.

I turned to the warriors alongside me, "Ready. Prepare shields. Pass it on." We were the closest to the gate and I would be the first up. Harald and Wills held their shield aloft. I hoped it would be high enough. Then there was a whoosh and a flash in the night sky as the fifteen arrows struck their target. I could hear the alarm from above me and also one in the distance. Now was not the time for caution and, placing one foot on Harald's knee and pulling on the shield, I began to ascend. I use Wills' knee and then I was on the shield. The battlement was level with my shoulder and I whispered, "Up!" It was a strange sensation rising up like that. I grasped the crenulations and pulled myself up. Soon others would follow but I needed to clear the walkway of any sentries. I drew my sword and gripped my shield. I could see that a kite shield would be better in a narrow space but I had to manage. There was no one in sight but I could hear the flames and the hiss as the sentries threw water onto the inferno which was raging. I could hear the shouts and then the screams as Branton's arrows thudded home. Glancing over my shoulder I saw Osbert and Ridley and I walked along the walkway. The old Roman stone steps descended to the ground level and I kept the sword at my side to gain as much surprise as possible. The stairs ended in a small guard room but the guards, I could see were peering through the slits in the door at Branton and his archers. There were eight of them. I turned and held up five fingers and then three; Osbert nodded and repeated the sign. I risked a glance into the city but it was mercifully empty, no one was rushing to the Petergate.

Outlaw

It was now or never and I stepped out and crossed to the far side of the gate and the man who was furthest away. My sword went through him before he even knew I was there. The man next to him turned in surprise and, as I withdrew my sword I head-butted him and, as he fell backwards, rammed my sword into his throat. The other six lay dead, for eight of us had managed to ascend the walls and we had had complete surprise. "Ridley, take some men up to the gatehouse and kill the guards there. Osbert let us get this door open." Even as we lifted the bar I heard the shouts from the city as a column of men appeared fifty paces away. It was too late to recall Ridley and, besides, we needed all of the guards dead. It seemed to take forever to lift it, even for two of us and then it was free and we dropped it. Osbert managed to open one door to let the others know we had succeeded. I turned just as the Norman warriors were within ten paces.

The leader was a knight with a kite shield and a mace, the ones with him all had spears and they outranged us for we had no axes. I rushed at the knight with my sword pointed at him and held above my shield. A round shield protects much of the body and his mace smashed harmlessly against the solid wood and iron structure. I did not try to hit him I slid my sword into the gap between his shield and his shoulder. He was wearing a gorget but it only deflected the blade and it slid along his neck, the blood showing that he was wounded. Before I could finish him off, the spearman next to him had thrust his spear at my arm and I was only saved by the metal plates. I sliced backhand at him and, as he had no gorget, took his head off in one sweep of my arm. The Norman knight staggered backwards clutching his neck and supported by two of his men.

I risked a glance to my left and saw Ridley, Osbert and the rest of my men dispatching the last of the column. As Branton and his men trooped in we took stock. Two of our men lay dead but the rest of us still stood. It seemed remarkably quiet although we could hear the noise from the Mickelgate. "Branton, cover our flanks. Osbert, detail four men to guard the gates. The rest of you, wedge!"

We had a choice, I could either take the men to aid the Danes over the Monkgate or help Sweyn at the Mickelgate. I was the decoy and I could do as I wished. The thought of brave warriors dying at the bridge decided me. There were twenty of us in the wedge and we filled the narrow streets with the six men at the rear. The rest of the men followed on behind. I felt elated as we trotted through the stone streets built a thousand years earlier by warriors who fought as we did. The Normans could not use their horses here! We did meet men as we ran through the five hundred paces of streets but they were all individuals who died with shocked expressions as the mailed warriors with the red horse shield appeared like wraiths from the grave. One warrior saw us and ran back to the gate which was close. I almost laughed as I heard him scream, "The ghost of Harold comes! Flee!"

The renegade Englishmen helped us more than had he fought with us for the defenders of the gate were already terrified before my wedge appeared suddenly from the side street. Relying on Branton to protest my flanks I roared, "Charge!" and ran straight at the centre of the gate. The Normans and Saxons there had never faced a charging wedge and they stood no chance as the combined weight and weapons of twenty-one warriors hit them and hit them hard. Even if we had not been striking them with our swords they could not have stood. The rest of my men formed a defensive circle behind us as Osbert and I opened the first gate. The second one showed that it had been damaged and when we opened it the Danes outside gave a huge roar and rushed in. Osbert and I stood aside to let them get their revenge on the defenders who had killed many of their comrades. I could see the bodies around the huge ram and others, wounded, lying next to the Mickelgate Bridge.

Sweyn strode up to me and clapped me on the back. "Once again I am indebted to you, Aelfraed Godwinson. You truly are a mighty warrior and your father, in Valhalla, will be proud of you."

We let the press of Danes rush into the fray. My men had done their part and I wished to have no more losses. Once the majority had entered I formed my men up. "Branton take your archers to the walls, kill any guards and then harry the rest."

"Ridley!"

"He has gone my lord. He followed Sweyn. He as not yet satiated his appetite for blood." Osbert looked sad and I could understand why. Ridley had turned from being a good warrior with a kind heart to a revenge filled killing machine. I pitied any Norman he met.

"The rest of you, form up behind Osbert and me. Our task is to protect the people." I headed for the Jewish quarter. I owed Rueben that much at least. Groups of Danes were busy fighting handfuls of Normans and renegades. They did not need our help and I pressed on. The bodies thinned out and I began to hope that the fighting had passed Reuben by but when I turned the corner I saw a crowd of Jorvik inhabitants with torches and homemade weapons. They were beating on Reuben's door.

"Come out you old Jew!"

"There's no one to look after you now. The Normans have gone!"

"Christ killer!"

I was suddenly angry. I had saved these people and they were turning on a harmless old man. I roared forward and smashed my shield into the three men I could reach. "Put your weapons down!"

One loutish looking man shouted, "Why? Who the fuck are you?"

His head came off in one blow. "I am Aelfraed Godwinson. I am the leader of the hooded men and I am the one who has helped free you from the Normans!" There was rage in my voice, in my face and in my actions. They shrank back, weapons and torches falling to the floor. "You could not fight the Normans yourselves, you let brave men die to do that and now you try to kill an old man who has only ever helped you. You all deserve to die!" I took one step forwards and they ran screaming. The street was empty.

"Well, I don't think they will be cheering you any time soon, my lord!"

"If they are the sort of people who we are dying for then we might as well leave for Byzantium now."

Osbert shook his head sadly, "But they are not. They are the people of the towns, the ones who look out for themselves only. We fight for those who lie at Coxold and Topcliffe."

Osbert truly understood me and I clapped my arm around him, "You are right and I urge you to remind me of that should I ever become enraged again."

"I am going to be a busy boy then eh?"

Outlaw

Reuben appeared and he was shaking, "Thank you, my lord! I thought my end had come."

"You are safe now, they will not return."

"No, my lord. I have seen their true feelings. I will leave for London on the morrow but I am in your debt." I knew then that Reuben meant more than he said; for a Jew, a debt was something honourable, my action had given me a sanctuary for life.

Leaving four men to guard Reuben while he prepared to leave we headed through the city to help Sweyn and Edgar with the scouring of the city. As we ran through I realised that I had not seen the Aetheling and wondered if he had been at the Monkgate. Dawn broke over the eastern walls and the trail of the Normans could be measured by their dead. As I passed the bodies, I noticed that there were few knights or Norman men at arms. The ones who had died had been like Tadgh, left guarding the horses and being guarded, in turn, by one of my men.

"Osbert, we will go to the Gillygate."

He looked at me shrewdly, "You know something, my lord?"

"We have seen few Normans yet and the only gate they could have used is the one we did not attack, the Gillygate." As soon as we neared the Gillygate we could see that there were no bodies and the gates were wide open. They had decided to abandon the city once we had entered. William of Perci was careful with his Norman lives. "Leave the men here to watch the gate and to get some food from the gate tower. Edward, you are in charge. Branton and Osbert come with me."

We trudged west towards the Monkgate. "I wonder where Lord Ridley is, my lord."

"My thoughts too, Branton. I prefer him to my right not off on his own on some sort of berserk death quest." Ridley had never loved a woman and the love he had had he had given to his land and his people. What the Normans had done was akin to the treatment of Ealdgyth. Osbert had said they had watched me, had I been as reckless? I suppose that going into the nest of Normans and killing their leaders was reckless but at the time I had not thought so. Perhaps Ridley felt the same.

The scene close to the Monkgate was one of carnage. We could see bodies, both Dane and Norman littering the streets. Here they

Outlaw

had fought hard. I spied Sweyn and Edgar standing with a group of warriors. We headed over. When we closed I could see that his face had none of the elation I expected but was grave. He walked towards me. "Your friend, Ridley. He is wounded." A chill ran through me. It was what I had feared. "He is a brave man. He came alone and fought with four Norman knights. Three of lie slain but he was given a fearful wound by the last one." He paused, "It was Perci."

I saw Ridley. He had been badly wounded. His face bore the scar of a sword along the cheek. It looked bad but it was the most minor of his wounds. Osbert knelt to bind the wound on his thigh where a sword thrust had gone through. Fortunately, the relatively small amount of blood told me that it was not mortal but I could see red seeping through his byrnie and there were damaged links. "Branton, let us take off his byrnie."

His eyes were closed but a half smile played upon his lips, "Be careful you don't damage it, old friend."

"As if I would." We continued to strip his body and I saw him wince at each movement. "And when you are well again I will be having words about the oath brother who leaves the shield wall in battle."

The old Ridley suddenly looked not pained but upset, "I am sorry my lord. The blood was in my head."

I took his helmet off and he opened his eyes, "I know my friend. I have been there and I should have had one of my men to protect you. Next time, eh?"

He coughed and blood oozed from his lips. "Will there be a next time?"

"There had better be. Who else will watch my right otherwise?"

When the mail shirt came off I could see that the sword had gone through his side. I touched, as gently as possible, the wound and Ridley bore it well, gritting his teeth. The ribs were broken but I could not tell what damage had been done inside. The important thing was to staunch the bleeding. "Branton, send a man for fire and then you go to Reuben, tell him what has happened and ask does he know of any medicines." I looked around the ground as Branton ran off and ripped the bottom half of the dead Norman's tunic. I pushed it hard against the wound, "Sorry this will hurt." I was speaking to no one for he had mercifully passed out. "Osbert, bring the men from the Gillygate." I looked up at Sweyn, "The Normans have fled King Sweyn and the city is yours."

"And we owe much to you and your gallant band for it was your attack that prompted our victory. You were the stone which began the rock fall and I am, once again, indebted to you."

"As am I, brother. The men who reached us told us of the valour of you and your men. I watched Lord Ridley and I have never seen such a fearless warrior."

"Aye brother and it is a lesson to be learned for this is the result of recklessness. Had he waited for us we would still have killed the Normans but he would not be close to death."

"If he is to die, it is a noble death that men will speak of for generations to come. And I think that he learned this from you, Lord Aelfraed."

I shook my head, "I would rather the Normans lived and Ridley was whole for this is not over yet and we will need brave warriors like Ridley. William will come, Edgar, and we will have to face him. We have bloodied his nose and we have yet to rip out his heart."

The venom in my voice made Edgar start back, "You are a fierce enemy."

"Aye remember that Edgar." I had not meant the threat but the actions of Edwin and Morcar had shown me that men's lust for power sometimes overrode their intentions. Branton arrived back first, "He gave me this balm, sir. He said that it will clean out the wound."

The pot he opened contained a small amount of a fragrant smelling paste. I removed the pad and blood still oozed. Ignoring the blood I opened the wound and I smeared the lotion deep into the wound and prayed that Reuben had saved Ridley's life. "And he gave me this powder. You mix a small amount with water and give it to him twice a day. It will ease the pain and make him sleep. He has given enough for four days." I nodded and he went to the nearest house. He had to kick in the door but he quickly returned and mixed the powder with the water. I held up Ridley's head and forced open his mouth. Branton looked at me and I nodded. He poured it into the open mouth. It remained there. Branton pinched his nose and with an involuntary cough, he consumed the medicine. Osbert arrived with the men at the same time as the warrior with the pot of fire.

"Osbert, make a litter. Edward, make the fire red hot." I took out my dagger and gave it to him, "I want this blade white hot."

Sweyn and Edgar had left us in the street which resembled a butcher's yard. The only ones who remained were my men. Counting the ones left at the gate there were forty of us now. We had done well but men had still died. "Here you are, my lord."

Edward held out the knife which smoked. "Hold his arms." I removed the pad and placed the flat of the blade onto the wound. There was a hissing and the smell of burning hairs and flesh but when I removed it there was no bleeding. "Put it back in the fire." I took the pad from his thigh and smeared more of the paste on that wound. When Edward handed me the blade I repeated the cauterisation. He no longer bled but his life was now in the hands of the Almighty. I put the last tiny portion of paste on the wounds on his face.

"Osbert, Branton, we need a roof and a kitchen. Find one."

Later, as we ate and drank, Branton told us of his meeting with Reuben. "He said the paste is an old remedy from his homeland but the powder comes from the Turks and was given to him by Aethelward. He was insistent that we only use it for a few days. He said no more."

I nodded, "If Ridley shows no sign of recovery in a few days then we will not need it anyway."

We rested in Jorvik for a few days. The fighting had been brief but hard and we all needed time to recover. Tadgh had proved a godsend for he knew Jorvik even better than we. His guard had admitted not watching him all the day and that proved, even to Osbert, that if he had wanted to run he could have done so and he was accepted. Some of Edgar's men also asked to join my company. I was too busy watching Ridley and delegated that to my sergeant. When he returned his face was a little dark. "Well," I asked, "are they men of my company now?"

"Aye sire, ten of them and good men too." He looked troubled.

"Come on man spit it out. Don't dance around with me we have known each other too long."

"The reason they wanted to join us is that they see no honour in serving Edgar. He kept his men back from the walls and only entered once we had won. They have spent the last two years avoiding fighting and they felt ashamed that Lord Ridley had been so badly wounded while they did nothing."

I was not surprised and it confirmed my view of the boy. Our father had not spent time with him; he had been his mother's boy and we all knew what that meant. It was a shame. I realised, at that moment, that he would never be king. Deep in my heart that was the instant that I knew the Normans had won. I spent the next year denying it to others but you cannot lie to yourself.

Sweyn and his army left Jorvik suddenly. We knew not why or where he went. There was an assumption that he had returned to Denmark. The Aetheling enjoyed the power of running Jorvik which in itself, sickened us. We were doubly grateful when Ridley awoke. We had fed him liquids whilst he slept and dressed his wounds but, on the fourth day after the battle, he opened his eyes.

"Am I dead?"

We were so pleased that he spoke but we could not control our laughter. "Very nearly old friend, very nearly but it must have been *wyrd* that decided you would live."

He nodded and tried to sit up. We helped him to an upright position. "I am starving and my head is ringing."

"Well, we will feed you and then, as soon as you are able, we will leave."

"Leave? Did we not capture the city?"

"We did but none of us like the stench!"

We spent another three days preparing to leave and what disturbed me the most was that Edgar never once came to see how Ridley was doing or to ask us our plans. It was almost as though we had done our part to capture the city for him and he no longer needed us. Sweyn had also deigned to bid us farewell. I resented both men for I felt used and that the lives of my men had been wasted. They had died for nothing. Ridley had almost died for a spoiled little boy's Christmas present.

As we left through the Petergate, still with its blackened burned gatehouse, I had no idea where we would be going. I just knew that I did not want to be in Jorvik and I wanted to be as far away as possible from my half brother. Osbert rode next to Ridley. He had watched him whilst I had slept and he had even more paternal feelings towards him than me. Branton rode next to me, his golden bracelet still on his arm.

"Well my lord, do you have any idea where we are going?" I shot him a dark look and he shrugged. "As we did not get a boat I assume it is not Byzantium and as we did not take the Gillygate then Scotland is not our destination."

I laughed. "You have the mind of a chess player, Branton. You analyse everything."

"True, it comes of being an archer. You and my brother just hit your enemies as hard as you can. Archers have to calculate wind, movement, even the weather and we have to estimate distances. "

I had not thought about it but it was a fact that his job was far harder than ours. "I am heading, since you ask, for Medelai. William will be heading north. When he fights Sweyn he will be at his weakest no matter if he wins or loses. That will be our chance to strike."

He looked back at the line of riders behind us. "With these fifty?"

"I was not boasting when I told Sweyn that you were all worth two of any other warriors. When William has fought, we will whittle his forces down and gather more volunteers. Who knows Hereward may prevail at Ely and increase our numbers? Malcolm may come from Scotland."

Branton shook his head, "The Scots are like the crows and ravens. They do not hunt like the kite or the eagle but they pick over the carcasses of those killed by true predators. He will only come when he thinks we are too weak to defend against him."

And, once again, Branton was proved right.

Chapter 14

Ridley was moving well and had regained much of his lost weight when the first refugees began to flood south. We had rested for two weeks awaiting the arrival of William but the March winds blew over a land devoid of armies. When the dam did burst it engulfed us all. Branton and Edward had been scouting the roads east of us, searching for signs of William and they returned with a gaggle of people from Persebrig. They were a pathetic group who had lost everything, their men had been slaughtered in an attempt to help their families to escape and the twenty or so who made it to Medelai with my archers were virtually all that remained of that once prosperous settlement.

As the people were fed, I asked Branton, "How did William evade our patrols?"

"He didn't my lord. This is the work of Sweyn and his Danes!"

The anger which erupted on my face made even the dour Branton take a step back. I was furious. My men had helped the Dane and he had repaid us by ravaging the very people we had sought to protect. "Get your brother and prepare the men we march north."

He looked at me, open-mouthed. "Against the Danish army?"

"Against any invader." I dismissed him with a wave. The Normans would have to wait; it was the ungrateful and deceitful Sweyn whom I would punish first.

"Yes, my lord?"

"The Danes are raping the land north of us. I have asked your brother to prepare the men. We ride north." Unlike his brother, Osbert just nodded.

"And Lord Ridley?"

I smiled a wan smile, "I do not think he would let us leave without him. We will just have to watch over him in his first combat."

"Much as we did with you, my lord."

"Aye, it seems that we are doomed to be a burden on you, Osbert."

"No, my lord, not a burden. We are all honoured to serve with such a noble and honourable man."

The river was half a day's ride north and we went armed for war. At the time I felt as though this would be the last ride of my company. I did not think that we could defeat Sweyn's army but we could, at least, bloody his nose and make him remember Aelfraed and his Housecarls. In the event, we never reached the river. Tadgh and another of the new men had been sent to Jorvik to bring back the men who had escorted Reuben south. They reached Medelai soon after we had left and, when we heard the thundering of their hooves, we all turned ready to face an ambush. When we saw that it was our six men we relaxed.

"My lord, King William is in Jorvik with his army. The Aetheling has fled to his sister in Scotland."

Ridley and Osbert closed with me. I already knew what Ridley wanted to do but I felt honour bound to ask them. "So, we have two enemies now. The question is who is the more dangerous?"

"The Normans!" Ridley was predictable, understandably so. I smiled and turned to Osbert.

"Well my lord, does this not suit us? William will have to fight the Danes and that means he will be weaker. That was your original plan was it not?"

"Aye, it was." I could see that Ridley itched to have his revenge on the Normans. "Do not worry old friend. We will fight the Normans but we will choose the time. We will head north-eastwards towards Marske. That way we will be afforded a view of the sea where, I am assuming the Danish ships will be waiting, and we may have an opportunity to strike at one or both of these enemies." The small port of Marske was as close to the mouth of the estuary as you could get. The land northwards was marshy and treacherous. We would be travelling along the escarpment which overlooked the Tees and we would be able to see the Danes. "Branton, take two men and head for Jorvik. Trail William and keep me informed of his movements. Edward, take two men and follow the Danes. We will camp in the hills above Marske."

As we crossed the land we saw the burnt out farmsteads which the Danes had left in their wake as they headed north, it was as though someone had scratched a line in the earth. I dreaded to think of the devastation he would have caused in the valley of the Tees which, so far, had been untouched by the Norman hand. We

Outlaw

camped at Othenesberg which had been a settlement for hundreds of years. As far as I knew it had been abandoned since the Norse had been driven from Jorvik but it had the best viewpoint and was highly defensible. The ditches and the huts still remained, although the roofs had fallen in. We used some of the huts for the horses while we repaired six of them for our use. Branton and Edward would have to come along the trail to reach Marske and that meant we could be easily found.

While Osbert organised and chivvied the men I took Ridley to the top of the cone shaped hill. We could see, to the north-west, the pall of smoke from burning buildings but the east looked as though it was untouched. As I peered towards the northern bank of the river I saw the Danish fleet, or at least part of it, lying at anchor. The Danes had obviously not left and the fact that they had anchored away from the southern bank showed that they were being cautious.

Ridley had still not said a great deal following his wounding. I took the bull by the horns and broached his apparent death wish, "Were you trying to die a warrior's death in Jorvik?"

He flashed me a look, partly of surprise at the sudden question and partly, because, I think, I had hit the mark. "I was killing our enemies. That is all."

"You can lie to others Ridley but there are two people to whom you cannot lie, me and yourself. What would Aethelward have said? Deserting your comrades to seek a pagan death?"

"I was killing our enemies."

"And what were the rest of us doing, eh?"

He looked shamefaced. "I feel guilty that I am alive and all those that we loved are dead. What is the point of it all eh, Aelfraed? We can never win and innocent, precious people die while bastards like Perci live. There is no God!"

I shrugged, "There may not be but the fact that I believe that the spirits of Nanna and Aethelward watch over me makes me think that there may be. Look, Ridley, those people who were killed by Perci meant a great deal to you. What about Osbert, Branton, Edward, me; do we mean nothing?"

Outlaw

He suddenly looked shocked and I saw understanding fill his open and honest face. "Of course you do! You know Aelfraed you have been like a brother to me!"

I touched his arm and said gently, "Then stay by my side next time. I feel safer with you to my right." His face filled with emotion and he just nodded. "Good, then let us descend for I see Branton has returned."

Osbert had pots bubbling away by the time we reached the camp. Branton hurried over with Osbert, "William is heading north towards the bridge at Persebrig."

I nodded, "And the Danish fleet is on the northern shore." I gazed westwards. What we needed was intelligence as to the size of William's army and his intentions. I needed to observe him closely. It was a risk, but one worth taking. "Tonight we will visit William's camp and see what we can discover."

Ridley and Osbert looked unhappy, "Is that wise, my lord?"

"You said yourself, Osbert, that we were outnumbered. We need every advantage we can get. Branton and I managed to infiltrate Ripon; a camp should be easier, especially at night. Are you game for it?"

Branton grinned, "Aye, I am that!"

"Good, then find us out two good horses and we will ride."

I covered my mail with my hooded tunic; it made us less visible but yet afforded the protection of mail. Branton always smiled at our mail. He maintained that without it he was too fast for anyone to hit him. Certainly, he had yet to suffer a wound whilst his brother and the other men at arms all bore the scars of combat, or perhaps he was just lucky.

We aimed to strike the Roman road short of Persebrig and then head north. The dusk had made us shadows and, by the time we were close to our prey, it would be dark. We saw the fires of their camp long before were close. There were men on both sides of the river which meant that they would not be fighting this night but tomorrow promised bloody combat. We halted a mile or so from the Norman camp. At least we assumed that it was the Norman one as it was south of the river. We hobbled our horses and tied them to a tree in the woods and well hidden from the road. We descended through the woods to the edge of the camp. The firelight showed us

Outlaw

that it was, indeed, the Norman camp. We edged our way to the east of the camp towards the river. There was a sandy little beach at Persebrig which meant you could walk, quite close to the bank and this way we hoped to be able to spy both camps.

As we walked I couldn't get rid of the feeling that something was not quite right. Normally, the night before a battle, there would be the sound of swords being sharpened and quiet reflective conversations. Here it seemed almost like a feast with loud laughs and cheers. I could not quite work out what was going on. The Roman bridge was a thousand years old and must have been a second one for we crossed the pillars of an older bridge. Fortunately, it afforded us a good view of the bridge and both camps. We lay next to the worn Romans stones and watched. The Danish camp appeared to be just as jolly and full of festivities as the Norman one. Was this something new? Party before you fight?

Branton nudged me and I leaned over, "There are no guards on the bridge." He whispered.

"What is going on? This makes no sense."

"Unless they are not here to fight." Branton's knowing look suddenly put everything into perspective. The two armies were not enemies, they were allies.

I gestured for him to follow me and we made our way along the darkened river bank to the side of the bridge where some Normans were talking. Infuriatingly, we could not understand a word. Suddenly Branton gripped my arm. I turned to look and he pointed at the bridge. There were Sweyn and his lieutenants. They did not look as though they feared the group of Normans who were less than thirty paces from us. I recognised most of the men with Sweyn for that had been at the conference before we took Jorvik. One of them, I could not remember his name, had been an Englishman who had once been a prisoner of the Normans and he now stood next to Sweyn.

Sweyn shook hands with a short stocky Norman and they both gave a cursory bow to the other. Then there was a silence. The man who spoke English said something to the stocky Norman and then turned to Sweyn, "King William says he is glad that there will be no hostilities between us for we both have the same roots in the north. " He then translated Sweyn's reply to the Norman. I heard

Outlaw

nothing for I was stunned. It was King William who stood there. If Branton had brought his bow then William would be dead. Of course, we would not survive either but...

"King William hopes that this coin will be sufficient."

I pricked my ears up and watched as Normans carried ten huge chests across the bridge. That was it. Sweyn was being bought off! The money which William had ripped from the poor inhabitants of England was buying off the Danes. The chests were obviously enough for the Normans followed the chests to the Danish camp and we were left alone again, in the dark. I had heard enough and we made our way back to the safety of the woods.

"That double-dealing bastard! Damn him and damn Edgar."

"It puts us in a difficult place then, my lord. We will not have a weakened William to deal with. We will have him and his army hunting us."

We mounted our horses and rode eastwards. "We will do what we did before we were duped by Sweyn and Edgar. We will fight from the woods and we will do all in our power to weaken William."

The only sounds, for a while, were clip-clop of the hooves. "In the end, my lord, it may be for nothing."

"So what are you saying? That I should submit?"

"Edwin and Morcar did so and they were given lands."

I stopped my horse and stared at the blackened shadow which was Branton. "Do you think I could do that? That would be a betrayal of all those who have died before now."

"It is an option which is open to you, my lord. Those who follow you have no choices, do we?"

Branton was right. They were not Housecarls and they were not bound by an oath. We could submit but I knew I never would; if only because Ridley would fight on and, probably, die. I would have to speak with the men once we reached camp for they had to know the truth. The truth was unpalatable but it had to be spoken. We could not win, ever. We would all die and we would not make a difference once we did end in some bloody, anonymous and soon forgotten battle.

We reached the camp just after dawn and Osbert had hot food waiting for us. I suspected that he and Ridley had spent most of the

Outlaw

night awake, worrying about us. Osbert was as sharp as a knife and one look at our faces told us that something was amiss. He did not say anything but he led our horses away as Ridley handed us our food. They both waited for me to speak. I did not want to speak for until I said the words then they were not true. I could almost feel Branton willing me to tell them. Eventually, I sighed, "Branton, gather the men together. I need to speak to them."

They gathered in silence around me sensing from my face that the news was not good. "Men, we came here to attack the Normans once they had fought the Danes. There will be no battle for William has bought off the Danes." I pointed to the river. "I fully expect to see the Danish fleet sailing eastwards later this day. It means that we will have the full army of William to contend with." I peered around their faces. "I have to tell you now that we have no hope of winning. We do not have the numbers to defeat the Normans and there is no one else. Once Hereward in Ely is defeated then that will be the end." I allowed this to sink in. I gave a half smile at the truculent look on Ridley's face. He would not be giving in! "I am telling you this because I will continue to fight, as I imagine will Lord Ridley." The smile appeared like a new dawn on Ridley's face."I have offered you coin before if you wished to leave my service and I do so again."

Edward stood and looked at the others. "Are you saying, my lord, that you do not wish to fight with us?"

"No Edward. I will always be proud to fight with you but if you remain I want you under no illusions. There is no hope."

He sniffed and sat down, "Well, that is all right then, for I stay."

There was a chorus of, "And me," which rippled through their ranks.

Osbert gave me a wry smile, "It seems you can't get rid of us then. So what do we do first?"

I had not thought that far ahead. I had assumed that they would be leaving. Branton said, "Well if you want my suggestion, they will have to travel south today to get back to Jorvik. The King is finishing his castle. Why don't we attack their rearguard, eh? Annoy them. They will not be expecting it for the enemy they were going to fight has gone."

Outlaw

Osbert and Ridley both nodded. "Break camp. Let's annoy some Normans."

We rode hard and with purpose. They were less than twenty miles from us and, riding along the edge of the hills we could see them as a black shadow crossing the land. Edward took eight archers to dog them a little closer while I rapidly came up with a plan to do more than annoy them. I want to leave as many dead as I could. We were converging with them and as the sun began to sink in the west, it hid us in the shadow and highlighted them. The men at the rear were the wagons and the light cavalry. They were moving at a slower speed than the foot soldiers before them and I could see a gap appearing. I suddenly realised that they were heading for Ripon. They would not be camping and would travel through the first hour of darkness. It made sense for it was a good road and a straight road. Better to sleep beneath a roof than a leaky tent.

"Branton, take the rest of the archers. Find Edward and, as soon as it is almost dark then shoot at the cavalry, not the horses, but the men."

"And if they chase us?"

"I am counting on that! When they chase you then ride north-west, towards Persebrig and then return to our camp near Medelai."

He hesitated, "And you, my lord?"

"I think we will see if we can capture those wagons."

When he rode off I turned to the company, "When the archers attack we will strike from this side. I want the drivers and the guards killing. We want whatever is in those wagons."

Ridley asked, "Why? What is in the wagons?"

"I have no idea but it must be important to the Normans or they would not guard it." I found myself grinning. I had worried and planned for so long to rid my land of the Normans and now that was no longer possible, it had freed us up and that, in itself, was a victory.

We halted less than a hundred paces away from the wagons but, in the gloom of dusk and with our hooded cloaks about us we were all but invisible. Suddenly I saw horsemen plucked from their mounts. There had been forty men guarding the wagons but suddenly there were just over twenty. Their leader roared an order and they galloped off in pursuit of Branton. We silently moved forwards. The attention of the wagon drivers and guards was, as I expected, to the west and the departing cavalry. The first that they knew of us was when our spears and swords hacked them from the six wagons. I did not even get to draw blood. Discarding the bodies we turned the wagons around. There was a road that led from just south of Catherick to Medelai; this turned into a woodman's trail which ended close to the camp. We could empty the wagons and then dispose of them in the Swale which ran nearby. We whipped the wagon horses a little harder than their drivers as we urged them north. I calculated that William would not notice the non-arrival of his wagons for at least an hour and then, by the time they had headed north we should have escaped.

Suddenly a party of riders loomed up on our left. To our relief, it was Branton and Edward. His teeth grinned white in the dark night, "All dead my lord! We thought you might need some help."

"Thank you, Branton. Keep your archers half a mile back and warn us of anyone heading north."

It was a nerve-wracking ride but that helped to keep me awake for I had not slept for two days. Ridley was in good spirits. At least four of the Normans had fallen to his mighty axe. We made it to camp, some time before the moon rose. The boxes from the wagons were manhandled for the last mile and then Osbert took the wagons to the high cliff overlooking the river and they were rolled in. They smashed on the rocks below. We took the horses with us and Edward and Branton masked our trail. Once in the camp, I just fell asleep, in my armour. Exhaustion took over.

We were like children as we opened the chests. I wondered if they contained money. Perhaps Sweyn had been bought off cheaply? In the event, they were even more valuable. Half of them contained mail armour, kite shields and swords while the other half had tunics and food. It was a treasure trove more valuable than gold for we were now, truly, outlaws. We could no longer ride into town to buy goods. We would have to steal and forage.

Osbert strode over to me as the men emptied the chests. "My lord, we need to think of security now. The Normans will have men looking for us. We are well hidden but we need a warning."

"I agree. What do you suggest?"

"Have eight men in pairs at the edge of the forest. If they see the enemy then one rides back here to warn us while the other watches them. If we split the men into two halves it will mean just one duty every four or five days; not too arduous."

"Good. Set it up." He started to walk away. "And Osbert, include Ridley and me." He went to the camp shaking his head. I went to Ridley, "Here Ridley, help me off with my armour."

He seemed almost disappointed, "Aren't we fighting today?"

"No Ridley. We have travelled late and the men are tired. Tired men make mistakes. We will attack when we are fresh."

As he helped me to pull my mail shirt off I explained about the watches, "That seems like a good idea but I for one want them to come here."

"They will come, Ridley, make no mistake. We have been a burr in the Norman's side since Senlac Hill. We have bloodied Aux Gemon's nose too many times and do not forget my moment of madness, Copsi."

The old Ridley grinned back at me, "It seems I am not the only one who has the red mist descend upon them then!"

As well as the sentries we also sent out patrols to watch the roads and so it was that a week after we had stolen the wagon we had word of the Normans. They burned Medelai to the ground and slaughtered every living thing. The scouts returned too late to prevent it but I mounted twenty men and rode south to ambush the perpetrators. I took a mixture of archers and men at arms. Ridley and Osbert did the same north of us.

As we headed towards the road I could see a number of columns of smoke on the horizon. There was more than a little mischief at Medelai that was certain. If the fire starters were heading south they would have to pass by Catherick and we waited in the thick woods to the east of the town and the road. Branton rode towards Catherick to see if they had gone there. When he returned his face was white. "What is amiss?"

"Catherick is no more. It is burned to the ground and the land littered with unburied bodies."

We did not know it then but this was the beginning of what came to be known as the harrying of the north when William killed everyone who lived north of Jorvik. He merely completed what Sweyn had started but, as with all things Norman, it was done with far more ruthless efficiency.

I addressed the men, "The Normans intend to slaughter us all. We take no prisoners."

The grim resolution on their faces told me that they understood. "Horsemen!"

The column of men rode down the road. There were thirty of them led by a knight. I nodded to Branton who loaded one of his precious knight killers. We waited until they were level with us and as soon as Branton's arrow had flown, the other archers loosed their missile and we charged. I rammed Boar Splitter into the side of the sergeant behind the knight before he had the chance to draw his weapon. We had the advantage for their shields were on the other side and, as they turned to face us we slashed and hacked at horses and men alike. Although we were outnumbered, Branton's archers could pick their victims off at will and we were in no mood for kindness. Soon there were thirty of their men dead on the ground but we had lost two and four more were wounded. In a war of attrition, we would lose. I did not doubt that for one moment; the question was, how many of the enemy could we take with us?

When we reached camp we found that Ridley and Osbert had also encountered William's men. The Bastard was making sure that the north would not rebel again, by killing everyone he found! Six more of our men lay dead close to the Tees. William could not afford to allow us to live. We had killed sixty of his men, including two knights and he began a sweep to destroy us.

The sentries saw the columns coming long before they reached the edge of the forest. He had brought over two thousand men; including fifty knights. We noticed that he had not brought his crossbowmen; the forest did not suit them. His men at arms rode but we were under no illusions, once they reached the forest they would dismount for the trees were no place for horses.

We held a short meeting, "My plan is to divide the men into three groups. Ridley and Osbert, you take one each and I will take the third. We will divide the archers. I will take Branton and Ridley, you can have Edward."

I paused and Osbert asked, quite mildly in the circumstances, "And we fight until we die?"

Although Ridley nodded, I shook my head. "No, we withdraw further north and west. I will use the five camp guards to move the horses close to Persebrig and the Roman Bridge. Those who survive meet there."

"And?"

"And then we decide what to do with whoever is left."

They nodded for we were now in the hands of the gods. I did not think that we could defeat two thousand men but, as Aethelward had often told me, three hundred Spartans had held off the largest army ever assembled. Who knew what we could do? "I will take the centre. Ridley, you will be a mile to my right and Osbert, a mile to my left. We should be able to slow them down for a while. And remember, when they are killing us, they cannot kill our people." I looked at each in turn and grasped their arms. "I will not say goodbye for I do not think it will end here in the forests west of Medelai. I will say that you are my brothers and it has been a privilege to fight alongside you." They nodded their goodbyes and we separated.

Branton and I headed due east with the other twelve warriors. I almost laughed at the pitiful numbers; six archers and eight warriors. Our only advantage was that they did not know where we were but their numbers meant we would hear them coming. "Branton, tell your archers to reserve their knight killers for the mailed warriors and be prepared to use your swords."

"Will we survive?"

I shrugged, "I know not but this seems as a good a place to die, in as good a company as it is possible. I think Aethelward and my father would approve."

He nodded, "At least we have a chance here but at Senlac, they were doomed from the first flight of the fyrd."

With our hooded tunics, we blended into the woodland well and I was not worried that they would see us first. One of the scouts held up his hand and we halted. I trusted my men and the sign meant that the enemy were close. I waved Branton forwards and then the rest of us hid in the undergrowth. I was amazed at how quickly Branton and his men disappeared. The forest was filled

Outlaw

with the sounds of silence and then we heard a scream, and another; suddenly the forest was filled with the noise of men as Branton and his archers ran through us. I had left Boar Splitter with my horse and I held Death Bringer. The comfortable, worn shaft seemed to be part of me. My shield was slung on my back and I was ready for death if it was my time. The knight who hurtled through the trees was intent on killing an archer. As I stepped out, I was already swinging my blade and the sharpened edge cut him in two so quickly that I swear he almost looked at me before death took him. The man at arms behind him was taken by the backswing; Death Bringer took his head. My third victim stopped and looked at the two corpses before him. His hesitation cost him his life. There were now lines of Normans but Branton and his archers shot volley after volley, thinning their ranks. "Back!"

The archers covered us as we ran through the trees to form up behind Branton. There were now but six of my men left. I had not seen the other two warriors fall, I hoped that they had had a good death for all of my men were as brothers to me. They were more cautious now and they used their numbers to try to flank us. I gestured for Branton to split his archers, three on each side and they ghosted away, suddenly invisible. I pointed to the ground and we all sank to our knees. The Normans were maintaining their eye level search and they saw what they expected to see, trees. I pressed myself as close to a tree as I could and I smelled the Norman before I saw him. I slid my dagger out and held it in my left hand. He was beyond me before he was aware of my presence, by which time the dagger had ripped out his throat and he had died a silent death. I waited until the next two men had passed beyond me before I stepped out to hack Death Bringer through one man's spine and then swing it upwards to split the other in two. I quickly ran towards the west and I felt the sword slice down to the place I had occupied. I turned quickly, just in time, to parry the sword aimed at my head. I lowered my head and drove the small spike into my opponent's face. I did not strike an eye but he fell backwards and I chopped at his bleeding face. The two men approaching me were wary of the whirling blade and so I charged one of them. The problem with forests is the roots of the trees and he fell over one. I stamped on his face and then whirled the axe at the man approaching my back. He died as the axe took off his head. I did not even look at the man on the floor I just hit him with the axe. I was suddenly alone with the corpses lying around me. I checked that no one was close and then I ran west. I almost tripped over Ralph's body; he had taken five Normans with him. "It was a good death, Ralph. I salute you."

Night was falling and, in the deep forests, the gloom became darker. I halted and waited behind a thick pine. Soon I heard noises behind me as the enemy made their way through the dead and the dying. I heard an occasional scream and a clash of metal on metal and still, I waited. The line of skirmishers nervously edged through the trees. I waited, almost holding my breath, as I saw them move westwards. I waited until I was certain that they were before me and then I stalked them. I slung Death Bringer and drew out my sword and shield. I saw dim shapes before me and knew that they were close. The knight who was at the rear had sounds masked by his helmet and mail coif. He never heard death approach as I walked behind him. There is a slit in a mail shirt and, approaching from the rear, it becomes an easy target. I slid the sword upwards through his body, directly into his heart. He fell with a soft sigh at my feet. Darkness was almost complete and I heard shouts in French. I crouched, waiting, for they would have to pass by me and I intended to kill as many as I could. The men at arms were easier to spot than the knights for they had white faces. I aimed my silent sword at their throats and they died silently, one by one. I could hear their terror as they shouted one to another and then the steady escape became a rout as they raced through the forests to escape the ghosts that were there. I lost count of the Normans who died at my hands. Sadly most were men at arms and not knights but the ones who died would never slaughter another villager again.

I found myself in the camp. I could see that there had been fighting there and I saw two of my archers, dead, but the Normans lay like leaves in autumn. I took the arrows from their quivers and bade them goodbye. I was tired but I knew that I would have a long walk to reach the horses. As I trudged through the forests, I saw no more dead but I could see that others had passed that way. I was cautious for I was not certain that all the Normans had fled. Perhaps some were waiting to ambush me as I had ambushed them.

Outlaw

Dawn broke and I was exhausted. My arms and legs felt leaden but still, I pushed on. The trees ended and I found myself looking at the ridge overlooking Persebrig. Would I find Normans there or the rest of my men?

Chapter 15

When I reached Persebrig I was as tired as I can ever remember. There were parts of the last few miles I cannot even remember. I rested against a tree and, suddenly, Branton appeared next to me. "We thought we had lost you, my lord."

I gave him a wan smile, "No Branton, I am still above ground but how, I do not know?"

They had built a small camp and it was big enough for the twelve of us who had reached journey's end. I saw Edward, Osbert, Tadgh, Ridley and the seven others. Only Branton and I had avoided wounds. I still do not know how. I suspect Nanna and Aethelward had been watching over me. I shook my head in the sadness of the deaths, "We did not do so well then?"

Osbert laughed, "My lord if that was the last act to the Red Horse Company then men will sing the saga for years to come. The forest is littered with Norman corpses. They call us the ghosts of Hastings and they fear us. They will not venture into those woods for many a year."

I looked at Ridley, "Truly?"

He smiled back at me, "Truly. I feel proud today to be an Englishmen for less than fifty men have killed over two hundred Normans. Many knights lie dead in the forests above Medelai."

"So we are all that is left?"

"Aye, my lord, and what a glorious death for all."

Branton put his arm around my shoulder. "I saw the web of death you wove in the forest, my lord. King Harold and your uncle would have been proud. I watched as men ran weeping from the monster of the forest. They fled from the Hooded Man."

I tried to laugh but I was too tired. "And now? What?"

"My lord, whatever you wish for you bear a charmed life and the Normans fear you. We may only be twelve in number but the Normans see a greater threat in the woods of the north."

We tended to the wounds we had suffered and took what rest we could on the bank of the river at Persebrig. Gradually we noticed people arriving, in ones and twos and sometimes in small family groups. At first, they were wary of armed men but the sight of the red horse on our shields encouraged them and they flocked to our

Outlaw

fire. We discovered that they were the remnants of those villages and farms in the east which had been destroyed by William and his men. The scale of the devastation was truly immense. Ripon had been sacked as had Thirsk and other large towns. It seemed, at the time, as though William was intent upon destroying the Saxons who lived in the north. The exhausted refugees slept knowing that they would be safe with us.

"What now then Aelfraed?"

"I do not know. I had thought to continue the fight but we have a duty to these people."

"There is always Dunelm, my lord."

Dunelm; I wondered how long that would survive if William was intent on destruction. The church of Cuthbert might provide a sanctuary that even a Norman would not violate. "That looks like the only option we have Osbert. We will leave tomorrow. Branton and I will scout south for I would not wish to be surprised while guarding these people."

Dressed in our tunics once more we headed back the way we had come. We also sought any horses and wounded warriors. The signs of our fighting were everywhere and we found many of our men with four or five bodies around them. My company had not died easily and I could see, from the disfigurement of the bodies that the Normans had made sure that they were all dead. By the time we had reached Medelai we had counted more than a hundred dead Normans but we had not seen any living. "Perhaps they have gone back to lick their wounds, my lord."

"No Branton, he will now be even more determined to destroy us. It is even more urgent that we deliver those refugees to safety before William comes after us."

My childhood home was now a shell of burnt out wood and stone. No one would live there again. I dismounted to walk once more amongst the buildings. Perhaps Nanna was watching over me for, as I stepped from my horse, the crossbow bolt flew over my head. Branton kicked his horse forward with his sword held before him. The man with the crossbow was torn between reloading and taking out his sword. In the end, he did neither and Branton ran him through. I quickly mounted again and drew my sword. It was an ambush and they had waited for us. The over-eager

Outlaw

crossbowman had triggered the attack prematurely. The Normans were hidden at the edge of the forest and I followed Branton to take the fight to them. They were all on foot and my long sword scythed down on either side of my horse's head as I cleaved my way through the terrified men at arms.

"Follow me!"

I decided to head south and strike the road for we needed to get north again as soon as possible. Suddenly, I caught sight of some mail and saw a knight. From his moustache I knew who it was, William of Perci. As usual, he was lurking at the rear of his men and I urged Sweyn through the trees, aiming at him. He was not expecting an attack from me and he frantically tried to turn his horse. In the end, he managed a half turn, which probably saved his life for my sword smashed at his shield and not the head I aimed at. He tried to kick his horse away from me but I stabbed downwards. The sharp point of the sword went through the upper part of his leg and into his horse. Both rider and horse crashed to the ground but before I could finish him off I heard Branton shout, "My lord, flee there are more men coming!"

Cursing Perci's luck I chopped at the spearman who bravely tried to defend the recumbent knight and then we were away from the ambush riding as quickly as we could. Once I was certain that there was no pursuit I halted to allow the horses to regain their wind. Branton was white and I saw the bolt sticking in his calf. "You are wounded. Let me look at it."

"We have not got the time, my lord."

I dismounted. "We will make the time." I took a leather lace from my satchel and tied it tightly around the leg above the bolt. The quarrel was in deep but they did not have barbed heads. I took one of Branton's arrows and gave it to him. "Bite down on that. This will hurt." He nodded as he put the arrow between his teeth. I grasped the end of the short bolt and turned it slightly one way and then the other. I heard a low moan as the movement sent waves of pain through my sergeant. Blood oozed out of the wound and I hoped that I had loosened it sufficiently. I tightened my grip and then tugged as hard as I could. The bolt popped out and the arrow snapped in Branton's teeth. I handed the bolt to him and then took out a piece of cloth. I wiped the blood away from the wound and then took out the small pot of Reuben's paste which I still carried. I smeared some on and then tied the cloth around it.

"That should do until we reach camp. Keep loosing and retying the lace or you will lose the leg." Unable to speak Branton nodded. "You lead and I will watch the rear."

A couple of times on the journey I thought he would slip off but he held on manfully. I had confidence in Reuben's paste, for it had saved Ridley's life but Branton had lost much blood. It was later afternoon when we rode into camp. The refugees had been fed and organised. I smiled when I saw Osbert's concern; the two bantered and bickered but Osbert looked after his younger brother like a mother hen and her chick.

Branton flashed a wan smile, "The revenge of the crossbow, eh Osbert?" He slid from the horse into his brother's arms, mercifully unconscious.

Osbert looked up at me, his face filled with distress. "I have bound the wound with Reuben's paste and he will live. He has lost much blood."

We laid him on the ground and covered him with a fur. "Will we be pursued?"

"Not for a day or two." Ridley wandered over. "They were waiting for us at Medelai. Perci!"

Ridley's eyes lit up, "Does he follow?"

"No, but he is badly wounded, he would be already dead now if it were not for the fact that we were outnumbered."

"I am glad, for I will be the one to kill him."

While Branton slept we rebound his wound and cleaned it up. We could see that it had not struck the bone and the vein had been missed by a fingernail. "It is the first wound he has sustained."

"I know Osbert; he has been lucky." I spread my arm around the men. "When you think how many times we fought and against whom then it is no surprise that we all bear scars. Remember Aethelward and his limp?"

He grinned, "Aye, now that was a bad wound. You could tell when it was damp for he would curse and shout at all."

"I know why he does that. The wound in my back always likes to tell me when the rain comes." I looked at the sleeping refugees. "Tomorrow Ridley and I will take Edward and the archers as a rearguard. You will take the refugees ahead." He looked at me as though he was going to argue but I held up my hand. "Branton will be with the refugees and you will watch them all. I do not think they will pursue us for they only saw Branton and myself. Besides, they would have to get Perci back to Jorvik. We will be safe for a day or so."

The journey was slow but uneventful. We picked up other homeless wanderers as we went for they had all come from the south to try to find a haven far from the Normans. The priests at Dunelm were sympathetic and I gave them coin for food but Father Norbert shrugged, "It is Christian and kind of you my lord but there is no food to be bought; no matter how much gold there is."

"I know Father. I will try to get some for you."

He looked at me strangely, "Where from? Will this be a miracle of the loaves and fishes again?"

I laughed, "No father more the miracle of the Men of the Hood and the Normans." He cocked an eye at me. "The Normans eat well!"

Branton refused to stay at Dunelm. We had managed to pick up another couple of volunteers, young men who wanted revenge. They were not trained warriors but beggars could not be choosers. There were few enough of us now to sit in a circle while I explained my ideas. "We are going south to rob the Normans of their food." Ridley grinned wolfishly. "Jorvik will be too heavily defended but I guess the Normans will be busy building their forts and castles. It seems to be their way. We do not have the luxury of a large number of archers so we will have to use stealth to achieve our ends."

The ever practical Osbert nodded, "How will we get the goods back here?"

"We won't. We will get them to Persebrig and I will ask the priests to collect them from there. That way we will be able to fight any pursuers and the priests can be the carters." I pointed at the horses. "We have enough horses for their riders now lie dead in the forests south of Persebrig. That is our advantage."

"It is a slim one."

"Aye Osbert but better a slim one than none at all."

Outlaw

Edward now assumed command of the five archers we had left. Our numbers were up to a score but Branton was wounded and five were young men, callow as warriors. We spent the next few days searching for any Normans who were foolish enough to wander into our land. We were heading for Topcliffe when Edward reported that he had seen a column of men with wagons heading north towards Medelai. Were they going to rebuild? I left Ridley and Osbert with the men and joined Edward. There were two wagons. They had ten men at arms walking close to them and ten outriders. Each wagon had two men but, although we were outnumbered, I could see neither knights nor crossbowmen. The best place for an ambush was where the road to Medelai left the Roman road. It twisted and turned through hedgerows and trees. We left one scout, an older experienced warrior called Aedgar, who was to keep watch on the column in case they deviated from their route.

We headed for the ambush point and I sent a rider towards Medelai to see if there were Normans there. It would not do to be caught between two such groups. "We will wait to the right of the road with the bulk of the men. Edward, you take the archers ahead of us and go to the left. When you fire I hope to draw their horsemen after you. If you ride then they will follow and we can attack…"

Suddenly, our scouts galloped in, "The Normans, they are not at Medelai. They are building a castle on the high rocks above the Swale."

"How many of them?" The place they spoke of was less than two miles away. With the small numbers at my disposal discretion might be a better option.

"There look to be no horsemen but about fifty-foot soldiers. They are still digging the ditch."

I smiled, "Well they cannot use our people to build their castles if they have killed them all. It seems that the Normans are a victim of their own success."

"We go ahead then, my lord?"

"We do, Osbert, and then we might return at night to give these Normans a visit from the ghost warriors."

Outlaw

Aedgar rode in soon after, "They are coming. About a mile behind me, my lord."

"Good, you join Edward." We waited in the trees. Branton was in no condition to fight so I gave him command of the new men. They would be used to plug any gaps. I was using Boar Splitter for I needed to be able to have a longer reach against the wagons. They had learned their lesson, following our previous ambushes and there were two riders well ahead of the column. Two more looked to be some way distant and the others were spread on either side. I turned to Osbert, "When we attack you take the rearguard. We don't want them to bring reinforcements."

He grinned, "It would be a long ride."

"You never know." The vanguard drew level with us and they halted, the lead rider almost sniffing the air. Had they seen or heard us? He said something to his companion who laughed and then they carried on. Edward would have to decide how to take out the two riders and launch his attack, I readied Boar Splitter and made sure that the strap on my shield was tight. The two daggers were in their scabbards above and below my arm and my sword had been oiled; it would slip easily from my scabbard.

I neither saw nor heard the arrows but two men at the head of the column fell. The outriders were too far away to see. Immediately the riders from our side galloped towards the danger and the foot soldiers closed with the wagons. We just leapt forwards, Ridley on the right, Osbert on the left and me in the middle. Boar Splitter sank easily into the neck of the first man and I twisted it to turn it and then pushed it through the driver of the second wagon. It went in so far that it struck his companion and I released it and drew my sword. I put one foot on the wagon and climbed on. The driver fell to the ground beneath the terrified horses and I despatched the wounded man. One of the riders had turned and charged towards the wagon, his spear held overhand. He hurled it at me from a distance of no more than five paces and I ducked behind my shield. Its point struck the boss and flew into the air. When I lowered the shield his sword point was slicing towards my head. His shield covered his body but he had no coif and my sword went straight through his neck.

Outlaw

And then it was over. We saw one rider, wounded; galloping away south but the others lay dead or dying. We removed the bodies and headed the wagons back towards the Roman road. Our casualties were light, in the scheme of things but our numbers were so few that every wound and death diminished us greatly. Two of the new men and one of my older warriors had perished. As we rode north I examined the content of the wagons. One was food while the other was tools and weapons; we would use the weapons. It was not perfect but it would have to do.

The priests were waiting for us at Persebrig. We gave them the wagons. "One of them contains tools, it may be some use. We will bring more directly to Dunelm when we get more." I turned us around and headed back to the new castle. I wanted to get there before they knew that their supplies would not reach them. My men were tired but, if we could hit them hard then we could rest for a few days before trying a third time to strike back.

We found a spot some eight hundred paces from the workings. It was close to the river and below the cliff. I chose it because it was the one side they would think they did not need to protect. I chose the best and fittest twelve to accompany me, leaving a sulky and unhappy Branton with the wounded, the new men and the horses. Osbert gave his brother little sympathy, "That'll teach you to be more careful."

"It was a crossbow bolt!"

Osbert grinned, "And if you had worn armour…"

We took no shields but swords, axes and daggers. Our two aims were terror and destruction; terrify the men to fear the night and slow down the building. We climbed the small hillside easily. There were many handholds and bushes to help us up. Later, when they had finished the building they would clear it but they had other priorities and problems to contend with. Edward and his lightly armed archers took out the five sentries by creeping up to them and slitting their throats. The builders and guards were all sleeping in tents. There were two braziers for the sentries to warm themselves upon and we took a burning brand each and spread out amongst the neatly ordered tents. I waved mine once and then plunged it into the tent. My sword and dagger were already out and I waited for the flames to catch. Suddenly there was a scream and a man's head appeared at the tent's entrance. I slashed my blade across his throat. The same reaction was repeated throughout the camp. The tents we had not burned were slow to wake and we raced along the sides slashing the ropes with our swords. It was all intended to cause confusion. Some warriors emerged, sleepily from their tents, swords in hands but, without a helmet and without armour they soon perished. I heard a shout in English and saw Tom, one of my warriors die with two men attacking him.

"Fall back!"

We had done all that we could and I watched as my men slipped away silently into the night. Then I saw that Ridley had not retreated and was fighting three men, his axe whirling around his head. To my horror, I saw two men stealthily approaching him from the rear. I dared not risk a warning shout and, instead, I ran towards them. My sword stabbed one in the back while my dagger ripped the throat out of the second, the warm blood covering my hand and splashing my face. "Ridley! Retreat!" I slashed at the man on his right who fell backwards his face a mask of terror. Ridley's axe split open the head of the warrior he was facing and the third just screamed and ran.

I grabbed Ridley's arm and pulled him away. He turned angrily and then saw it was me. His expression changed to an apologetic, wan smile and we fled. When we reached the horses Osbert was watching for us nervously. "We thought you had fallen."

I shook my head. "Ridley here decided to take on half the Norman army. Luckily they were not as brave as they thought and they ran."

Osbert and the men burst out laughing. "And I can see why my lord. Your face is a mask of blood; you look as though you have come from a pit in hell."

I went to the river and, as a shaft of moonlight lit it up I saw that I did indeed look as though I have been slaughtering animals. I shrugged, "It all adds to the legend and I think we will have achieved our aim. They will not sleep easy here again."

We rode north again. The new Norman castle was too close to our old camp and we would be at risk if we stayed there. Osbert suggested our eastern camp. "I think not. We need to be as close to the river as we can be. We are too few to defend against large numbers. We will return to Persebrig. The deserted Roman ruins will give us shelter and an escape route."

"Escape to where Aelfraed?"

Ridley had been more of his old self since his bloodfest. "North to Scotland."

I saw the glance exchanged between the brothers and Ridley. "What is in Scotland, my lord?"

I could almost see their thoughts and hear their conversations when I was not present. They worried about Gytha and how I would react to her infidelity. To them, Scotland was as much a danger as England. "Firstly Edgar is there and he and I have some issues to settle. Secondly, we have money there. Branton brought me the promissory note from Reuben, remember and finally, it is the one place we can take ship should the Normans get too close."

Branton looked uncomfortable. "Leave England? Why?"

I waved my arm at the handful of men who rode in a ragged line behind me, "Because this is all that is left to fight the Normans and," I pointed to the shells of houses we were passing, "because this is not England any more. England is the people and they have been slaughtered by the Normans who bring a new style of war to our land."

When we reached the river we collapsed to the ground. A lack of food and sleep meant that we were living on our last reserves of energy. I took Ridley to one side. "Come old friend; let us do as we did as young men and hunt. The men need food and we owe them that much, at least."

He gave me a funny look and shook his head. "If we are talking debts…oh never mind. Aye, let us hunt."

We took off our byrnies and took two of the horses we had left behind. Osbert opened an eye as we passed him. "We are going hunting Osbert. I do not think the Normans will reach us today and we need food." He started to rise, "No stay. We will need your energy later."

We crossed the old Roman bridge and headed away from the road and what passed for civilisation now. Ridley was the better shot and he took his bow. I trusted in Boar Splitter. I had killed deer with it before; it all depended upon how close you could get to the beasts before they smelled you. I found myself oddly excited.

Outlaw

This was the first time, in a long time, I had not been hunting my fellow man. Perhaps, too, it was because I was with Ridley again and we were young boys again in the woods above Medelai. This was not the thick woodland of the land further south. This was shallow grassy valleys with tree-lined bottoms and we made good time as we headed for a spot we knew where the deer gathered to graze during the day. We rode west for a while as the wind was blowing east to west and then we cut south. Once we lost sight of the road, Ridley strung his bow and nocked an arrow. We would have to leave the horses soon and we needed to be ready. When you do something, like hunting, regularly with a close friend, then you do not need words. Ridley just dismounted and tied his horse to a tree in the small copse sheltered on the northern side of the dale. I hefted my spear. I was travelling light and we descended to the stream we could hear bubbling away before us.

We were silent as we scanned the ground for tracks. The earth was muddy in places but the deer tracks would stand out, even in the grass. Ridley froze, like a good hunting dog and pointed. I saw that the deer had begun walking east; they too were trying to stay upwind of any predators. We both stepped into the water, for the sound of the stream would mask any noises we might make and the deer would stand out more. Ridley stopped again as we saw the small herd ahead of us. There was an old stag, with five does and three young. With luck, we would take two and have food for a week. I readied Boar Splitter but the range was too great for a throw; I would have to hope they fled close by me and then I might take one. The arrow flew true and took the doe in the neck. It lurched away east along with the rest of the herd. The old stag though did the opposite. He charged Ridley. As Ridley reached around quickly to notch another arrow he slipped in the water and I saw that he would not make it to safety in time. "Down!" Holding the spear before me I ran as fast as I could to reach the beast before it struck Ridley. Its head was down and its antlers pointed at the helpless Ridley who had drawn his dagger prepared to fight to the last for life. Its preoccupation with Ridley cost the old stag his life and I pushed the sharp head of Boar splitter deep into the beast's chest just as it prepared to strike Ridley. The blow turned his head and Ridley ripped his knife across the neck of the dying animal.

With a soft sigh and a gushing fountain of blood, it collapsed into the stream.

I helped up Ridley. The only thing he had injured was his pride. He nodded at the spear, "Deer Killer now eh?"

"No, it is still Boar Splitter I think."

Laughing we hefted the stag onto Ridley's shoulders and then walked along the valley to find the doe. I managed to manhandle it onto my back and we struggled back to the horses. With our kills over the horse's necks, we rode east again. We would feed the men.

It was the horses who warned us of the danger. They whinnied. That meant strange horses or men. We were still south of the river in the woods above the bridge and we could see the smoke rising from Osbert's campfire. We threw the carcasses to the ground and prepared our weapons. If all was well we could return for the deer but if not we would need to fight. Ridley drew his sword and I took the lead. The trail masked us from observation but also prevented us from having a clear view of the ruins. Suddenly we heard a shout and a scream; throwing caution to the wind we kicked our horses on and tumbled down the slope. There were ten Norman horse led by a knight and they were galloping across the bridge. I could see Aedgar lying slumped over the bridge and there looked to be much blood about him. The only advantage the two of us had was that they did not know we were behind them. The momentum of the slope helped us to gain on them. I could see my men fighting desperately against the knight who had just raised his sword to strike down the sentry. Branton and Edward must have had time to reach their bows for the knight fell with two shafts sticking from his chest. The other horsemen slowed and I thrust Boar Splitter into the unprotected back of one of the rearmost men. Ridley's sword took his head from his shoulders and the two men in front of them made the mistake of turning. They saw the blood-covered iron weapons which ended their lives. Osbert had managed to organise some sort of defence and the other six soon fell.

It was heart-breaking to see the remnants of my once proud company. The knight and his men had killed many before we had seen them off. "Ridley, stand guard on the bridge. Osbert, check the wounded."

Outlaw

I dismounted and went to the bodies of the Normans. The knight still lived although I could see the life oozing from him in deep red rivulets. I took his helmet from his head and pushed by the coif; he was a young man, barely eighteen at most. He tried to grin and opened his mouth to speak. To my amazement, he spoke English, not well but he spoke it, "I so nearly had you Lord Aelfraed. I nearly killed the hero of Stamford. God watches over…" and then he died. He had been a brave warrior. I was now a trophy to be hunted. My name and my reputation had been the cause of the deaths of many of my men.

Osbert stood over me and I looked up. "How many of our men fell?"

"It would be easier to count the living. There are seven of us."

I stood and looked. Tadgh, Edward, Branton and Aidan were all that remained of my warriors. We buried the last of the hooded men in a patch of wooded ground in the lee of the ruins. The ceremony was largely silent as we said goodbye to those who had fought with us for the last few years. The Normans were brave men too but we just laid their bodies in lines. When their comrades came for them they would bury them.

Once we had recovered the deer it was dark and we cooked all the meat up. We were not hungry but human nature dictated that we forced ourselves to eat. No one spoke until Osbert said, "North then my lord?"

"North? Aye. I think William wants the outlaws."

"I think Aelfraed he just wants to kill. Do you think he will just stop at this river? No. He will keep coming until the whole of old Northumbria is his. Malcolm had better watch his borders."

Ridley was right. These Normans were not like the old Northumbrians. They used horses and could move swiftly in small armoured conroi. They were swift enough and well armed enough to control large areas, especially sallying from their castles. We had copied them, using the captured horses and that was why we had lasted so long but our numbers had become too few for us to be effective and they were both right; we would have to head north to the land of the Scot.

Chapter 16

We left the next day. With the Norman's horses, we could travel swiftly but I decided not to take the Roman Road for we knew not where William would send his men. "We will ride to Dunelm first and deliver the horses to the refugees and then we will take the coastal route."

Osbert looked sceptical. That will take longer, my lord."

"True, but we need to evade the Norman hunters," I remembered the look in the young knight's face; every Norman north of Jorvik who was not massacring the poor of the land would be hunting us. The road was empty as we twisted through the wooded valleys north of the Tees. Every farmstead and village we saw was burnt out and flocks of crows and ravens feasted on the corpses. We proceeded cautiously for the last time we had ridden north there had been no sign of destruction on this scale. This time there was no column of smoke to warn us of the presence of the Normans. As we reached the ridge which overlooked the valley we could see the ant-like figures that were the Normans, busily building yet another castle. Down towards the river, we could see flocks of crows and birds; we had seen enough to know that the refugees we had saved had been slaughtered. I felt as low then as at any time. What had been the point of saving them? Better we had let them run, some might have survived.

Osbert peered towards the mound as though trying to count the warriors while Ridley put his hand on my shoulder. "It looks like we will be taking the coastal route then."

Now that we knew they were north of the Tees it became even more dangerous for us. Edward and Tadgh rode as scouts ahead and behind us. Each night's camp meant we had to use sentries. We had surprised others; it would be ironic to be caught napping ourselves. All of this meant that we were tired.

When we reached the Tyne we saw that this was the limit of Norman expansion. There were still villages that were happily working, oblivious to their impending doom. Osbert pointed east, "There is no bridge for fifteen miles or so. We have to rejoin the Roman Road and use the Roman Bridge."

Outlaw

I nodded. Once we crossed the bridge we would be safe for we would be close enough to Malcolm's land then to know that William would not risk a confrontation. We trudged wearily northwards. The weariness was induced, I think, that we finally knew we had been defeated. We saw the stonework in the distance- even after a thousand years, the Roman's hand could still be seen across the land. The buttressed pillars looked solid enough and we looked forward to a camp that would be safer than those we had recently endured. Perhaps we were tired, I don't know, but the ambush which hit us could have been planned by us. The first we knew was when Edward flew backwards from his horse. Even from thirty paces, we could see the white feathered bolt sticking from his chest. I swung my shield around just in time to hear the bolt ping off the boss. "Charge them!"

I knew that the last thing they would expect would be for us to charge them and, besides, those who had used crossbows would take some time to reload them. The three crossbowmen who had hit us were crouched next to the bridge. I speared one as he frantically tried to reload the cumbersome weapon. Ridley's axe smashed the skull of a second and the third was despatched by Osbert. The Normans had made the mistake of not having others beyond the bridge; they had counted on our turning back into their horses. I glanced over my shoulder and saw a column of men rapidly mounting their horses from their hiding places. Aidan's lifeless body was being dragged along by his horse for his foot was still stuck in the stirrup. The others appeared to be uninjured. Once we reached the other side we halted to allow Tadgh and Branton to reach us. When Branton did he turned and took out his bow. He quickly strung it as Tadgh thundered over the bridge. Branton calmly nocked a mail killer and aimed at the knight who was eagerly racing to the other side of the bridge. The range was but forty paces and the arrow smacked him firmly in his open mouth and he was propelled backwards. His body and his rearing horse caused confusion and the Normans halted. We turned and raced into the forest which climbed northwards behind us.

I urged our mounts up the steep slope through the tightly packed trees. We were in single file and there were now but five of us. There looked to be at least a score of Normans behind us and they would struggle to reach us, or so I hoped. At least they could not use their crossbows in the woods and I would still back us to defeat them in hand to hand combat. Suddenly, the land flattened out, as did the trees and we were on the old road which ran from coast to coast. Before us was the old Roman wall; derelict but still an obstacle. I reined in and turned. The Normans were at least a hundred paces away. Osbert pointed east, "There is a gate a mile or so that way. To the west, it is a sheer drop."

That decided us and I kicked my horse along the road to the east. We made better time but so would the Normans and they could use their numbers to cut our escape route. "Osbert, take the lead!"

There was little point in my leading as I did not know where this gate was. Osbert flashed alongside me and I kicked Sweyn on. The Normans were now less than forty paces from Tadgh whose horse was labouring somewhat. Osbert left the road and dropped down a small slope. He rode hard and opened a slight gap. His horse leapt one of the ditches and I followed suit. Then the land began to rise and I saw the stone wall of an old Roman fort on the skyline. Our horses were tiring as they laboured up the hill. Behind us, the armoured horsemen had slowed but the lighter cavalrymen had begun to gain on Tadgh who was now less than thirty paces behind him. I saw him look up at me and wave then he turned his horse.

"No!"

His sword was out and he struck two attackers before they knew what was happening. His took the one on his right and, continuing his swing, the one on his left. His mount crashed into another two and then they were lying in a heap. Tadgh was on his feet slashing away for all he was worth.

"Come on, my lord! Do not let his sacrifice be in vain."

I urged Sweyn towards the walls but I could not tear my eyes from Tadgh's last stand. He could not defend against the mailed men who speared him as he stood amidst the bodies of the men and the horses he had killed. So Tadgh, who had changed sides, ended his life by buying us enough time to reach the gate. I saluted him and thanked *wyrd* for bringing us together. It was not a straight ride to the gate and there was debris on the ground. I hoped it would slow them up. I was now thirty paces behind the rest and when I reached the gate I saw Branton and Ridley with nocked bows. As soon as I was through they loosed and I heard a neigh and a scream which told me they had struck flesh. Beyond the gate was open moorland and there, a mile away, was the security of another forest but this one stretched all the way to Scotland.

As we rode into the forest I looked behind us; our pursuers, all ten of them were about a mile back but still intent on following us. "I don't know about you three but I don't fancy having to keep watching over my shoulder for these."

Ridley dismounted. "Let's end it."

"Branton, you and Ridley use your bows. Wait until they are less than ten paces from the trees. Osbert, take your axe and go behind the trees to the left."

With the horses hidden we watched as they thundered up the slope leading to the forest trail in which we hid. I had Death Bringer and Osbert had his trusty axe. I was counting on the fact that they would be keen to close with us and assume that we would have fled. They were all mailed and they had their shields strapped to their backs. They held their spears in their right hands. Although Ridley and Branton only had a couple of knight killers with them I hoped that Osbert and I could do the most damage.

Ridley's arrow flew a moment before Branton's. They took the third pair of warriors down. At the same time, I swung Death Bringer and hacked upwards through the neck of the first rider's horse. He soared over the headless mount and crashed with a sickening thud somewhere behind me. I had no time to see what had occurred for the second man lowered his lance to spear me in the chest. I reached forward and grabbed the spearhead in my mailed fist. As he stabbed at me I pulled forwards and a surprised Norman crashed to the ground next to me. I swung Death Bringer one handed to decapitate the prostrate figure. I turned, quickly to see the last two men fall to Ridley and Branton's arrows.

I heard a moan from one of the Normans but before I could react, Ridley leapt forwards, drew his dagger and slit the man's throat. "That is for Coxold!"

Branton ran by me to grab his brother who had suffered a wound to the leg. One of the lances had pierced it, just above the knee. It looked nasty and bled heavily but it looked as though it was not serious. Branton quickly stripped the armour and tunic from Osbert

Outlaw

and, taking a water skin from his horse cleansed the wound. I searched in my satchel and I found a tiny morsel of Reuben's paste. I gave it to Branton and then joined Ridley to search the bodies. There were some young men amongst the dead and they looked to be of noble birth from their fair skin and fine undergarments. They had died in their quest for fame; they had wanted to be the ones who killed Aelfraed, the last Northumbrian, but they had failed.

We left the bodies where they lay. We had no time to bury them and we knew not how many other hunters were following. We managed to get a white-faced Osbert onto the back of his mount and, leading the four best Norman horses, we headed north.

Because of Osbert's wound, we had to take it slower than we would have liked. It amused me to see Branton being the mother hen; normally it was the other way around. Ridley seemed more at peace with himself. The slaughter of the ten Normans seemed to be a mark in the sand. For myself, I was leaving England reluctantly but the persistent chase by young Norman warriors keen to make a name by killing the notorious outlaw showed me that it would have been only a matter of time before my luck ran out and I did not wish to die just yet. I had no idea what my destiny was but I was certain it was not to die in a northern forest pierced, like a wild boar, by Norman lances. I was still a young man and I knew that neither Ridley nor myself had reached our prime as warriors. The wounds we had sustained had not slowed us up. I suppose, had we been older, then the wounds might have had a greater effect but when you are young the wounds do not impact quite as much.

We bypassed the towns and we reached the estuary which led to Fife. Ridley looked at me strangely, "Why do we go to Fife, Aelfraed? Do you feel the need for more pain?"

"No Ridley. I was just as guilty as the Lady Gytha. I lay with Ealdgyth did I not? I need to see my son and then say goodbye to them both."

Branton and Osbert exchanged looks. Ridley looked across the water to the ferry which slowly made its way across the choppy waters. "And then Aelfraed; what do we do?"

Ridley was still Ridley; he was still the man who followed me no matter where I went. It was a great responsibility. I wondered

Outlaw

what it would be like to travel alone. I had always had him by my side. I asked myself, was it fair? I said nothing for I had not yet decided. I had a vague idea what I wished but that was all. We left one of the horses with the ferryman as payment for the ride with the promise of another one when we returned south.

The Scots looked at us strangely, as we rode north of the river, for we were well armed and bore many marks of war. Since the Normans had arrived in England the border had been quiet and it amused me that they had not yet met the killing machine that was the Norman army. When they did then they would know what hardship was. Calum's castle showed all the signs of having been improved. I wondered whom he feared. As we rode up the road I saw the drawbridge raised and armed men appear on the ramparts. I wondered, briefly, if some other Scot had taken the castle and if so where were my wife and son.

Ridley turned to me, "Do you think they know who we are then?"

Osbert gave a wry laugh, "I think, my lord, that they know exactly who we are and that is why they prepare for war."

Branton saw my confusion, "I think the Thegn of Fife fears you have come for revenge."

It all became clear. We had been so used to war and dressing for a war that we did not know what we looked like. I shook my head, "Let us look peaceful then." I spread my arms out, as did the others and we rode towards the motte. The archers on the walls never once took their attention from us but I saw the drawbridge lower and the gate open. Calum, Thegn of Fife appeared with six mailed and armed warriors behind him.

I dismounted and approached him. "This is a strange welcome for someone you promised eternal friendship to." The confused look on his face almost made me laugh out loud. It was then I realised that my world had been dominated by war and rebellion, Calum's had been dominated by a new spouse and a fear that her former husband would come seeking revenge. In the scheme of things, Gytha's infidelity meant nothing. "If you worry that I come for revenge then allay your fears. Had I wanted you dead then you would be, believe me. I have fought and killed better men than those who stand behind you."

Outlaw

One of them started forwards and I heard Ridley's sword slide from his scabbard. Calum held up his hand, "Peace, Hamish. He comes in peace. Sheath your weapon." He strode up to me and embraced me. When his head was next to mine he whispered, "I am sorry. We did not mean it to happen."

I held him at arm's length. "Then I am sad that you did not think to tell me and face me like a man. Were you so afeared of me?"

Again his men bristled with indignation at the insult but Calum held up his hand. He smiled sadly at me, "Feared the greatest warrior in England? Of course, I was afraid." He saw my look of doubt. "I have spoken with the Aetheling and heard the tales of your deeds. And we receive word from the refugees who flee north. There is a mighty price on your head, old friend. The Bastard fears you!"

We were allowed into the castle although the bodyguards of the Thegn cast us murderous looks. Having had the Normans try to kill me for the last few years the enmity of the Scots did not worry me. Calum's Steward took us to a smaller version of the warrior hall. We were to be kept alone, that much was obvious. It did not worry me; we would be there for a short time only. Once I had seen my son and said goodbye to Gytha then I would leave. I was still uncertain as to my final destination but I knew that it would be neither England nor Scotland. One other place it would not be would be Sicily and southern Italy for they too were riddled with the curse of the Norman.

Calum had a bathhouse which he had built for Ealdgyth who loved such things. I made sure that I had one for I disliked the smell I had developed; it was a mixture of sweat and dried blood. I knew that it would soon come to me again but, when I met my son again, I would not stink like some animal.

As soon as I dressed and re-entered our quarters, I could smell the other three. I could not help the involuntary wrinkle of the nose. Ridley laughed, "I believe our lord thinks we smell a little unpleasant."

Partly to cover my embarrassment but mainly because I was waiting for an opportunity to speak with my friends I held up my hand. "No, Ridley. I am no longer a lord. What am I lord of? My horse, Sweyn?"

Ridley looked puzzled but Branton shook his head. "You will always be our lord."

"Like the hundreds of our comrades who now lie dead? No, this is a time for new beginnings and a new way of working. I am leaving this island."

"And going where?"

"Byzantium." They all looked in surprise at me although I think Branton had an inkling of what I meant for he nodded slightly.

"Why Byzantium?"

"I spoke with Reuben and he told me that many warriors who survived Senlac Hill joined the Varangian Guard and they serve Emperor Romanos. Since we slaughtered so many at Stamford Bridge the Emperor needs other axe-wielding warriors to defend him."

"And you, my lord, have a promissory note for Constantinople."

"I do Branton."

"I will follow you there."

"No, Ridley, you can come with me but as a friend and not as a follower."

Ridley looked puzzled, "He means, my lord, that you have to choose."

"Correct Osbert, as do you and Branton." The two brothers looked at each other and I knew then that they had discussed the situation. "If you were to stay here I would not blame you." They looked at the ground, shamefaced. "Do not feel that way. I could not have had two more loyal warriors to fight alongside me but I go to a strange place and the journey to reach it will be hard. If you come with me Ridley then you must be prepared for dangers that we have never faced before."

"Aelfraed, I have followed you since I was smaller than your sword. I will follow you till the end of my days."

"Thank you old friend, I am glad. And you Osbert, Branton; what are your plans?"

"No, my lord, we are English and we will stay here but it has been an honour to serve you."

"That is good; I am happy for I can say all my goodbyes at once and begin anew. We will leave in the morning for Eidyn Din and I will collect the money from the Scottish promissory note then we will take a ship."

That part of my life was sorted but I dreaded meeting my son and Gytha; would the boy run in fear from me? I shook my head. I had stood in a shield wall and faced innumerable enemies and yet I was afraid of a boy and his mother. Ridley put his hand on my shoulder. "Come Aelfraed, we will all go to meet with the Lady Gytha."

I suspect that they had all been waiting some time to greet us. We took no weapons for I did not wish to terrify them all again. There was a roaring fire and they were seated around the table. I saw no guards but I think they were within calling distance. Harold looked to have grown. He had been little more than a walking baby the last time I had seen him but now he was recognisable as a boy. He smiled shyly at me as I entered and I breathed a sigh of relief; at least he had not run. Gytha looked as lovely as ever and I saw that she was with child.

I bowed and kissed her hand, "My lady."

She burst into tears and threw her arms around me. "Oh Aelfraed, I am so sorry for…"

I held her away from me and put my hand on her lips. "It was *wyrd*. It is in the past and it is forgotten." I suddenly remembered Ealdgyth and Aethelward, Thomas and Sarah. "We should not be thinking of us but those that have died, Ealdgyth, Aethelward, Thomas and Sarah."

She suddenly became tearful, "Thomas and Sarah? I didn't know."

I realised then that she would have heard of the death of the Queen but why would anyone have told her of two servants and their death? We sat and we told her of Topcliffe and Coxold and the deaths, slaughter and rapes. It was hard telling the tale and I saw Ridley's eyes well up.

"We did not know. We heard that the Normans had to put down rebellions."

I snorted, "Rebellions? Hah! Traitors like Edgar and those less than useless brothers of Ealdgyth. No, the Normans did not have to do much; it was the Earls and the Aetheling who destroyed England."

Outlaw

I saw my son, out of the corner of my eye, staring intently at me. I so wanted to pick him up in my arms and take him but I knew I could not. I had given up that right when I chose to fight the enemies of my father.

"We have heard that William has destroyed many towns in Northumbria," I wondered where the Thegn of Fife had gained his knowledge.

"We thought the people had fled."

"No. I am afraid that they died." I looked at Calum. "Should they come north to fight you then I warn you it will be a bitter war and the Normans are no respecters of women and children."

Gytha put a protective arm around Harold and I saw her eyes fill with tears, "Where are Harold and Ulf?"

Gytha looked at Calum in panic and he reddened and then began to bluster, "Er, well when Edgar, their half brother arrived he took them with him to the court of King Malcolm."

I stiffened. Edgar was treacherous and deceitful. "You let that renegade take Ealdgyth's sons? When they were left here under your care."

"I wanted to keep them here but Edgar was insistent."

I shook my head. They were both weak-willed empty vessels and I was tempted to take Harold with me. "Where are they now?"

Calum shrugged apologetically, "Still at the court I believe."

I stood up and walked towards him. He recoiled in fear. "Liar! You know where they are and what has happened to them!"

The door suddenly burst open and six guards entered with swords at the ready. Ridley and the others immediately turned to face them but my dagger was out and pressed against Calum's throat, "Tell your men to drop their weapons or by all I hold dear you will die! Do it!"

Gytha's voice, suddenly pathetic screamed, "Aelfraed! Please!"

I pressed harder and a tendril of blood oozed out. "Drop your weapons!"

I heard the metal thump to the ground, "Disarm them and then tie them up." I glanced over my shoulder. "If they give you any trouble then kill one!" My voice suddenly sounded merciless and I saw that the Normans had made me so, along with Edgar, Edwin and Morcar. "Now I am already an outlaw. I have nothing to lose

Outlaw

so tell me what I want to know or this castle will become a charnel house."

"They are dead! Edgar said they died on the road but I know that he killed them."

At that moment I wanted to kill Calum but I knew that I could not care for my son in my absence."You were always a weak-willed bastard and you should die for what you have done but my friends and I are leaving tonight and someone needs to watch over my son but if you ever fail in your duty then I will return and you will die. Do you understand me?"

He nodded, "I will, I promise."

"And to remind you of that promise." I took the knife and ran it down his cheek. It was not a deep wound but it bled profusely. Gytha screamed and raced to him to staunch the bleeding.

I went over to Harold who looked terrified. "My son. I may never see you again but know this, your father loves you but I cannot stay for you would be hunted. Your grandfather was a king and a great warrior. Your father fought the Normans. Do not be like this apology for a man. Be a man." My men had bound the guards and gagged them. "Tie this spineless reptile up. Osbert, Branton, fetch our gear and meet me at the gate."

When Ridley had tied Calum up. I took Gytha in my arms. "I did love you once but I love you no longer and I release you from your vow. If you wish to marry this man then do so. Ridley, go and secure the gate." He nodded and left. "I am leaving this land and I will never see you again but if you hold me at all dear then you will tell our son the truth about his father, Aelfraed, son of Harold Godwinson."

She nodded and then threw her arms around me. She kissed me and then said, "I did love you Aelfraed but you loved England more and I will tell our son of his father. The only warrior William the Conqueror feared."

Once outside I saw that the two guards by the gate had been disabled by Ridley. I hoped he had not killed them; we had enough blood on our hands. Osbert and Branton were grinning like children as they rode up with our horses and gear. "Like old times my lord!"

Outlaw

"When do we have new times? Let us ride for the Thegn may decide to send his men after us."

Ridley quickly mounted and we raced through the open gate and over the drawbridge. Scotland did not have the anarchy of Northumbria and the garrison was not as alert as a Norman one would have been and we were soon racing down the road towards the ferry.

"What if the ferry is on the other side?"

"Then, Branton, we will have a long ride around the estuary." Having said my goodbyes I felt almost light-headed. It was as though every tie holding me to this island had been severed and, for the first time in my life I would be free.

Nanna, Aelfraed or perhaps just wyrd, were watching over me that evening for the ferry was still there. The ferryman looked at us, "Well that was a short visit! You can't have your horse back you know."

"Get us across quickly ferryman and there is a gold piece for you."

He looked beyond me to the north and the castle of the Thegn. He grinned, "Like that is it? Push off, lads. We eat well tonight."

We were halfway across when the gaggle of riders reined up at the landing stage. The ferryman shook his head, "I can see you have been pissing off the Thegn. Ah well, he is a tight bastard anyway. He pays in copper, not gold!" He bit the gold piece I had given him and whistled happily as the southern shore loomed up.

I felt safer on the other side. "We will head to Leith and find the Jew Reuben told us of and then we will say goodbye." As we rode along the coastal road, with the sun setting at our backs I could feel the sadness in the brothers. Having taken the decision to stay, they were now thinking of life without Aelfraed and Ridley. I know that for I was thinking the same about them. We had endured much together. All of us had almost touched death and yet we, alone of all our company, had survived. We did not break our thoughts with useless words but enjoyed the memories of times past.

Leith was a busy port and I could see many ships at the wharf. I left Ridley and the others with the horses while I went to the commercial quarter of the port. I asked where the Jews lived and the answers showed me that they were held in disdain here too. I shook my head; without their usury then businesses would not prosper. I saw the sign of a money lender and went in. "I seek Isaac."

The hooded eyes gave nothing away but I could see suspicion lurking in them. "Why?"

"Reuben of Jorvik told me I could redeem this promissory note."

I handed it over and he pulled a candle over to read it carefully. Suddenly his eyes lit up and a smile appeared on his face. "I am Aaron, Isaac's brother. He is away on business but I can help you." He went to the rear of the building and said something in his own language. A gaggle of faces appeared. "This is the warrior who saved Reuben of Jorvik. Here is the only Christian warrior to stand up for our people."

They all wanted to touch me as though I was special. It felt strange. Aaron allowed it for a while and then shooed them all away. "I will get your money now, my lord." As he counted it out he asked, "You are leaving?"

"I am leaving Aaron."

"That is wise. We have heard that King William has put a high price on your head and that of your Hooded Men." He shook his head. "He is so afraid of you he has ordered your name to be struck from every document. You and your men are now the Hooded Men." He rolled his eyes, "As though that wipes you from our memory." He leaned forwards. "There are men coming north, for it is known that your wife, forgive me, lives close by." His eyes looked sad and pleading. "I would take the first boat you can my lord." He smiled as he handed over the money in two bags. "Reuben has spread your name throughout our people. Wherever you travel you can use your note to get funds." He scribbled something on the note and handed it back to me. "I am honoured to have met you."

I slipped quickly back to the port where I found the others. "It seems that William is a little bitter about us." I handed one of the bags to Osbert, "Here you may need this."

He tried to refuse it, "No my lord, it is your money."

"It is our money and I would not have this were it not for you two and the men who died for us. Take it for them. You may be wiser to travel on a ship with us for the Normans are coming here."

Outlaw

Branton laughed, "Without you two my lord, no-one will know us. We will head west and then south. It is Aelfraed and Ridley who are the named outlaws. We are just the Hooded Men."

I nodded and embraced each of them in turn. "Take the horses, we will not be needing them and Godspeed."

Ridley took his farewell and then Osbert and Branton saluted us both and rode off west. We never saw either of them again but I hope they had good lives for they were honourable men and they deserved it.

"Well Ridley, this is it. We leave this land. Did you find out the destinations of any of the ships?"

As we hefted our bags containing our gear he said, "Aye and there are none for Constantinople. Most go to Jorvik or London and one goes to the land of the Danes."

"Then that is the one for us."

He looked appalled. "That liar? You would go to his land?"

"The Jew told me to take the first boat. It happens to go to Denmark. *Wyrd*! Besides, he said once that he owed you and me for saving his men at Jorvik. Let us see. Besides that, old friend, the world is filled with people who want to kill us. And Denmark is the shortest sea crossing. Let us find a berth on that ship. We sail to Denmark."

Striding along the quayside I felt my heart lighten as my old friend and I set off to conquer the world or at least see a greater part of it.

The End

Historical note

The events around Edwin, Morcar and Edgar are largely true. They did submit and then rebel. Edgar did ally with King Sweyn of Denmark and invade Northumbria, attacking Jorvik. Edith and Ealdgyth both disappeared from history after Harold died. I have merely speculated. William did spend a long time back in Normandy and eventually returned in 1067. He appointed Copsi as Earl even though he had fought with Tostig. The motivations of both men are interesting.

There is a deserted medieval village called Griff close to Helmsley. I did no make it up. It was deserted sometime after the invasion. William of Perci was given Topcliffe and huge estates in North Yorkshire. He was nicknamed Aux Gemons because of his long moustaches.

Edgar did invite Sweyn of Denmark to invade England; they captured York and then ravaged the countryside. When William came north he bought off Sweyn with the money he had raised through taxes and then punished the people of the north by slaughtering them! Edgar fled to Scotland where his sister had married King Malcolm and then William completely emptied the land north of York; killing every man woman and child. William (who was known as the Bastard) tried to wipe Anglo-Saxon England from the map. His genocide did not work and the language of England still has many Anglo-Saxon words. For a good book on this try Melvyn Bragg's "The Adventure of English". The reason why English did not die out is because the Norman women used Anglo-Saxon wet nurses for their children and they spoke English to the Norman children. Within a hundred or so years the nobility were using English again.

Ealdgyth, Ulf and Harold all disappeared from history following the Battle of Hastings. This is my version of their lives. The Varangian Guard was originally filled with men from the Rus, (Russian Vikings and Swedes) but following Hastings, the numbers were swelled with Anglo-Saxon warriors fleeing the Norman tyranny.

Outlaw

Edgar the Aetheling did flee to Scotland where he stayed with his sister, the wife of Malcolm Canmore. Morcar and Edwin both died in captivity. William, wisely, never trusted them again!

The next and last book in the series will be Varangian and it should be out in Spring 2013 when Ridley and Aelfraed journey to Constantinople.

Characters and places in the novel

Fictional characters are in italics.

Aelfe Saxon-Elf
Aelfraed-Descendant of Alfred the Great's son
Aethelward-Aelfraed's uncle
Alfred-King of Wessex
Branton-Osbert's brother, an archer
Byrnie-Armoured coat
Catherick-Catterick North Yorkshire
Conroi-Knights who follow a leader
Danegeld-Bribe paid to Danes by English kings
Dunelm-Durham
Ealdgyth-Wife of King Harold
Eidyn Dun-Edinburgh
Gammer-Old woman or mother
Guy of Evreux-Norman knight
Gytha-relative of the Earl of Hereford and wife of Aelfraed
Hetaireia-Imperial bodyguard of the Byzantine Emperor
King Sweyn King of the Danes
Leat-An open stretch of water close to a river
Legacaestir-Chester
Maeresea-River Mersey
Malcolm Canmore-King of Scotland
Mara-Delamere forest Cheshire
Medelai-Middleham North Yorkshire
Othenesberg-Roseberry Topping, Cleveland
Osbert-Sergeant at arms of Aelfraed
Oswald-Priest at Topcliffe
Persebrig-Piercebridge
Reuben-Jewish money lender
Ridley-Housecarl of the Earl
Strategos-A Byzantine general
Thingman-Housecarls of the English Royal family until 1051
Ulf-Housecarl killed at Senlac Hill
Wight-Spirit
Witenagemot-The council of England which chose the king
Wyrd-fate

Outlaw
Other books by Griff Hosker

If you enjoyed reading this book, then why not read another one by the author?

Ancient History

The Sword of Cartimandua Series
(Germania and Britannia 50 A.D. – 128 A.D.)
Ulpius Felix- Roman Warrior (prequel)
The Sword of Cartimandua
The Horse Warriors
Invasion Caledonia
Roman Retreat
Revolt of the Red Witch
Druid's Gold
Trajan's Hunters
The Last Frontier
Hero of Rome
Roman Hawk
Roman Treachery
Roman Wall
Roman Courage

The Wolf Warrior series
(Britain in the late 6th Century)
Saxon Dawn
Saxon Revenge
Saxon England
Saxon Blood
Saxon Slayer
Saxon Slaughter
Saxon Bane
Saxon Fall: Rise of the Warlord
Saxon Throne
Saxon Sword

Outlaw

Medieval History

The Dragon Heart Series
Viking Slave
Viking Warrior
Viking Jarl
Viking Kingdom
Viking Wolf
Viking War
Viking Sword
Viking Wrath
Viking Raid
Viking Legend
Viking Vengeance
Viking Dragon
Viking Treasure
Viking Enemy
Viking Witch
Viking Blood
Viking Weregeld
Viking Storm
Viking Warband
Viking Shadow
Viking Legacy
Viking Clan
Viking Bravery

The Norman Genesis Series
Hrolf the Viking
Horseman
The Battle for a Home
Revenge of the Franks
The Land of the Northmen
Ragnvald Hrolfsson
Brothers in Blood
Lord of Rouen
Drekar in the Seine
Duke of Normandy

Outlaw

The Duke and the King

Danelaw
(England and Denmark in the 11th Century)
Dragon Sword
Oathsword

New World Series
Blood on the Blade
Across the Seas
The Savage Wilderness
The Bear and the Wolf
Erik The Navigator

The Vengeance Trail

The Reconquista Chronicles
Castilian Knight
El Campeador
The Lord of Valencia

The Aelfraed Series
(Britain and Byzantium 1050 A.D. - 1085 A.D.)
Housecarl
Outlaw
Varangian

The Anarchy Series England 1120-1180
English Knight
Knight of the Empress
Northern Knight
Baron of the North
Earl
King Henry's Champion
The King is Dead
Warlord of the North
Enemy at the Gate

Outlaw
The Fallen Crown
Warlord's War
Kingmaker
Henry II
Crusader
The Welsh Marches
Irish War
Poisonous Plots
The Princes' Revolt
Earl Marshal
The Perfect Knight

Border Knight
1182-1300
Sword for Hire
Return of the Knight
Baron's War
Magna Carta
Welsh Wars
Henry III
The Bloody Border
Baron's Crusade
Sentinel of the North
War in the West
Debt of Honour
The Blood of the Warlord

Sir John Hawkwood Series
France and Italy 1339- 1387
Crécy: The Age of the Archer
Man At Arms
The White Company
Leader of Men

Lord Edward's Archer
Lord Edward's Archer
King in Waiting
An Archer's Crusade

Outlaw
Targets of Treachery
The Great Cause (April 2022)

Struggle for a Crown
1360- 1485
Blood on the Crown
To Murder a King
The Throne
King Henry IV
The Road to Agincourt
St Crispin's Day
The Battle for France
The Last Knight
Queen's Knight

Tales from the Sword I
(Short stories from the Medieval period)

Tudor Warrior series
England and Scotland in the late 14th and early 15th century
Tudor Warrior

Conquistador
England and America in the 16th Century
Conquistador

Modern History

The Napoleonic Horseman Series
Chasseur à Cheval
Napoleon's Guard
British Light Dragoon
Soldier Spy
1808: The Road to Coruña
Talavera
The Lines of Torres Vedras
Bloody Badajoz
The Road to France

Outlaw

Waterloo

The Lucky Jack American Civil War series
Rebel Raiders
Confederate Rangers
The Road to Gettysburg

The British Ace Series
1914
1915 Fokker Scourge
1916 Angels over the Somme
1917 Eagles Fall
1918 We will remember them
From Arctic Snow to Desert Sand
Wings over Persia

**Combined Operations series
1940-1945**
Commando
Raider
Behind Enemy Lines
Dieppe
Toehold in Europe
Sword Beach
Breakout
The Battle for Antwerp
King Tiger
Beyond the Rhine
Korea
Korean Winter

Tales from the Sword II
(Short stories from the Modern period)

Other Books
Great Granny's Ghost (Aimed at 9-14-year-old young people)

Outlaw

For more information on all of the books then please visit the author's website at www.griffhosker.com where there is a link to contact him or visit his Facebook page: GriffHosker at Sword Books

Ancient History

The Sword of Cartimandua Series
(Germania and Britannia 50 A.D. – 128 A.D.)
Ulpius Felix- Roman Warrior (prequel)
The Sword of Cartimandua
The Horse Warriors
Invasion Caledonia
Roman Retreat
Revolt of the Red Witch
Druid's Gold
Trajan's Hunters
The Last Frontier
Hero of Rome
Roman Hawk
Roman Treachery
Roman Wall
Roman Courage

The Wolf Warrior series
(Britain in the late 6th Century)
Saxon Dawn
Saxon Revenge
Saxon England
Saxon Blood
Saxon Slayer
Saxon Slaughter
Saxon Bane
Saxon Fall: Rise of the Warlord
Saxon Throne
Saxon Sword

Medieval History

Outlaw

The Dragon Heart Series
Viking Slave
Viking Warrior
Viking Jarl
Viking Kingdom
Viking Wolf
Viking War
Viking Sword
Viking Wrath
Viking Raid
Viking Legend
Viking Vengeance
Viking Dragon
Viking Treasure
Viking Enemy
Viking Witch
Viking Blood
Viking Weregeld
Viking Storm
Viking Warband
Viking Shadow
Viking Legacy
Viking Clan
Viking Bravery

The Norman Genesis Series
Hrolf the Viking
Horseman
The Battle for a Home
Revenge of the Franks
The Land of the Northmen
Ragnvald Hrolfsson
Brothers in Blood
Lord of Rouen
Drekar in the Seine
Duke of Normandy
The Duke and the King

Outlaw

Danelaw
(England and Denmark in the 11th Century)
Dragon Sword
Oathsword

New World Series
Blood on the Blade
Across the Seas
The Savage Wilderness
The Bear and the Wolf
Erik The Navigator

The Vengeance Trail

The Reconquista Chronicles
Castilian Knight
El Campeador
The Lord of Valencia

The Aelfraed Series
(Britain and Byzantium 1050 A.D. - 1085 A.D.)
Housecarl
Outlaw
Varangian

The Anarchy Series England 1120-1180
English Knight
Knight of the Empress
Northern Knight
Baron of the North
Earl
King Henry's Champion
The King is Dead
Warlord of the North
Enemy at the Gate
The Fallen Crown
Warlord's War

Outlaw

Kingmaker
Henry II
Crusader
The Welsh Marches
Irish War
Poisonous Plots
The Princes' Revolt
Earl Marshal
The Perfect Knight

Border Knight
1182-1300
Sword for Hire
Return of the Knight
Baron's War
Magna Carta
Welsh Wars
Henry III
The Bloody Border
Baron's Crusade
Sentinel of the North
War in the West
Debt of Honour
The Blood of the Warlord

Sir John Hawkwood Series
France and Italy 1339- 1387
Crécy: The Age of the Archer
Man At Arms
The White Company
Leader of Men

Lord Edward's Archer
Lord Edward's Archer
King in Waiting
An Archer's Crusade
Targets of Treachery
The Great Cause (April 2022)

Outlaw

**Struggle for a Crown
1360- 1485**
Blood on the Crown
To Murder a King
The Throne
King Henry IV
The Road to Agincourt
St Crispin's Day
The Battle for France
The Last Knight
Queen's Knight

Tales from the Sword I
(Short stories from the Medieval period)

**Tudor Warrior series
England and Scotland in the late 14th and early 15th century**
Tudor Warrior

**Conquistador
England and America in the 16th Century**
Conquistador

Modern History

The Napoleonic Horseman Series
Chasseur à Cheval
Napoleon's Guard
British Light Dragoon
Soldier Spy
1808: The Road to Coruña
Talavera
The Lines of Torres Vedras
Bloody Badajoz
The Road to France
Waterloo

Outlaw

The Lucky Jack American Civil War series
Rebel Raiders
Confederate Rangers
The Road to Gettysburg

The British Ace Series
1914
1915 Fokker Scourge
1916 Angels over the Somme
1917 Eagles Fall
1918 We will remember them
From Arctic Snow to Desert Sand
Wings over Persia

**Combined Operations series
1940-1945**
Commando
Raider
Behind Enemy Lines
Dieppe
Toehold in Europe
Sword Beach
Breakout
The Battle for Antwerp
King Tiger
Beyond the Rhine
Korea
Korean Winter

Tales from the Sword II
(Short stories from the Modern period)

Other Books
Great Granny's Ghost (Aimed at 9-14-year-old young people)

For more information on all of the books then please visit the author's website at www.griffhosker.com where there is a link to

Outlaw

contact him or visit his Facebook page: GriffHosker at Sword Books

Printed in Dunstable, United Kingdom